KAREN CLARKE lives in Buckinghamshire with her husband and three grown-up children, where she writes romantic comedy novels and psychological suspense.

When she's not writing, she reads a lot, enjoys walking – which is good for plot-wrangling and ideas, watching Netflix, baking and eating cakes. And then more walking to work off the cakes.

AMANDA BRITTANY lives in Hertfordshire with her husband and two dogs. She is the bestselling author of *Her Last Lie* and *Tell the Truth*, and her third psychological thriller, *Traces of Her*, was published in October 2019. Her debut, *Her Last Lie*, has raised almost £8,000 so far for Cancer Research UK from her ebook royalties, in memory of her sister.

When she's not writing, Amanda loves reading, walking, travelling and going to the theatre.

The Secret Sister

K A CLARKE AND A J BRITTANY

ONE PLACE. MANY STORIES

HQ
An imprint of HarperCollins*Publishers* Ltd
1 London Bridge Street
London SE1 9GF

First published in Great Britain by
HQ, an imprint of HarperCollins*Publishers* Ltd 2020
2

ISBN: 9780008376253

MIX
Paper from
responsible sources
FSC
www.fsc.org
FSC™ C007454

This book is produced from independently certified FSC™ paper
to ensure responsible forest management.

For more information visit: www.harpercollins.co.uk/green

Printed and bound in Great Britain by
CPI Group (UK) Ltd, Croydon CR0 4YY

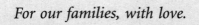

For our families, with love.

Prologue

Ella

When you've led a charmed life, I suppose it's inevitable that it'll fall apart at some point.

It happened to me after my mother died, though her death was the catalyst, not the cause.

Mum had been ill for a while and had come to terms with dying. She'd lived to see me happily married, and to meet her precious granddaughter. I thought we'd had time to say all the things that mattered.

When the end came it was peaceful, with her family gathered around, and I was holding her hand.

It was much later, while clearing out her bedroom, that I realised I hadn't known my mother as well as I thought I had.

The one thing that *really* mattered had been left unsaid.

Chapter 1

Colleen

Saturday

The sun woke me, slanting through the half-open curtains, hurting my eyes. I rolled out of bed, pulled my hoodie on over my pants, and padded to the window.

My brain pulsed against my skull. I felt sick and fragile. It had been years since I'd suffered a hangover, but I'd never forgotten the feeling.

The view from the ground-floor window of the guesthouse was nothing special – an area for cars, a scruffy garden with plastic furniture and faded umbrellas – but there was something soothing about the silence. Apart from the occasional cry of a seagull it was a respite from my shite-awful life.

I squinted up at the sky as the sun grew bigger and rounder – a shiny ball of hope. It would disappear within hours, if the puffy grey clouds approaching were anything to go by. Hope never stayed around long.

A solitary magpie landed on the window ledge with a thud

and a flap of wings, and I jumped. I'd been on hyper-alert since leaving my husband, nerves jangling at the slightest thing. I prayed Celia wouldn't tell Jake where to find me – not that she cared. The woman I'd called mother for thirty-three years had long since lost interest in me.

I turned and scanned the room, trying to work out how I got so pissed the night before that I now barely remembered arriving.

A folder on the bedside table informed me the guesthouse was close to the Atlantic Ocean, near Rosses Point, and a forty-minute walk to Sligo.

I turned to look at Gabriel, sprawled face down on the crumpled bed, taking in his narrow shoulders, his flop of lank blond hair. Hopefully, he would be out for hours.

A flashback of me talking too much, and later my words slurring into an incomprehensible blur filled my head.

What had I said to him?

I eyed his open wallet on the floor, stuffed with a wad of euros. A table by the door was littered with rolling tobacco, two empty bottles of wine and half a line of cocaine. I etched a finger round my nostrils, praying I hadn't taken any. I'd been clean since meeting my husband, Jake, fifteen years ago.

How had I let this happen?

My heart pounded as I tried to recall the night before. But, despite raking around my head for clues, I could barely remember a thing, just tiny bursts of memory that floated in and out in disjointed flashes. 'But I don't drink,' I could hear myself saying in a silly flirtatious voice that didn't suit me, laughing as a large glass of wine was pushed in front of me. 'Not anymore.'

I heaved with self-disgust as my eyes skittered around, looking for my rucksack, noticing a row of cheap-looking seascapes, fixed to the wall with nails in case some loser tried to take off with them.

Had Gabriel booked us into this horrible dump?

I couldn't remember.

There was a laptop on the dressing table, its charge light

flashing, and a rubber plant in a plastic pot on the floor, starved of everything it needed, but somehow surviving.

I finally spotted my rucksack, lying on the floor beneath a pillow. I grabbed it and headed into an adjoining bathroom that looked as if it hadn't been updated since the Seventies. I closed the door quietly, filled a tumbler with water and gulped it down as I stared at my pallid, blotchy reflection in the mirror above the sink. Already, I didn't look like me. I hadn't worn a hoodie before, for a start. Jake would never have approved.

I retrieved the black hair dye and scissors I'd bought the day before, and taking a length of my hair between my fingers, snipped it off. Another clump followed, and another. I daren't look at the honey-coloured strands of hair in the sink in case I cried.

My eyes stung as I mixed the dye and pulled on the plastic gloves. Once I'd massaged the lotion into my hair, I thought I might puke and hung over the toilet, but after retching several times, nothing happened. I rose and sat on the edge of the bath, waiting, striving to make sense of everything, trying to work out how I got here. I pummelled my temples. *Still nothing.* Gabriel certainly hadn't forced me to drink wine. I could see myself, willingly knocking it back. Perhaps Jake had been right. Perhaps he was the only person who could stop me from self-destructing. I'd proved him right within a day of leaving.

Twenty minutes later, I rinsed off the dye and studied myself again. My hair was so dark my skin looked like Snow White's, my freckles more distinctive.

Jake won't recognise me now.

I threw the remnants of the dye in the wicker bin then took a lukewarm shower. Afterwards, I pulled on black skinny jeans and a black T-shirt. I didn't bother with a bra.

Jake would call me a tramp. He knew I'd gone. He'd already cancelled the credit cards, and texted me.

Where the hell are you?

I returned to the bedroom, opened Gabriel's wallet and took

out the wad of notes. There must have been over a thousand euros. It would help me get by until I found my father. What little money I'd withdrawn from a cashpoint before Jake cottoned on wouldn't go far.

Gabriel was snoring into his pillow, his spine rising and falling. Had we had sex? Surely I'd have remembered that.

He suddenly swung his arm above his head and it landed with a thud on the pillow, making me jump. A flash of memory of his arm tightly round me, him whispering, 'I love you, Colleen.'

Had that happened?

I shoved the money back in his wallet and left it on the table.

After pulling my hoodie back on, I pushed my feet into my trainers, grabbed my rucksack, and left without looking back.

Thick clouds gathered as I walked towards Sligo, and heavy spots of rain began to fall. A bus drew up at a shelter, and I ran and jumped on it. It was empty, apart from an old lady talking to herself.

As the bus revved a man leapt on, tall and slim with dark hair slicked to his head. My heart began to hammer against my ribs. I dragged up my hood, and slid down in my seat, but the man wasn't Jake. Apart from his build and hair colour, he looked nothing like him. My heartbeat slowed as he sat in front of me and took out his phone.

Before I walked out yesterday, I'd felt sure Jake had been following me for months. 'Are you having an affair?' he'd asked more than once, as though something had happened to raise his suspicions.

I'd wanted to say, 'When? When the hell do you ever let me out of your sight long enough to meet anyone?'

My phone vibrated in my pocket, making me jump. I pulled it out and saw Gabriel's name flash up. Christ, I'd given him my number. I declined the call and within seconds a text came through:

Hey gorgeous. Shall we meet in the same bar tonight in Sligo? xx

6

'Not a chance in hell,' I whispered, typing a reply.

It was a mistake, Gabriel. I'm sorry.

I deleted his contact details, just in case.

My head pounded as the bus rocked and jolted on its way, and I prayed I wouldn't throw up. I hadn't even got a bag to be sick in, just the hood of my jacket, which would be all kinds of messy. I breathed deeply, fighting nausea, watching the sea through the window, spreading endlessly.

Rain speckled the window like tears, blurring the view. I gripped the necklace – a letter 'B' – that I always wore, and rested my head on the glass. I closed my eyes, but the sound of the man in front watching videos on YouTube on his phone and shifting in his seat prevented me from dozing.

As the bus stopped in Sligo its exhaust backfired, jolting me alert. It had been dark when I arrived the evening before and I hadn't appreciated the colourful buildings curving around the banks of the River Garavogue. A smile tugged at my mouth. This was the town where everything would change.

I jumped from the bus, bought a local paper from a stand, and searched the pages for somewhere to stay.

The cheapest place I could find was a bedsit, near the town centre.

'It's yours if you want it,' said the man who answered the phone, with very little charm. 'You can rent on a day-to-day basis.'

It was obviously basic, probably terrible, but it didn't matter. I was in Sligo, where I needed to be. This was where I would find Reagan, my father. Everything would be better then. I'd have someone on my side, to look out for me, protect me – maybe convince Jake I didn't want to be with him anymore.

'Leave her alone, you controlling bastard,' I imagined my father saying.

Words I could never quite say myself.

As I headed towards the bedsit address, the rain eased off

and my thoughts drifted to Celia. I couldn't call her my mother anymore. Not after what she'd told me two weeks ago, during one of my rare visits.

'It's time you knew the truth, Colleen.' That's how she'd started the conversation, out of the blue.

We'd become estranged over the years, but I made the effort to see her now and then. We would sit in her dark kitchen – it was always dark, even with the lights on – and she would make tea, a mug for me, and always a cup and saucer for her. We'd sit at the old pine table, barely saying a word, until it was time for me to leave.

But it had been different this time.

'I'm not your real mother,' she'd said, fiddling with her spoon, not looking at me. There was no preamble. No preparation. The words sounded surreal, as though she was trying them out to see what they sounded like. As if it was a game. But Celia never played games.

'What are you on about?' I said, with a laugh that didn't sound like mine – not that I laughed often.

She put down her spoon. 'She died six months ago,' she said. 'Your real mother.'

Just like that.

I'd stared at her for what felt like an hour. She kept biting her lower lip with her small teeth, her eyes looking anywhere but at me.

'And you tell me this now?' My brain couldn't form a coherent thought. 'Now I'm thirty-three?' I paused. 'When my real mother is *dead*? Christ, Mam.'

'Don't blaspheme, Colleen.'

Seconds passed. I rose and began pacing, questions flooding my mind. *Who was my father? Why did my mother leave me with Celia? Was Bryony adopted too?* But I knew better than to mention my sister.

'I only found out myself because her death was reported in

a magazine.' Celia's voice cut through my frantic thoughts, and I stopped pacing. 'She, Anna, is ... was ... a successful artist.'

I sank back down in the chair. 'Go on.'

'I should have told you a long time ago, I know that,' she said, her fingers twisting together. 'I should have given you a chance to find her.'

'Too right, you should have.' My heart was beating so hard I was surprised she couldn't hear it.

'I'm sorry.' Her eyes shimmered with tears, but this was nothing new. Celia spent nearly every moment on the edge of a nervous breakdown. And the truth was, now her words were sinking in, finding out Celia wasn't my biological mother wasn't such a shock, not really. It explained so much.

'I wouldn't have wanted to find her,' I said, anger bubbling up. 'Any mother who could give up a child—'

'But you don't know why, Colleen,' Celia cut in. Her voice was soft, and her green eyes – eyes I'd thought were like mine – darted around the kitchen as if looking for a quick escape. She rose from the table, smoothed her apron, and went to look out at the garden. It had grown wild since her second husband walked out, years ago, but she had recently cultivated a little vegetable patch. It had made me wonder if she was improving, if her depression of so many years was finally lifting. 'I want to tell you who your da is too,' she said, not turning. 'It's time you knew everything.'

'Jesus, you're full of news today,' I said, my mind reeling. I'd always believed Celia's first husband – the man we'd lived with in Cork until I was five – had been that man: my father. But Celia was about to destroy that belief too.

She crossed to a kitchen drawer, opened it, and took out a photo. 'His name is Reagan Brody.'

'Wasn't Brody your maiden name?'

She nodded and sat back down. 'Reagan's my brother,' she said. 'He lived abroad for a long time, but he's back now. He's living in Sligo.'

'Your brother?' I cried, covering my mouth.

She nodded, her straight grey hair hanging limply on either side of her face.

'So, I'd have called him Uncle and Da, had I ever met him?' My voice was rising. 'What a bloody mess. Jesus Christ.'

'Please don't take the Lord's name in vain, Colleen.'

'So he – my father – knew where to find me all along?' I snatched the photo, hands shaking. It was too much to take in. I stared at his face, trying to convince myself there'd been a terrible mistake. Unable to take in that he was part of the family, and yet he'd never bothered to contact me.

'We thought it was for the best,' said Celia, her voice calm.

As I stared at his image, something tugged at my memory. His tanned face, that fair unruly hair, his cheery smile. He looked familiar. Or maybe it was just that I'd inherited *his* green eyes, not Celia's.

I felt so many things, all blended together so they were indistinguishable, my mind buzzing with thoughts. But Celia closed off after her confession, as she so often did; never quite living in the real world.

Yesterday, after I walked out on Jake, I went round to see her to say goodbye and let her know where I was heading. She'd slipped a piece of paper into my hand.

'I've never used it,' she said, as I read the email address she'd written down. 'It's Reagan's. He sent it to me a couple of years back, in case I needed to get hold of him.'

She clammed up again after that. I wasn't even sure she'd heard me tell her where I was going.

Now, after settling into the bedsit, which was as grubby as I'd feared, I pulled out a bottle of vodka I'd picked up at a nearby off-licence. It wasn't a good idea, but I still had a throbbing hangover from the night before. I would only have the one little drink, something to smooth the jagged edges, while I thought about finding my father.

Chapter 2

Ella

'I didn't realise Mum had so much stuff.' The heap of clothes, shoes and boxes looked wrong in the middle of the bedroom.

Greg came through from the landing, running his hands through his light brown hair. 'That's because it was all hidden in cupboards and drawers for years,' he said, reasonably. 'And don't forget there's at least thirty years' worth here.'

'Oh God.' I covered my face with my hands. My earlier optimism that I could clear out her things without feeling upset was fading fast. I wished she hadn't insisted that I do it. 'Where am I supposed to put it all?'

Greg came over and pressed a kiss on top of my head. 'Unless there's anything you want to keep, bag up the clothes and shoes for the charity shop. We can shred or burn any paperwork that's not relevant.'

'It sounds so clinical,' I said, dropping my hands. 'I wish I could just leave everything as it was.'

'She knew your dad wouldn't be able to cope with it,' Greg reminded me. He was unusually dishevelled, his hair falling over his forehead. 'Remember you said he's been sleeping on the sofa.'

'But why get rid of it all?' I was suddenly close to tears. 'I thought he'd want to keep Mum's things around him.'

'That doesn't work for everyone.' Greg tilted my chin with his fingers, his hazel eyes sympathetic. 'After my dad died, Mum couldn't bear the reminders. That's why she sold the house and moved abroad.'

'Jesus.' I shook my head, taking in the familiar sight of him. He hadn't changed much in the six years we'd been together, but lately I'd noticed a deepening of lines around his eyes and a hint of grey at his temples. At thirty-three, he was starting to look older than his years, and I wondered – not for the first time – whether I should have encouraged him to chase a partnership at Sheridan-Hope, the London law firm where he worked. The company specialised in media cases, and his job involved gruelling hours, but I worried if he didn't push himself, he'd get left behind.

It was the first Saturday morning we'd spent together in ages and I'd been surprised, but grateful, that he'd offered to help me out with Mum's things. 'I can't imagine getting rid of all traces of you if you died,' I said.

His face relaxed into a smile. 'I'll take some of her books down to the car.' He reached for my hand just as I stepped away and so he scratched his elbow instead. 'Do you want some coffee?'

'Please.' On a sigh, I turned back to the muddle I'd made, while Greg picked up a box of paperbacks and padded downstairs.

I crossed to the bed and picked up a heavy black coat, holding it to my face. It didn't smell of anything. I couldn't ever remember Mum wearing it. She hadn't thrown anything away for years and most of her clothes looked dated, the lengths and collars all wrong, the fabrics faded from washing.

As I folded the coat, ready to add to a bag stuffed with skirts and sweaters, I felt a crackle of paper in one of the pockets. Digging my hand inside, I touched something soft and pulled out

12

a yellowing receipt. The print was worn, but I could make out the words *Annie's Tea Room*, and the date: nearly twenty-eight years ago. She'd bought a cup of tea and a buttered scone, which had cost £1. She must have been there on her own, and I wondered if it had been during a trip to York to visit Aunt Tess.

I crumpled the receipt into the pocket of my jeans and thrust the coat in the bag, anxious to get the job over with, but as I turned my attention to a pile of shoes a burst of childish laughter caught my attention.

I moved to the window and looked out to see Dad pushing Maisie on the swing that used to be mine at the bottom of the garden. She was kicking her sturdy legs, her dark curls dancing around her face, eyes wide with delight.

I pressed my forehead to the glass, clouding it with my breath. Maisie looked so like Greg, my own freckled skin and straight fair hair having passed her by. At the age of three, there was already something of Mum in her smile and clear calm gaze.

I pushed open the window to let the warm June breeze flow in, bringing with it a layered mix of scents from the garden. Mum used to love sitting out there with her easel, painting. Neither of my parents had been keen on gardening, but before he died my grandfather had taken care of things, and since then a local gardener had kept it in shape.

It was good to see Dad, if not smiling, at least looking less tense. He hadn't coped well with Mum's death just after Christmas, six months ago. He was angry that she'd been taken too soon – which of course she had.

Sometimes he seemed angry with me too. I'd catch him watching me, grey eyes narrowed like a sniper's, and wondered if I reminded him of her – though I looked more like him than Mum. I'd asked him once what was wrong and he dropped his gaze and said curtly, 'Isn't it obvious? I've lost the best thing that ever happened to me,' which had left me wondering where I stood in his affections.

13

I glanced sideways at a silver-framed photo of them on the windowsill; Mum, an elegant figure in an A-line denim skirt and flowery blouse, smiling with friendly reserve, and Dad in his rimless glasses, an old wool jacket over a checked shirt, looking every inch the college lecturer he was. I'd taken the picture with a new camera on my sixteenth birthday, and they looked relaxed and happy.

Dad had been strong during Mum's illness, but since her death seemed half the man he'd been. The double chin he'd developed over the years had vanished and his clothes hung off his lanky frame. Even his reddish hair looked thin and lifeless and he'd grown a straggly beard that aged him. Worse, he'd applied for early retirement from the university, and spent most of his days either walking Charlie, his old spaniel, or slumped in an armchair in front of the television.

Eyes stinging, I turned back to the job I'd begun two hours ago. At least the wardrobe was empty now, apart from Dad's few clothes. They looked lonely, taking up barely any space.

As I went to close the door, my eye was drawn to a shoebox I'd missed on the floor of the wardrobe, at the back. I bent to retrieve it, impatiently pushing my hair back, and carried it to the bed. I sat on the floral duvet, wondering whether Mum had kept her wedding shoes in the box. It was a nice cream one, with a silver band around it, and a picture on the side of some strappy, open-toed shoes in her size.

Hoping for a glimpse of a younger mother on her wedding day, I removed the lid and peered inside, hit by a musty smell. There weren't any shoes, but my initial disappointment gave way to an unexpected burst of excitement as I delved inside and drew out a faded Polaroid photograph. It was of Mum, cradling a newborn baby wrapped in a lacy white shawl. She looked different than in other photos I'd seen of her with me when I was a baby. She was wide-eyed, her black hair a wild mass of tangled curls around her heart-shaped face. I couldn't make out what she was wearing. It

14

looked like a nightdress, and she was sitting on a bed that could have been anywhere.

Why wasn't the photo in the album with all the others? Why shove it in a shoebox? I flipped the photo over and read the words scrawled on the back in blue ink.

Colleen.

My heart gave a thud.

Colleen?

So, the baby wasn't me.

I looked closer, but there were no discerning features, apart from a swirl of fair hair. Could it be Aunt Tess's baby, Mum's niece? But her name was Rosa, after their mother.

I plucked out a tiny wristband, almost identical to the one I'd kept after leaving hospital with Maisie. Only this one had *Colleen Brody* written on it, along with a date of birth: five years before I was born.

I felt as if someone had squeezed all the breath out of my lungs.

A vision of Mum, just before she died, swam into my head. She'd started apologising to Dad and me, her eyes cloudy from the morphine. 'I'm so sorry,' she kept saying, clutching at our hands, blinking too much, as if she was trying to bring us into focus. 'I should have fought harder. I'm so sorry. Forgive me, please forgive me.' We'd assumed she was talking about the cancer that had fatally spread.

'Oh my God.' Forcing myself to breathe, I dug out a square, dog-eared envelope addressed to Anna Harrison. *Mum's maiden name.* The address on the front was my grandparents' house in Hampshire, where she'd grown up.

The letter was crumpled, and soft with use, and the writing was tiny and sloping – almost impossible to decipher. The word *Reagan* leapt out. A man's name. Irish? My eyes jumped to the address at the top of the page. *Cork, Ireland.* Underneath, were the words:

Anna, I thought you should have Celia's new address. She doesn't want any contact right now, but might change her mind. We did the right thing, you know. She'll have a good home with a mother who loves her. I've been abroad more or less since you left and will be returning to America at the weekend. Hope all's well and that you're on your way to becoming a famous artist! Reagan. PS: The baby's well.

The words slammed into me like a punch. I stood up, my thoughts simmering and darting, and finally grasped the only possible conclusion – the one I'd suspected the second I saw the picture of a mum I barely recognised, holding a baby that wasn't me.

'Ella, what is it?' Greg manifested in front of me, coffee slopping out of the mug he was holding onto the cream carpet. 'What's wrong?'

'Nothing,' I managed, knowing how crazy I must look, standing there clutching a wristband and a letter in one hand, and waving a photograph with the other. 'Oh, Greg,' I spluttered, laughing and crying at the same time. 'You'll never guess what.'

His look of bemusement only made me laugh harder, even though my eyes were leaking tears. 'What? What is it, Ella?'

'Something wonderful,' I burst out. 'Greg, I have a sister.'

Chapter 3

Ella

'I can't believe it.' Greg studied the photo with a furrowed brow, turning it over and over, as if doing so would reveal answers. 'It doesn't make sense.'

'Why not?' I said, dropping back on the bed. 'Do you remember I told you how Mum kept apologising right at the end? Well, I think this is what she was talking about.' My cheeks were burning, as though I were running a fever. 'I think she had a baby girl before me and gave her up for adoption.'

Greg threw me a perplexed look. 'But why didn't she ever say anything?' He'd been close to my mum. They'd shared a dry sense of humour, as well as a love of art, and would sometimes meet for coffee in the city if it was one of her days at the gallery where she occasionally worked before she became too ill.

'I don't know,' I said, not wanting to dwell on the 'why'.

'Maybe it's a friend's baby.'

I jabbed the letter I was holding. 'It says in here, "we did the right thing",' I repeated. I'd read it out once, but unusually for Greg, he hadn't taken it in. As a lawyer, he was used to absorbing all sorts of confidences, but perhaps this was too personal. 'I think she had a baby with this Reagan and they gave her up for adoption.'

'It doesn't seem like something she would do, that's all.' Shaking his head, Greg looked down at the garden. 'Do you think your dad knows?'

'Probably not.' I tried to imagine it. There'd always been something self-contained about Mum that suggested she might be good at keeping secrets, and Dad had a jealous streak. 'If it happened before they met, she might not have wanted him to know.'

'Pretty big secret to keep from your husband.' Greg's tone held an undercurrent that annoyed me, considering he'd once kept a secret of his own for months. 'What if this Colleen had tried to find her?' he continued. 'How would your mum have explained that?'

'Well, maybe he does know,' I said, changing tack. 'I'm just getting to grips with all this.' I gave an incredulous half-laugh. 'Perhaps they made a pact never to talk about it.'

He glanced at the photo again. 'So, she's your half-sister.'

'She's still my sister, Greg.' I couldn't hide the bite in my voice. 'I want to find her.'

'Whoa, hang on.' He came and sat beside me, dislodging the shoebox, which slid off the bed and scattered its contents on the floor. 'Let's take a minute to think this through.' He reached for my hand. 'You've had a shock,' he said with a worried smile. 'Christ, even I can't take it in.'

'It's more of a nice surprise than a shock.' I pulled away from him, poking around my feelings. It was as if a switch had been flicked inside me, lights going on. I wanted to bounce on the bed, to run up and down, to rush off and find her immediately. 'It's a *wonderful* surprise.'

'Aren't you angry with your mum?' He picked up the letter and squinted at the tiny script. 'This writing's awful.'

'Maybe she didn't want to hurt me and Dad,' I said, chewing my thumbnail – a childhood habit I couldn't shake. 'Or buried the memories so deep she kind of forgot.'

18

'Forgot?' Greg pulled a face. 'Would you forget if you'd given Maisie away?'

'It sounds awful when you put it like that,' I said, suppressing a flutter of anxiety.

'Why do you think she did it?'

'I don't know, Greg.' There would be plenty of time to consider why Mum had hidden something so important – so life-changing. Right now, all I could think about was how I'd longed for a sibling growing up, and now it appeared I had one; half-sister or not, we shared a mother. We had her blood running through our veins. 'Oh, Greg, this is the best news I've had in ages.' Unable to sit still any longer, I skirted the mess on the floor and dashed to the window, my heart beating too fast. 'Maisie has an auntie,' I said, watching my daughter circling the lawn, her arms stretched out to the sides. Charlie was chasing her, his pink tongue lolling out, while Dad watched, hands dug deep in his corduroy trouser pockets. Seeming to sense my gaze, he turned and raised his arm in a wave.

'I need to talk to Dad,' I said, with a rising sense of urgency. 'Now.'

'Ella, wait.' Greg's hands circled my upper arms. 'You're getting ahead of yourself,' he said. 'Your dad's still grieving, and there's a lot we don't know. There'll be hoops to jump through before you can think of finding this … finding her.'

'Colleen,' I said, already possessive of her name, liking the feel of it on my tongue. *My sister, Colleen.*

'She might not be called that anymore.' He turned me to face him, sounding more like his assured self now that the shock was wearing off. 'Most adoptive parents give the child a new name.'

'I didn't think of that.' I felt a sagging inside. 'There must be a record somewhere, of the adoption.'

Greg hesitated. 'Yes … if it was done formally,' he said, sliding his hands down my arms and wrapping his fingers around mine. 'The truth is, Ella, we don't know what happened back then. It could have been a casual arrangement, or money might have changed hands.'

'Oh, don't say that.' I wrenched away from him. Squatting down, I began rifling through the items on the carpet. 'There might be something else here.'

There was a tortoiseshell hair slide, a train ticket, a theatre programme, a pressed rose – its crispy petals the colour of blood – but apart from the wristband, photograph and letter, there was nothing else linking Mum to the baby.

I read the letter again, my eyes sliding over the words, and turned it over as if there might be some new ones on the other side. 'I could write to this address,' I said, looking up at Greg. 'Explain who I am.'

'They've probably moved by now. That letter was written years ago, and they might not want to be found.' He knelt beside me, a dark stain on his jeans where the coffee he'd brought me had spilled. 'She might not even be alive, Ella.' His voice was sombre and I felt a pinch of hatred at him for spoiling things.

'You've got a sister and a brother,' I said. 'You've no idea about being an only child.'

'Hey, steady on.' He held up his palms. 'You've always gone on about what a happy childhood you had. Don't start twisting things.'

'But I still used to wish I had a big sister.' I wanted him to throw caution to the wind, to be excited for me, instead of the voice of reason. 'I just want to try and find her, that's all.'

'I *will* help, of course I will.' He plucked the letter from my hand, his gaze unbearably gentle. 'But maybe we should sleep on it first.'

'I'm not going to change my mind,' I said, my brain tingling with questions. Did she look like me, or Mum? Or her father, Reagan? Was she happy; married with children? Tall or short? Outgoing or quiet?

I leaned against the bed and hugged my knees. 'This kind

of makes up for losing Mum.' I felt a wobble in the pit of my stomach as I said it.

Greg's eyebrows lifted. 'You think you're owed a sister to make up for losing your mother?'

'Why not?' I countered. 'There's a kind of balance, don't you think?'

He exhaled, seeming lost for words. 'I think you've had a shock.' He rose and dusted his hands on his jeans. 'I'll go and make some more coffee while you finish up here.' He touched my hair. 'We'll talk again at home.'

I sat for a while when he'd gone, listening to him moving in the kitchen below, calling something to Dad through the window, and I heard the low rumble of Dad's response. Greg was right, this wasn't something to be rushed into, but nearly thirty years had gone by without me knowing my sister and I couldn't bear to waste another minute.

I tried to locate some outrage – some horror even – but the truth was, I felt elated. Feelings that had been lying dormant since Mum's funeral were flowing back to life. I could feel the blood fizzing through my veins, like champagne. I wanted to know … *everything*.

Scrambling up, I rummaged past the detritus on the bed for my bag and yanked out my phone. After switching it on, I drummed my fingers while it connected to the inefficient Wi-Fi, then signed in to my Facebook account.

I tapped in *Colleen Brody Ireland* knowing it was silly – pointless, in fact. It was an Irish name, there were bound to be hundreds and I remembered Greg's comment about her maybe having a different name altogether.

A whole list of Colleens sprang up and my breathing grew shallow as I scrolled through them, hands shaking. There was a learning consultant, a teacher, an artist and a lifeguard. One was even a man, and several of them were too old. A couple had no identity at all – no photos, no details, just a blank avatar.

I mainly used social media for keeping up with old friends and for networking in my job as a food photographer, but I hadn't posted anything for a while. My profile picture was a professional shot that deepened my eyes to a smoky grey and made the most of my cheekbones. My hair looked sleek and shiny and my smile mysterious; not like my usual sunny self – 'sunny' being the word most often used to describe me.

I wondered what Colleen did for a living. The possibilities seemed endless.

Reluctant to log off, I scrolled up and down the list again more slowly, examining each face. One in particular leapt out. I hadn't looked properly the first time, but now I felt a flash of recognition. *It's her.*

She was gazing directly at the camera with a serious expression, and something about her reminded me of Mum – the same long straight nose and curve of her upper lip. Her hair was the same pale honey-blonde shade as mine, but wavy where mine was straight. She looked about the right age too and although it could have been an old photo, I felt a deep connection in the pit of my stomach that was almost chemical.

This is my sister.

My fingers felt fat and clumsy as I tried to access her page, but it was set to private.

Downstairs, Maisie was calling. 'Mummy, Mummy, I want you!'

'Coming, darling!' I was rigid with excitement and couldn't stop looking at the picture, searching for clues to her personality. Who had taken the picture? A husband, a relative, or had she taken it herself?

I clicked on the message box and quickly typed: *You don't know me, but I need to talk to you. I think we might be related.* I hesitated. What if she didn't know she was adopted? It might come as a massive shock for her and her family. I didn't want to be responsible for dropping such a bombshell, but what else could I do?

Go through the proper channels, I imagined Greg saying.

'Mummeeee!' Footsteps pattered up the stairs.

'Won't be a minute!' I chewed my knuckle then typed *Please, please reply to this. I have reason to believe you're my sister.* Oh God, what if it was the wrong Colleen?

But somehow, I knew that it wasn't.

I pressed Send, and was almost sent flying as Maisie charged in and flung herself at me.

'Mummy, I missed you,' she said, winding her arms around my neck as I fell back and I held her close, breathing in her smell of sunshine and innocence, wondering for the first time how Mum could have given up a child, whatever the circumstances.

'I missed you too,' I said, nuzzling her neck until she giggled, quelling a surge of apprehension when Greg appeared with more coffee. He wouldn't approve of what I'd done. The thought of keeping something from him was a new one and not entirely unpleasant.

'Still not finished?' he said, eyeing the clothes-strewn room.

I settled for widening my eyes in a way that made him smile.

'Don't worry, I'll give you a hand,' he said, ruffling Maisie's hair. It was almost as if our previous conversation hadn't happened. 'We'll be finished in an hour.'

'Grandpa's making a peanut butter sambich,' Maisie said, leaping up and throwing herself at her grandfather as he appeared in the doorway.

'It's ready,' he said, smiling thinly as she let go of his legs and ran along the landing. He looked tired, deep lines bracketing his mouth. 'I don't know where she gets her energy.'

'From Greg,' I said lightly, as he put the coffee on the bedside table.

Dad avoided looking at the paraphernalia on the bed and floor and it hit me afresh how sad it was that he wanted to get rid of Mum's things. He'd loved her so deeply, almost painfully. I'd sometimes felt left out when I was younger. Though he'd been affectionate enough with me, Mum had been his world in the same way I'd been hers.

'What's that?' he said, spotting the open shoebox.

I caught Greg's horrified stare and looked away.

'Just some of Mum's bits and bobs,' I improvised, smiling. 'Hair slides and … jewellery – costume stuff, not the nice bits.' I snatched up the lid and placed it back on the box. My heart was banging my chest hard enough to leap out. 'Nothing important.'

His gaze landed on the letter, which I'd forgotten to put back. 'That's mine,' I said, slipping it in my bag.

He was clutching the doorframe, the tendons in his hands standing out, but he didn't respond.

'Let's get that sandwich,' Greg said, moving onto the landing and scooping Maisie up as she passed.

'What's wrong, Dad?' I said, when they'd gone downstairs.

'Why do you keep asking me that?' The edge in his voice made me flinch. Mum's death had roughened his boundaries. He never used to speak to me like that. He glanced at my phone, where my Facebook page was displayed, and I had to resist the urge to switch it off.

'I was just checking my messages.'

He hesitated. 'I'm going out for a bit. Lock up when you leave, Ellie.' He spoke more gently, reverting to my childhood name. 'Thanks for doing this, I know it can't be easy.'

'It's OK,' I said, but we both knew it wasn't.

I sat on the edge of the bed when he'd gone, sipping my luke-warm coffee, feeling adrift in the sea of my mother's belongings.

Slowly, the elation I'd felt ebbed away and I had the feeling my life was about to slide out of control.

Chapter 4

Colleen

I woke, my nose pressed against the wall as though I was trapped in a box, the smell of damp invading my nostrils.

'Christ,' I groaned, yanking myself away, coughing as I dragged myself to a sitting position on the single bed.

An empty vodka bottle lay on the floor, and my head felt as if it had been kicked several times.

You're useless, Colleen. Can you really not survive without Jake?

It was raining again, and almost dark outside. I'd wasted a whole day when I should have been searching for my father.

I climbed from the bed and lurched into the bathroom. The state of it told me I'd be cleaner if I didn't wash, but still I turned on the tap, which shuddered and spluttered before a burst of clear water shot out. I splashed my face and cleaned my teeth with my finger, studying the strange person staring back at me from the grimy, rust-tinged mirror.

It's you, Colleen. Look at the state of you.

I ripped my gaze away from my reflection, pulled up my T-shirt and squirted my armpits with deodorant. That was as fresh as I was going to get.

Back in the bedroom, I pulled on my jeans and dropped onto the edge of the bed, my headache receding to a dull throb. After a few moments, I dug into my rucksack for Reagan's – my father's – email address and my phone. But it was no good. I felt trapped in this dive. I needed to get out, needed headspace. I grabbed my jacket and left the room.

The narrow communal staircase smelt of sweat, pee and stale cigarettes, a long way from my perfect house in Waterford, with its airy rooms and minimalist furnishings chosen by Jake to showcase his good taste, kept pristine by my constant cleaning.

Am I doing the right thing? Was living with Jake so awful? At least there, I'd had everything I needed.

The landlord – a man in his sixties – was sorting through some mail by the front door. When I'd booked in that morning, he barely met my eyes – had about as much charisma as a cockroach – but now he turned, ogling me as he rubbed his bristly chin, the smell of whisky oozing from his pores.

'Evening, gorgeous,' he said, and dried his wet lips on the back of his hand. 'Where are you off to, all dressed up like a stick of liquorice?'

I didn't answer, just hurried out through the door, letting it slam behind me.

The rain hit my face, sharp and stinging, as I headed down the road, huddled into my hoodie, glancing back every few moments. And despite feeling better for getting out of the dingy room, I still couldn't shake the feeling that Jake was following me. That Celia had let it slip that I was heading for Sligo, and he was here hiding somewhere in the shadows.

I found a quiet café on a quiet back street lined with terraced houses, and once inside, ordered a black coffee, sat in the corner, and opened up my phone.

It took a while to set up an email address. I'd never had one of my own, had shared an account with Jake. My words were his words, he told me once. I knew he read my emails anyway, so I rarely sent any.

I hadn't planned what I would say to Reagan. Should I call him Da? Father? Dad? Reagan? Should I begin with, 'I'm the daughter you abandoned'?

I imagined over and over his reaction when he realised who the email was from. I dreamed he would lean back in his chair and say, 'Thank God she's found me. Thank God I've found my Colleen. Now I can be a proper father to her.' But deep down, I knew he could have found me any time, if he'd wanted to.

'Awful day, isn't it?' An Eastern European voice interrupted my thoughts, making me jump. I turned to see a man in his late twenties, dark hair pushed back from a pale, serious face, hands stuffed in his jean pockets. He sat down at the table next to me, despite the café being almost empty, and I wanted to tell him to piss off. The words were so close I could taste them.

I turned and caught his gaze, and Jake's ice-blue eyes and disapproving stare seemed to superimpose over his face. I looked away quickly, a clammy, suffocating feeling making me shudder. It was too hot in the café. I should leave – get out of here.

'You're being ridiculous,' I told myself, and inhaled deeply. Fingers trembling on the screen, I created an email account. I pulled out Reagan's email address and keyed it in, and then leaving the subject box empty, began typing.

I'm not even sure where to begin. My name is Colleen, and your sister Celia told me I'm your daughter. I was hoping we might meet. I have so much I want to tell you – so much I need to ask you. I'm in Sligo now.

I pressed Send before I could change my mind, imagining him sitting at a huge wooden desk, a golden retriever at his feet, opening my message immediately and drafting a reply.

I waited and waited, killing time on YouTube – something I'd

27

often done on my phone if I couldn't sleep, my earphones pressed in so Jake couldn't hear.

Bored of waiting for a reply, I clicked on Facebook and signed in to the lonely profile I set up the night after Celia's confession, thinking if I used Reagan's surname, he might find me. But he hadn't. Not that it mattered now.

'You've got message,' the Eastern European said, leaning over my shoulder and pointing at my phone screen, his cheap aftershave too strong.

I turned and glared. 'Please leave me alone.'

He lifted his palms and looked away. 'I was trying to help. You people, you do not check other folder, that is all.'

'I don't need your help,' I said. *I don't need anybody but Reagan.*

I turned back to the screen and clicked on the message he'd pointed out. It was from someone called Ella Matthews. I didn't recognise the name, but clicked on her profile. She was about my age, maybe younger, and the photo looked like something from a magazine. She was pretty and her pale face held a broad smile, but she seemed slightly closed off. There was a sprinkling of freckles across her nose, a bit like mine, and her hair draped round her shoulders, fair, straight and shiny. Mine had a natural kink, though Jake had always liked me to straighten it. I'd barely got enough to straighten now. *He wouldn't like that.*

Ella Matthews' cover photo was a cluster of raspberries on a white oblong plate, alongside a slab of blue cheese, and some nuts. *Bizarre.* I opened her message and read:

You don't know me, but I need to talk to you. I think we might be related. Please, please reply to this. I have reason to believe you're my sister.

I read it again. She had to be kidding me. Christ, I didn't need this kind of spam. Yet something about her words – about her – stirred my curiosity, and I was aware my pulse was racing. I was being foolish. She'd probably mistaken me for someone else.

And whatever the reason, I was in Sligo to find my father, and couldn't afford to get distracted. I had to stay focused.

With agitated fingers, I flicked back to my email account, and felt my stomach roll over. Reagan had replied.

'Thank all the saints,' I said, too loudly, my eyes scanning the large font.

Colleen, I'm in New York at the moment, but I would very much like to meet you. I'll be back in Ireland soon and will be in touch.

I clasped my chest, tears filling my eyes as I began typing again, my fingers stumbling over the keyboard.

That would be grand. I can't wait to see you. x

Adrenalin rushed through my body as I waited for his reply, but when it didn't come my euphoria dimmed to confused impatience. Maybe I was expecting too much, too soon.

I returned to Facebook to close it down, but something made me read the message from Ella Matthews again, and I felt an urge to respond – to find out what game this woman was playing. Maybe, while I waited to reunite with my father, I'd play a few of my own.

I'm intrigued. Why would you think I'm your sister?

Chapter 5

Ella

'Sure you're OK?' asked Greg, when we'd finished loading the boot of the car and wrestled a tired and tearful Maisie into her car seat. She wanted to play with Charlie, but he'd grown tired of her constantly grabbing his tail and ears.

'I'm fine,' I said. For a moment my chest tightened and my breathing speeded up, but I fought the feeling back.

'What did your dad say, earlier?'

'Not much.' I handed Maisie the old, blue teddy Mum had bought for her first birthday, its once soft fur matted and faded to grey. 'He seemed weary and cross,' I said with a pang, recalling his expression in the bedroom doorway.

'No change there then.' Greg started the car engine and pulled carefully out of the drive. 'Where did he go, anyway?'

I shrugged, not wanting to dwell on Dad's mood. I'd done little else for months, and he'd made it clear I couldn't help him. Seeing Maisie clearly offered some light relief, but he seemed to struggle around me. After Mum's funeral I'd asked him if he'd like to come and stay with us, and he'd stared at me, seeming baffled.

'Why would I want to do that?' It was as though I'd suggested he start dating again right away. 'I'm perfectly capable of looking after myself.'

I hadn't argued, but made a point of driving to Buckinghamshire most weekends, to keep an eye on him.

We fell silent on the drive back to Surrey and Maisie slept, her face bathed intermittently in yellow light from passing cars as darkness fell. I watched her, parcelling up my thoughts and questions about Mum and pushing them to be back of my mind.

Back at our converted schoolhouse, I carried her indoors and up the stairs, and spent some time tucking her teddy-patterned duvet around her and clearing away her toys, before changing into a pair of fleecy pyjama bottoms and a vest top.

I was delaying the moment I would have to talk to Greg. Did I need to tell him about the message I'd sent Colleen, and spoil the mood? Despite the strangeness of the day, I'd felt closer to him than I had in ages. It had reminded me of the early days of our relationship, when we couldn't stand being apart and spent every spare moment together.

We'd met at a mutual client's in Shoreditch, where Greg was sorting out a contractual glitch, and I was photographing wedding cakes for a food magazine. After almost colliding in the corridor we kept sidestepping in the same direction in an effort to dodge each other, and in the end Greg had said with a smile that made my heart leap, 'Shall we dance?'

He'd made a decent stab at moonwalking across the shiny floor and I laughed as I hurried away. I'd just ended a relationship that was going nowhere and wasn't looking for another, but found myself recalling his smile for the rest of the day.

He invited me to dinner the following evening, having prised my details from the client, and we talked and laughed until the restaurant closed, both aware of a simmering chemistry between us. He didn't play games. He called when he said he would, making it clear that I mattered. Two years later, we married in my local church and had been happy to spend as much time as possible in each other's company – until lately.

I'd put the growing distance between us down to work and becoming parents, but there were other reasons too, which I didn't want to examine too closely.

'She's worn out,' Greg said through a yawn as I came downstairs. He was on the sofa, hands laced behind his head, feet up on the coffee table. I thought he'd be worrying about work, busily checking his emails, but he seemed content to be home. 'I bet she sleeps through the night.'

'You know I don't mind her getting into our bed.'

Maisie had dislodged the armchair cushions during a bouncing session that morning, and I fidgeted them back into place before crossing to the window. I twitched aside the curtain, but it was too dark to see the garden I'd fallen in love with the first time we viewed the house.

'It'll be lovely out there in summer,' I'd said, visions of lazy, sunshiny days, the baby playing on a blanket on the lawn, floating through my mind.

'And a nightmare to maintain,' Greg had responded with a grin, but I could tell he loved the house too. It was huge compared to the cramped London flat we'd shared for the last two years. The previous owners had restored and extended the house before moving abroad. 'It'll be an easy commute to work,' he'd added, a glint in his eyes.

We moved in three months later.

'Come and talk to me,' Greg said now and I turned to see him patting the sofa. He often asked me to stop moving for five minutes, but sitting still was something that didn't come easily. If I stayed still, things I didn't want to think about seeped into my head.

The TV screen was blank and I was tempted to switch it on to deflect his attention. 'It's been quite a day,' he added, clearly in the mood for my company.

A strange, panicky sensation rose in my ribcage. I moved to sit beside him and he drew me into a hug. He smelt warm and musky, and looked handsome in the khaki T-shirt that complemented his tan. He nuzzled my ear, and when I looked up there was no mistaking the desire in his long-lashed eyes.

I immediately pulled away and sprang to my feet. 'I think I'll get Mum's things in from the car, ready for the attic.'

Greg's smile slipped. 'It's a bit late,' he said, not quite masking his disappointment.

'It's only nine o'clock.' I glanced about for the car keys, even though I knew they were in the blue bowl on the table in the hallway. 'I can't bear to leave it all out there.'

'You don't have to.' A crease appeared between his eyebrows. 'I do understand, Ella.'

'I know you do.' My eyes flew to my bag on the floor. Would she have replied yet?

'What's going on?' Greg sat forward, resting his elbows on his knees, and gave me the mock-stern look that used to make me smile.

'I think I've found Colleen,' I blurted out, knowing there was no point not telling him.

I dived for my bag and retrieved my phone, the excitement from earlier pounding back as I fumbled to get the screen up.

Greg rose. 'How is that even possible?'

'Facebook,' I said. I pulled out a chair and sat at the dining table. Its polished surface was smudged with Maisie's fingerprints, but for once I didn't care enough to reach for a cloth to clean it. 'Look.' I showed him the page in a way that reminded me of Maisie, brandishing her paintings for approval. 'It's definitely her.'

Greg leaned across me, examining her profile, his expression tight with concentration. 'She does look a bit like your mum,' he admitted. 'The hair colour, and something about the shape of her mouth.'

'Told you.' My face split into a grin.

'I think you might be right,' he said, sounding dazed, and the fact that he agreed with me was a shock – as though I hadn't quite believed it before. Turning back to the screen, he narrowed his eyes. 'She looks a bit like you too, with the freckles. Very attractive.' A feeling rose inside me and fizzled out before I could name it. 'Though, the camera could be lying,' he continued. 'She might have a squint, or a moustache, or be unnaturally short.'

'Greg,' I scolded, nudging his arm with my shoulder. 'Look, she still lives in Ireland.' I jabbed the screen. 'I could go there,' I said. 'We could all go, have a holiday. We haven't been away for ages. Or, she could come here. On her own at first, so we can get to know each other, and then she could come with her family, if she has one, and—'

'Ella, for God's sake!' Half laughing, Greg pulled up a chair and sat down, his eyes still fixed to the photo of Colleen. 'You're getting carried away,' he said. 'You haven't even spoken to her yet.'

'I sent her a message.'

'What?' His head whipped round.

'Just asking her to contact me,' I said, quickly. 'That I had reason to believe she was my sister.'

'Oh, Ella.' He sat back, rubbing a hand over his face. 'That's a bit strong.'

'I know, I know. I got carried away.' I glanced at the screen again, hoping she'd replied, knowing it was too soon. She might not go online much, for all I knew. 'I didn't know how else to put it.'

Greg puffed out his cheeks and exhaled. 'I suppose all you can do is wait,' he said.

'What if she doesn't reply?' It was both unthinkable that she wouldn't, and a distinct possibility that made me feel a little nauseous.

'To be honest, it might be for the best,' he said. 'It was a bit reckless, rushing in like that, without thinking it through.' He spoke in the tone I'd heard him use on the phone to clients, and

I felt a pang that he wasn't being more supportive. 'Now, what about some dinner?'

Greg ordered in a Chinese, and afterwards I brought in some bags from the car and dumped them in the hall. Every five minutes, I checked Facebook, but still there was no response.

It wasn't until the following day, after breakfast, while Greg was transferring Mum's things to the attic and Maisie was trying to coax in the cat from next door, that I logged on and noticed a message in a folder I didn't usually check.

My stomach tipped. 'She's replied!' I shouted, running into the hall and back again. I stared at the screen, chewing my thumbnail.

Greg appeared, in ancient tracksuit bottoms, pushing his hair off his forehead. 'You'd better read it then,' he said.

The realisation that reading the message would change *everything* punched a shot of adrenalin into my system. Leaning forward, I tapped the screen. There were only two sentences.

I'm intrigued. Why would you think I'm your sister?

Ignoring Greg's plea to think before I replied, and Maisie's demand for milk for the cat, my fingers danced over the keys, almost of their own volition.

I was going through my mother's things and found a photo of her holding a baby, and a wristband with your name and a date of birth. There was a letter too, with an Irish address for someone called Celia, from a man called Reagan. I think he must be your father. My mother – our mother – was called Anna Davis. Her maiden name was Harrison. I added several phone numbers she could reach me on. *I'd love to talk to you.*

I sent it before I could change my mind, feeling breathless, as though I'd been running. I turned to look at Greg. He was holding Maisie, staring at me as if a stranger had wandered in, and I snatched up my jacket and said, 'Who wants to go to the park?'

Chapter 6

Colleen

Sunday

The August sky had cleared of dark clouds, and the sun was out, making me feel woozy as I trawled the Sligo streets, searching for a job to replenish my dwindling funds.

I was tired, and bored of seeing happy tourists breathing in the sights of the town as though they owned them. Seeing couples waltz into posh hotels, wearing big smiles and carrying expensive cases, reminded me of my old life, and I wondered what was going on behind those smiles. Were those women as desperate as I had been?

I'd given myself another massive hangover by drinking myself stupid the night before. It was for the last time, I told myself. Alcohol didn't solve anything. It never had and never would.

As I rounded a corner, Ella Matthews' message leapt into my head.

You don't know me, but I need to talk to you. I think we might

36

be related. *Please, please reply to this. I have reason to believe you're my sister.*

The word *sister* brought Bryony into my head. I pushed her out; forced myself not to think about her.

If this Ella really was another sister, how the hell would she fit into my life? Had Anna and Reagan had another daughter and kept her? I clenched my fist and punched a brick wall, scraping my knuckles. *How could they?*

As I examined the damage to my hand, the green door of the pub I'd found myself next to opened and a bloke stumbled onto the pavement, stinking of beer.

'Cheer up, it may never happen,' he said, giving me a toothless grin.

'It already has,' I said. 'Not that it's any of your bloody business.'

He stopped and stared. His eyes were kind, and with a hint of sadness in his voice he said, 'Life can get better, love.'

I raked around for an abusive retort but no words came, and as he went on his way, tears burned my eyelids.

I took a deep breath, my mind back on Ella Matthews. *My sister?* I bit the inside of my mouth and tasted blood. I had no reason to think her message was anything more than mistaken identity, and part of me regretted my stupid reply.

I looked about me. A rainbow stretched over the river in the distance, which reflected the pale blue sky. It was beautiful here.

I turned back to the pub, and was about to walk on when my eyes fell on a notice on the window: *Bar Staff Wanted.* I stepped towards the door, Celia's soft voice nagging in my head. 'Keep away from sin, Colleen.' *She should have practised what she preached.*

Up to the age of five, I'd lived with Celia in a big house in a pleasant tree-lined suburb in Cork. We'd never gone short of anything. My father, or the man I thought was my father, was a kind, well-spoken Englishman, who left early every morning in his grey pinstriped suit, for work in the city. As an adult, I'd never been able to visualise his face, only his dark, neatly cut hair

37

and that pinstriped suit. Celia was attractive back then, small and slim, with hair the colour of chestnuts.

'Bye, little one,' the man I called Da would say to me as he left each day, kissing my forehead.

'Bye, Da,' I'd say, wrapping my arms around his legs.

When I was five, Terry came to our house to do some odd jobs. He'd arrive when the man I called Da wasn't there, and ruffle my hair with his big, rough hand. With a wink he'd say, 'How are you, cutie-pie?'

I would laugh and reply, 'I'm OK, muscle man.' I'd heard Celia call him that.

He would always leave before the man I called Da returned.

When I was six, Celia and I moved to Waterford with Terry, and I never saw the man I'd called Da again.

Terry stopped calling me cutie-pie, no longer ruffling my hair and winking, and I stopped calling him muscle man. I resented how much Celia seemed to love him, but at least he'd made her happy – for a while.

I opened the pub door, sucked in a breath and entered. The smell of ale and remnants of a Sunday roast hit me in a wave. Several punters sat at the bar on stools and others around wooden tables. Nobody looked up. A blackboard on the rough brick wall advertised food: sausage and mash, steak and ale pie, fish and chips. Nothing classy. A folk band called The Fox Trotters played there every Friday.

A woman in her fifties with a mass of red hair and a garishly made-up face, smiled from behind the counter as I approached. 'What can I get you?'

I pointed to the window. 'You've advertised for staff.'

She nodded and smiled again. She had lipstick on her teeth. 'Have you worked in a pub before?'

'Yes,' I said. It wasn't a lie. I'd worked behind a bar when I was seventeen. I'd lied about my age back then. They never questioned me and paid cash in hand.

'It's every evening from seven until eleven,' the woman said, her hand on her hip as she looked me up and down. 'We're pretty desperate. When can you start?'

I shrugged. 'Whenever you need me.'

'Tomorrow?'

I nodded. 'Sure.'

'I'll just need your details and a couple of references.'

My insides froze, but I managed a casual shrug. 'I can give you my details. But it's been a while since I worked.'

'I'm sorry,' she said, shaking her head so her hair bounced. 'We really do need references. I took the last one on trust, and had to sack him for having his hand in the till.'

Tears of frustration flooded my eyes. 'But I need this job.'

Looking concerned, the woman came out from behind the bar. 'Are you OK?' She put her solid arm around my shoulders. I wanted to shake it off, but knew she was just being kind. 'Alfie,' she called to a man at the other end of the bar.

He turned and smiled. 'Yes, Sandra, my darling?' He looked to be in his thirties, with sandy hair curling over the collar of his polo shirt.

'Can you take charge for a bit, love?'

He came over. 'Anything for you, Sandra.' He had an open face; direct blue eyes behind geeky, dark-rimmed glasses, and a relaxed, confident expression. 'You're the boss.'

Sandra ushered me to a tiny office at the back of the pub and gestured for me to sit down on a black swivel chair.

'So, what's your name, love?' she said.

'Colleen. But I'm fine, honestly,' I said, drying my eyes with my hand. 'I really need a job.'

'Well, Colleen,' she said, handing me a tissue from a box on the cluttered table. 'I'm Sandra, as you've probably gathered.' She took my hand, running her fingers over my knuckles, which were grazed and bloody from where I'd hit the wall. 'Why not tell your Auntie Sandra who you're running from?'

I wrestled with whether or not to tell her the truth. 'My husband, Jake,' I said, making myself look into her pale grey eyes, with their lavishly shadowed lids. 'He abuses me, uses me as a punchbag.' I looked down at my hands. 'I just want to make a fresh start, that's all.'

I looked up to see Alfie in the doorway, holding a checked tea towel. 'The pump needs changing,' he said, and smiled at me with friendly interest.

'It'll have to wait.' Sandra shooed him away with a flick of her hand, and once he'd gone, pinned me down with a direct gaze. 'I'll give you a new start,' she said at last. 'But first, I'll get you a nice cup of tea.'

The warming tea, and Sandra's kindness, made me feel a bit better and I was glad she didn't press for more information, content to give me a rundown of what my job would entail.

As we headed back into the bar, which thronged with evening drinkers jostling for attention, I allowed myself to believe for a moment that everything would be OK.

'Be here at ten to seven tomorrow.' Sandra resumed her place behind the bar, and I nodded and made to leave. 'Wait, love,' she added, producing a notebook and a pen. 'Jot down where you're staying, and your mobile number, in case we need to get hold of you.'

She thrust the pad towards me, and I felt suddenly uneasy about giving out my contact details. Sandra's gaze sharpened as I hesitated, so I picked up the pen and wrote my address and mobile number, and handed her the notepad, which she placed by the till. 'Thanks, love.'

On my way back to the bedsit, I detoured into the internet café, hoping my father had sent another email. He hadn't. But there was another Facebook message from Ella Matthews:

I was going through my mother's things and found a photo of her holding a baby, and a wristband with your name and a date of birth. There was a letter too, with an Irish address for someone called Celia, from a man called Reagan. I think he must be your father. My mother – our mother – was called Anna Davis. Her maiden name was Harrison.

My pulse began to throb as I read it again, then a third time. Suddenly there was no doubt in my mind.

I had a sister, and she wanted to find me.

Chapter 7

Ella

Monday

It was a soft and balmy morning with a promise of summer. As I rubbed Maisie's fingerprints from the patio doors, as quickly as she added more, I found myself thinking of Colleen again, picturing her reaction to my message and willing her to reply. I'd almost expected her to phone right away, but Greg pointed out she could be accessing her Facebook account from anywhere in the world.

'She might be in Australia,' he'd said, and I had to convince him I wouldn't do anything rash and would put it out of my mind – as if I could.

Now, he paused in the doorway on his way to work, looking smooth in a navy linen jacket, cream shirt and dark trousers, his hair swept neatly back. 'It's amazing, really,' he said, rubbing his clean-shaven chin. 'To think you've had a half-sister all this time.'

I couldn't quite work out his tone. 'Sister,' I said automatically. 'And yes, it is amazing.'

'Can I have a sister?' Maisie piped up.

I put down my cloth and swung her into my arms. 'Maybe, one day.' I didn't look at Greg as I spoke. He'd wanted another baby straight away, but I'd been keen to pick up the threads of my career and return some order to my life, which had felt upended after Mum's ovarian cancer diagnosis.

Once Greg had left for work – much later than usual – and I'd dropped Maisie at the nursery at the end of our road, I headed to Battersea, where my agent had booked me to photograph a new restaurant called Fresh, for an upmarket food magazine.

I arrived in record time and parked round the back. The two-storey building overlooked the dock, where sunlight sparkled off the water. The exterior looked industrial, but inside was charmingly rustic, and the owners were young and enthusiastic.

The food stylist was already there along with a young lighting assistant I hadn't met before, called Ben. After introductions, and a chat with the clients over coffee, we ran through the shooting order.

While the chef prepped some dishes from the menu, I set up my camera and took a few shots of the interior, making the most of the natural light pouring through the metal-framed windows. The familiar routine was soothing and Ben, who had a hipster beard and highlighted quiff, was touchingly eager to learn, noting my every move.

'How did you become a food photographer?'

'I've always loved taking pictures,' I said, and explained how I'd won a photography competition at school aged fourteen, and after getting a degree had headed to London to work as a photographer's assistant.

'One of the jobs was a recipe book by a television chef and I got to eat all the food afterwards.' I smiled, remembering. 'It kind of snowballed from there,' I went on. 'I signed with an agent soon after and here I am.' I didn't add that photographing

43

food had never been my intention; that I'd planned to specialise in portraits, or even landscapes – the sort of pictures Mum had loved to paint – but I'd somehow got stuck and lost the drive to change things.

'Cool.' Ben's brown eyes were wide and admiring. 'You make it sound easy.'

'The business was less competitive then,' I warned him.

'I want to work in films, eventually.'

They all wanted to work in films, eventually. I wished him luck, my mind drifting back to Colleen, trying to guess what she did for a living and whether we shared any traits. Perhaps she was creative, like Mum. I'd wanted to be an artist too, but that particular gene had passed me by. My attempts at school had been laughably bad, yet through a lens I could capture a scene the way Mum had done with a paintbrush.

Maybe Colleen was my polar opposite – practical, or sporty.

I grew impatient, longing for the shoot to be over so I could check for messages. As soon as there was a natural break, I grabbed my bag and headed outside. Ben looked as if he might follow, so I pulled out my phone and pressed it to my ear as I sat at one of the mosaic-topped tables by the water.

The sun had strengthened and I pulled up the sleeves of my fine-knit jumper, enjoying the warmth on my arms. With almost unbearable anticipation, I checked my phone for missed calls or messages. *Nothing*. No response on Facebook either.

I let out a breath. I'd probably frightened her off with my last message. Maybe the shock had been too great. Or, I needed something stronger to convince her we were related.

I rifled through my bag for the letter from Mum's shoebox that I'd slipped inside, thinking I could scan or photograph it as proof. It wasn't there. I emptied my bag on the table and sifted through the contents: my phone, a pink frilly sock of Maisie's, a memory stick, one of Greg's cufflinks and the usual mix of lip gloss, diary, tissues, hand cream.

I checked all the pockets, but they were empty, apart from some old cinema tickets.

My heart stalled.

Perhaps the letter had slipped out and Dad had found it.

I picked up my phone and called his number. It rang for a long time and I wondered what he was doing. After years as a lecturer, shrouded in academia, how on earth did he fill his time?

I was about to ring off when he answered.

'Hi, Dad.'

'Ella.' He sounded irritated. 'What is it?'

He'd never been great on the phone. Whenever I called home, after moving to London, he would quickly pass the handset to Mum, once he'd established I was fine.

'I just wondered how you were.'

Was that a sigh?

'I'm the same as I was on Saturday, Ella, and I expect I'll be the same tomorrow.'

What did that mean? I nibbled my thumbnail. Was he clinically depressed? He'd been given a leaflet about bereavement after Mum died and was offered counselling, but it hadn't gone down well.

'As if talking endlessly about my feelings is going to bring her back,' he'd stormed, tearing up the leaflet and throwing it in the fire.

'I was wondering if you found my letter,' I said, deciding to plunge right in and get it over with. 'I can't find it in my bag.'

'Letter?' His voice had a suspicious edge and I wished I hadn't mentioned it. He might decide to look for it now. 'What letter?'

'It's OK, I just found it,' I lied, forcing a laugh. 'It was in my camera bag.'

'What's so important about it?'

'It was an appointment, that's all.' I felt my face burn. 'Dentist. I might need a filling.'

When he didn't reply, I pictured him in his armchair, where he used to take up residence after work in the evenings. But instead of a small glass of brandy, and his and Mum's favourite opera playing softly, he'd have a cup of black coffee and a newspaper on his lap, folded open at the crossword, which he would start but never complete. I had no idea how to reach him. 'Dad,' I began. 'Did Mum …?'

'Did she what?'

I knew I couldn't ask him about the shoebox. 'Did she ever express a wish about what to do with her stuff?'

'Why are you asking me?' He sounded disappointed, as if he'd hoped I was done with it. 'Her sister will want some – you know what she's like.'

I suddenly wondered if Aunt Tess had known about Colleen, but dismissed the thought straight away. Tess was great fun, but loved to gossip. She would never have kept such a big secret. 'I've put most of it in the attic.'

'I don't care what you do with it,' Dad said. 'I found some of her old paintings in the shed, ones she never showed. You can take those too, if you like.'

I suppressed a surge of annoyance, reminding myself he couldn't help his attitude and that grief took many forms. 'Fine.' I glanced at my watch. 'I'd better go, Dad, I'm working.'

'Bye,' he said and hung up.

I stared at my phone, my insides churning. I suddenly, desperately, wanted my old life back. The one with Mum in it, her soft eyes smiling, and a husband who supported me, no matter what. The one where I didn't know I had a sister.

A barge glided by, laughter trailing in its wake, and I recalled a boating holiday with Mum and Dad when I was ten. Would it have been more fun if I'd had a sister? My childhood would have been so different with a playmate and confidante.

'Tess and I used to fight like cat and dog,' I remembered Mum telling me once, when I demanded a sibling. 'There's no guarantee you'd get on.' Had she been reassuring me, or herself? I knew it was pointless speculating, but now I'd started, I couldn't seem to stop.

46

'The food's ready,' said a voice behind me. It was the client, her face pink and shiny, eyes bright with purpose. Gathering my things, I pasted on a smile and followed her in.

I'd just finished photographing a plate of rose-pink lamb with polenta and spinach, and a dainty bowl of seafood, when a beep from my bag alerted me to a text.

'I'd better get that,' I said, to no one in particular. 'It might be the nursery.'

Stepping over to the window, my pulse gave a little leap when I saw the message was from Greg. *I know you're working but wanted to let you know, I've found out where Colleen lives.*

Chapter 8

Colleen

I'd refused to let Ella's message sink in the night before. Instead, I'd bought another bottle of vodka to numb all the feelings I didn't want to deal with.

Now, curled under my grubby duvet in the middle of the afternoon, I found myself crying for the sister I had lost – my real sister. The sister I'd loved and would never see again. I didn't want another sister in my life, but there was no doubt Ella Matthews was who she said she was. She knew too much. She'd mentioned Reagan, and her mother's name was Anna.

A flood of memory surged back; long forgotten, buried under so much shite. I'd heard the name Anna years before Celia's shock revelation. I must have been about five when Celia had opened the door of our house in Cork.

'Celia,' the woman on the doorstep had said in a funny voice. She was tall, pretty, with dark curly hair.

I'd stared at her from where I was sitting in the hallway, setting out dolls and soft toys for a tea party. I remember them arguing. Celia threatening to call the Gardaí.

'Please, I just want to see her, that's all,' the woman had cried, and I scrambled to my feet, grabbing my blue teddy and hugging it to me.

'You signed her away,' Celia had screamed, before the door slammed.

The knocking that followed made me cry. I'd thought it would never stop. Celia covered her ears, her own tears sliding down her pale cheeks. She scooped me up and raced up two flights of stairs.

'Teddy!' I called, as my soft toy dropped from my hand and bounced down the steps.

I'd asked Celia who the lady was, but she said it didn't matter – that we wouldn't be seeing her again.

As the memories dissolved, I buried myself deeper in the bed, my head throbbing, my throat sore and dry. *She signed me away.*

Later, I stuck my hand out and seized my phone. It was 3 p.m. Reluctantly, I emerged from under the duvet and dragged myself up. There was a carrier bag on the floor containing cleaning fluid, a pack of cheap cloths and an uneaten egg sandwich I'd bought the night before. With a surge of determination, I grabbed the cleaning stuff and headed for the filthy bathroom. I was used to cleaning, making everything shiny, although never with a hangover.

I knelt and squirted the liquid around the bath and began rubbing it in, my mind spinning. Ella had included her mobile number. Should I ring her? Meet her? Would it mess up everything with Reagan?

I almost laughed. Jake would have hated that I'd discovered two new relatives. It had suited him, having me to himself.

I rinsed the bath, put in the plug and ran the water. It was tepid, but I needed to feel clean.

When the water was deep enough, I undressed and stepped in. Taking a deep breath, I lowered myself under the water. I could hold my breath for ages. I'd taught myself how to after Bryony died.

As I lay there, submerged in the water, I wondered, not for the first time, how it would feel to never come up again. Would it be a release?

An image of Jake swam into my head and my eyes sprang open. Someone was standing over the bath, his shape distorted by the water.

I shot up, gulping air, sending a tide of water splashing over the side.

'Jesus, get out, get the fuck out!' I screamed, recognising the landlord and covering my boobs with my arm. 'What are you doing in here?'

'I knocked,' he said, not moving, eyes at chest level.

'And did you hear me say come in?' I was still yelling as I scrambled out, reaching for my towel and wrapping it around me. 'Jesus! You could have given me a heart attack.'

He shrugged, and lowering his eyes at last, fiddled with the keys on his belt. 'Somebody's downstairs, asking for you.' He took a handkerchief from his cardigan pocket and blew his nose. 'Some bloke.'

My heart thumped. 'What does he look like?'

Before he could reply, the door opened, and Alfie from the pub stepped inside. I couldn't fathom what he was doing here. It was as though my bathroom had turned into Piccadilly Circus.

'Is everything OK?' he said. 'I was downstairs, hoping to speak to you, and heard you yelling.'

'Oh, for Christ's sake.' I tightened my towel, wishing it was longer and covered my legs. 'Why don't you call some people in off the street, so everyone can see Colleen having a bloody bath?'

The landlord tore his gaze away and left, muttering under his breath, and Alfie shrugged and followed. As he closed the bathroom door, I heard him whisper, 'Sorry.'

I got dressed and sat on the toilet seat, my head in my hands.

I was already a wreck, and now the old git downstairs had seen me naked. Could things get any worse?

*

'Hi,' Alfie said, as I came out of the bathroom. He was sitting on my bed, feet up, as though I'd invited him to stay.

I opened my mouth to ask what the hell he was doing there and tell him to piss off, but before I could say anything, he smiled and said, 'I thought you might fancy an all-day breakfast.'

'I'm not hungry.' Finding my comb, I dragged it through my short, wet hair.

'But you have to eat, don't you?' he said. 'I'm not being funny, but you look like you haven't had a decent meal in ages.'

'I eat.' I looked at the sandwich on the floor. 'Not that it's any of your business.'

'No, you're right,' he said, rising and backing towards the door, zipping up his chunky cardigan. 'Sorry. I just … well, I thought as we're going to be working together it might be nice to …' His words trailed off, and he gave an apologetic smile.

Something unfurled inside me. 'Sure, why not?' I grabbed my hoodie and disconnected my phone from where it had been charging, before shoving it in my pocket. 'I guess I do need to eat.' It would be good to know someone in Sligo besides Sandra.

'So what are you doing in this part of the world?' Alfie said, once we were seated opposite each other in a steamy café a couple of streets away. He was tucking into a fry-up, and I was pulling apart a bacon sandwich, trying to decide what to tell him. Part of me wanted to offload to this stranger with his quirky glasses and a smile that said he was a good guy, but something stopped me.

'You go first,' I said.

'OK.' He paused for a moment. 'Well, I live in Drumcliff, not far from here.'

'The final resting place of Yeats.'

'Indeed.' He lifted an eyebrow. 'You know your poets?'

'Not really,' I said, shaking my head. 'But I have been to Drumcliff before, or the outskirts, anyway.' I looked down, aware I'd said too much already. 'It was a very long time ago. I barely remember.' I took a bite of my sandwich and swallowed. 'So do you live with your wife?' I felt myself blush. I rarely blushed.

Alfie shook his head, a piece of sausage suspended on his fork. Not quite meeting my eyes, he said, 'I'm not married.'

'Do you work in the pub full time?' I tried and failed to recall the last time I'd made small talk like this with a man. A good-looking man at that. Jake would never have allowed it.

'I'm actually a freelance web designer,' Alfie said, after taking a swig of builder's strength tea. 'But being my own boss is a bit hit and miss. That's why I work at the pub.' He paused, and put down his knife and fork. Counting on his fingers, he said, 'I have one sister, two cats, a mum, a gran and a Fiat 500.'

I laughed; a sound I hadn't heard in a while. There was something reassuring about Alfie, something that made me certain I was safe in his company.

'So you're married,' he said, in a deliberately casual way.

I nodded. 'His name's Jake, we got married when I was eighteen.'

'That's very young,' he said.

I didn't want to go into all that. 'Yeah, but it's over now.'

'He sounds like a bastard, if you don't mind me saying.' Alfie's cheeks reddened. 'I couldn't help but overhear what you said to Sandra at the pub,' he admitted. 'Men should never hit women.'

'I'd rather not talk about it,' I said, pushing my plate away. I rose. 'Actually, I have to be somewhere.'

'Was it something I said?' He looked concerned. I felt bad.

'Not at all, I'm fine, Alfie, honestly.' But I was far from it. I should never have agreed to come out with him. I didn't want to lie to him, but couldn't face going into the truth. 'I'll see you later, yeah?'

'Listen, if you ever need a friendly ear, I'm here.'

I could see he meant it. 'Thanks,' I said. First Sandra, and now Alfie. I wondered if everyone in Sligo was this kind. Maybe my luck was changing.

Alfie resumed his breakfast. 'Quiz night tonight,' he called, as I opened the door to leave. 'Should be fun.'

'See you later, then.'

Back at the flat I poured what was left of the vodka into a mug, and opened my phone.

I checked to see if Reagan had replied – he hadn't – then I signed in to Facebook, my curiosity about Ella rising with every gulp. I took a deep breath and replied.

I can't believe we're sisters. That's amazing. You look stunning in your picture, by the way. We have the same freckles. Did you notice?

I paused. If I said I was in Sligo, would she come over? She obviously wanted to meet me, but I needed time to think. I was in Sligo for Reagan. Did I really need the distraction of Ella?

I'm in America at the moment, I typed. If Reagan was in America, I could be too. I glanced at my watch, as I fiddled with my necklace, wondering about the time difference. Was it the middle of the night over there? Would Ella notice?

Oh God, I wasn't thinking straight. I took another gulp of vodka, before continuing the message.

I'd love to hear more about you. I love travelling and I'm very sporty, a bit of an adrenalin junkie, to be honest. I'm always jumping out of aeroplanes. I had a happy childhood with my adoptive parents, and work as a film editor.

I laughed at my words, unsure where the lies were coming from. I'd never dreamed or wanted to be a film editor. In fact, I wasn't sure I'd ever had any dreams of my own. Was I inventing someone Ella might like and want as a sister? Someone far removed from who I really was? Or was I just playing games?

I'd love to hear more about Anna – particularly why she gave me up and kept you.

Too harsh. I deleted the last line.

I'd love to learn more about Anna, I began again. *You talk about her in the past tense.*

I smiled. I already knew her mother – our mother – was dead.

I'd love to get to know you better once I'm back. Are you married? Is he handsome? Do you have children? So many questions! I finished and found myself laughing. *Your loving sister, Colleen x*

I pressed Send.

'Are you married?' I whispered. 'Is he handsome?'

Fifteen minutes passed as I stared at my phone, an unexpected feeling of anticipation creeping over me, as I realised I wanted her to reply.

I decided to text the number she'd sent me.

This is my number, Ella. I've messaged you on Facebook, but we can text too if you like. Colleen x

Chapter 9

Ella

'How did you find out?' I asked Greg the second he came through the door that evening.

After reading his message at the restaurant I'd tried to call him, but it went straight to voicemail. I'd returned to the shoot on autopilot, my mind buzzing. The fact Greg had found an address for Colleen suddenly made her more real somehow. I could meet her, get to know her, make her part of my life, and I couldn't wait to start.

Greg hung up his jacket and dropped his laptop bag at the foot of the stairs. 'Give me a second,' he said, rather tersely. He was home earlier than usual and picked up Maisie, swinging her round until she squealed. 'What's for dinner?' he said. 'I'm starving.'

'Never mind dinner. I can't believe you've left me hanging for hours,' I said. 'Couldn't you have called me back?'

'I knew you were busy, and anyway, it wasn't something we could discuss easily over the phone.' He hoisted Maisie onto his shoulders and strode into the kitchen, pretending to look outraged when he realised the oven was cold. 'I fancied roast chicken with all the trimmings,' he said, spinning around, while Maisie shrieked and clutched at his hair.

'Ha, ha, very funny.' I grabbed a couple of ready meals from the fridge and slid them into the microwave. It was a running joke that although I photographed food for a living, I'd never quite mastered the art of cooking it.

'Now tell me,' I prodded Greg, once Maisie was settled with her colouring book and crayons, and we were sitting at the dining table with our supermarket 'finest' shepherd's pie and glasses of wine. I couldn't remember the last time we'd eaten together this early in the evening. 'Where does Colleen live?'

Greg played at sipping his wine and savouring his first mouthful of dinner. He closed his eyes and smacked his lips together.

'Greg!' He appeared to be enjoying himself a bit too much. 'Tell me, or I'll stab you with my fork.'

'Not in front of Maisie,' he said with a grin. He put down his glass and leaned closer. 'A bloke at work has got this new facial recognition app. They're normally pretty bad, bringing up all kinds of weird and wonderful people, but because the Facebook photo of Colleen was so clear, it brought up one of her with her husband at an official-looking function. He's called Jake Harper, he's a surgeon, and they live in Waterford.'

'Oh my God.' I was silent for a moment, trying to take it in. 'Where's Waterford?'

'It's a county in southeast Ireland,' he said, looking gratified at my response, and I briefly wondered whether his reluctance yesterday had been more about him wanting to take control of the situation.

'Waterford,' I repeated, feeling stunned. *I have a sister. She lives in Waterford, with her husband, Jake. My brother-in-law.*

'It looks like a nice place.' Greg finished his wine and sat forward again, helping himself to my untouched plate of food. 'Founded by the Vikings.'

I couldn't stop smiling. 'Do they have children?'

His eyebrows dipped. 'Not that I know of.'

'Do you have an exact address?'

After a moment's hesitation, he nodded, a lock of hair falling forward, giving him a rakish look. 'They're on the electoral roll.'

I slumped back in my chair. 'What did people do before the internet was invented?' I said, shaking my head. 'Mum could have found her any time, if she'd wanted.'

'Well, she clearly didn't want to.'

I couldn't think about that. I tucked Greg's words to the back of my mind and fired up my laptop. I wanted to see a picture of Waterford for myself. I wanted to see Colleen again. 'Can I look at the photo of them?'

'If you want to.' Greg joined me on the sofa, pulling Maisie onto his lap. 'He works at a hospital over there, and he's written a couple of papers, medical stuff, so his name was linked to those.' He blew a raspberry on Maisie's neck and she wriggled.

'Daddy, you stop it.' She giggled, clambering across him to grab my laptop. 'Want to see penguins,' she said, trying to swivel the screen to face her. She was obsessed with penguins, after seeing a film about them at nursery.

'Not just now, darling,' I said, wrenching the laptop out of her sticky grasp. 'Finish colouring in your lovely picture.'

'Don't want to.' She stuck her bottom lip out and folded her arms, glowering at me. 'Want penguins.' Her eyes were dark smudges in her oval face.

'Someone's tired,' I said.

'I think it might be time for a bath.' Greg gathered her against his chest. 'We can play submarines.'

She cheered up instantly. 'Yay! Sumbarines,' she said, getting the word wrong in a way that made me smile. She was so adorable. *How could Mum have given her daughter away?* I quickly banished the thought and opened my laptop as Greg and Maisie headed upstairs.

'Don't go online until we're done,' he called, as if it had just occurred to him. 'I want to be with you when you do.'

But it was too late. Instead of looking for the picture of Colleen with her husband, I logged straight in to Facebook. 'Greg, she's replied!' I shouted, and he thundered back with Maisie on his back.

'You are joking?'

'No, I'm not!' I pointed to the screen. 'Look!'

He hushed Maisie, who was protesting and pulling at his shirt as he sat beside me. 'What does she say?' he said, sounding almost cross. He had such a straightforward relationship with his own siblings that my discovery that Colleen existed must seem like a television drama.

Choosing to ignore his tone, I opened up her message, my eyes dancing over the words twice to take them in properly. 'Oh God, Greg, she sounds amazing.' A stinging behind my nose signalled tears. 'She's seems to have taken the news in her stride, even though she didn't know about me.'

'Let's have a look.' Greg leaned over, eyes scanning the message already imprinted on my brain. 'She didn't know about your mum either, by the sound of it.' I felt him glance at me. 'I knew it would be too much,' he said flatly. 'I told you to take it slowly.'

'I can't believe she's really there.' I wiped away a tear with my finger.

'Actually, she isn't,' Greg pointed out, jiggling Maisie on his lap. 'She's travelling. She's not even in the country at the moment.'

'But she'll be back soon.' I began reading bits aloud. 'She's a film editor! And she's quite sporty, always jumping out of aeroplanes.' I glanced at Greg, but couldn't read his expression, and wondered why he'd bothered to tell me he'd found her address, if he was worried about me finding her. 'She's nothing like me,' I said, feeling an odd little ache inside as my eyes were drawn back to the screen. It wasn't as if Colleen and I were twins, but I'd hoped we'd have more in common.

'You both have freckles,' Greg said, grudgingly.

I managed a smile. 'She'll be sad to hear that Mum has …
passed away.' I still couldn't bring myself to say 'dead'. 'She's bound
to want to meet her.'

'Not necessarily. Not if her adoptive parents were good people.'
Greg looked at Maisie, who'd wriggled off his lap and gone back
to her colouring, the tip of her tongue poking out in concentration. 'She might not even be interested in knowing about her
birth parents.'

I knew he was probably just trying to help, to save me from
getting hurt – I couldn't think of any other reason for the reluctance that had crept into his voice – but I felt as if I was on a
roller coaster that had already started to climb. 'I have to reply,'
I said, making my mind up. Colleen had forwarded her mobile
number, but if she was travelling it would be easier to communicate online until she returned.

'I'll get Maisie ready for bed.' Greg stood abruptly and I felt
a chill where he'd been sitting. 'Say night, night to Mummy.' He
dangled Maisie in front of me, as if to remind me of what was
important – not that I needed reminding. I rubbed noses with
my daughter and exchanged ten kisses, and promised to go up
and read her a story as soon as she'd had her bath. 'Are you
coming to help?'

'I'll be up shortly,' I said, choosing not to ignore the challenge
in his voice, and once they'd left, opened up Facebook once more
and began to write, my heart keeping rhythm with my fingers.

*Thank you so much for replying, Colleen. You sound so calm
about it all! I think I'm still in shock to be honest, but VERY excited
about us getting to know each other. Your life sounds quite different
from mine. Perhaps you take after your father :o) I'm afraid our
mother passed away a few months ago, after a long illness. That's
how I came across you, while going through her things. I miss her
very much. She was a wonderful person.* Tears threatened again,
but I blinked them away. *I don't know why she gave you up, but
there must have been a strong reason. I so hope you had a happy*

childhood. I was worried my news would cause some sort of fallout, and I'm happy that's not the case.

My hands faltered as something occurred to me. Nowhere in her message had she mentioned her husband, Jake. Perhaps they were divorced and that was why she was in America. Or maybe her job took her to different countries and they spent a lot of time apart. Recalling Greg's creeping reluctance, doubt whispered through my mind, and switching to Google, I typed in her married name and added *film editor*. It would be interesting to see if any well-known films had her name attached, but there was only one Colleen Harper, linked to a film in 2003 I'd never heard of, listed as 'miscellaneous crew'. There was no image, so I had no idea whether or not it was her, but the date probably ruled her out. She'd have been still in her teens back then, but maybe she worked under a different name.

On impulse, I tried *Colleen Harper skydiving*, knowing it was silly, and wasn't surprised when nothing relevant came up, and when I added Waterford, Ireland, for my next search, the only result was a collection of crystal drinkware. I chewed my lip for a moment. It was unusual for someone Colleen's age to not have an internet presence, other than a Facebook account, but not impossible, and there could be a good reason why. I was probably searching the wrong name. Switching back to my message, I carried on writing.

I am married, by the way, and yes, he's very handsome, but I would say that. He's called Greg, and we have a three-year-old daughter called Maisie and we live in Surrey. I'm so looking forward to you coming back from America, and hope we can get together when you do. Have you worked on any films I've heard of, by the way?! What name do you go by, these days? Are you married? Decided not to ask about children – it could be a sensitive topic for all I knew – I looked again at how she'd signed off: *Your loving sister, Colleen x*

She sounded so caring. Maybe she'd felt an instant connection, as I had. I liked that she'd said 'sister' instead of half-sister. It had to be a good sign. When I thought of how it could have gone … I shuddered, imagining a very different message – one telling me to shove off and that she didn't want anything to do with me, and before I could overthink it quickly typed: *Look forward to hearing more from my brand-new sister! Love, Ella x*

It sounded a bit twee, and not very me, but it would be easier once we'd met to put real meaning behind my words. At the moment she was still an abstract, a wonderful discovery – a possibility, rather than a living, breathing person.

After I'd pressed Send I sat back, feeling drained. Outside, the light was fading and I got up and drew the curtains and switched on the television, with a sudden longing for normality. But the sound was too intrusive so I turned it off again. I thought about work, and a couple of jobs I had lined up, but they seemed trivial and insubstantial.

Recalling Greg's subdued reaction, after his initial rush of enthusiasm at finding out where Colleen lived, I made my way upstairs, where Maisie was splashing in the bath, and Greg was making submarine sounds. I'd intended to join them, but found myself circling the bedroom instead, arms wrapped around my waist, heart leaping and racing as my thoughts circled like birds. The sooner I met Colleen the better, because I couldn't focus on anything else until I did.

Chapter 10

Colleen

'Colleen.' Alfie raised his hand and threw me a cheerful smile as I came through the door of the pub. 'Good to see you.'

I'd had a couple of shots of vodka before I left the bedsit, so everything seemed louder and brighter than it had the day before.

'Hi,' I said, heading towards the bar. 'Where's Sandra?'

'She's out back on the phone,' he said, as he pulled a pint for a grey-haired man, leaning on the counter. 'She'll be through in a minute.'

I hung my hoodie on a hook out the back and joined Alfie behind the bar. 'So, what should I do?' I said with a nervous shrug. It had been years since I'd worked in a pub, or with people. I was out of my depth already.

Alfie took five euros from his customer and turned to the till. 'Just give me a hand behind here. Any problems, just yell.'

'Sounds like a plan,' I said, serving a youngish woman who wanted a large white wine. I had to ask Alfie how much to pour, how much it cost and how to use the till. He was patient with me and once I got into the role the evening flew by and I began to relax. At half past eight, Alfie took to the mic for the quiz night. He was a natural, with a boyish charm that appealed to me, and the punters loved him. He had great timing, and I realised I hadn't laughed so much in years. I even knew the answers to some of the questions. I felt normal, free, like any other woman having a laugh, if only for a short while.

After the quiz, Alfie made us some coffee, saying he never drank when he was working, as he had to drive back to Drumcliff. I realised I hadn't thought about having another vodka, despite being surrounded by alcohol. He kept up a steady stream of chatter, telling me funny stories about some of the regulars, keeping things light, as if he sensed it was all I could cope with.

Sandra looked over at us talking, narrowing her heavily made-up eyes, and after the pub closed and Alfie had gone down to the cellar to grab a crate of wine, she came over.

'So, how was your first evening, Colleen?' Her tone had a bit of an edge and I worried I'd made a complete mess of things.

'I think it was fine,' I said, pulling a glass from the dishwasher and wiping it with a tea towel. 'You tell me.'

'You're good with the customers and I'm pleased to have you on board.' She lowered her voice. 'I saw you laughing with our Alfie,' she added, nodding towards the cellar door. 'You like him.'

It wasn't a question. I felt my face flush. 'He's good fun.'

'He is that.' She lifted an over-plucked eyebrow. 'Just be careful, love,' she said. 'You've been through a lot. I wouldn't want you to get hurt.'

'He's a nice guy, that's all.' It was annoying, having to defend myself, but I told myself she meant well.

'And there's something else, Colleen.' She rested her hand on my arm. 'Something I've debated whether to tell you, for fear you might take off. But I don't see that I have a choice.'

'What is it?' Her expression worried me.

'A man came in here after you left yesterday.' She leaned in and I could smell the cloying sweetness of her breath, could see clumps of mascara thickening her lashes. 'He was asking after you.'

My heart thumped against my ribs. 'What man?'

'It was your husband, Colleen. He wanted to know what you were doing here.'

The glass I was holding slipped through my fingers and smashed, shards of glass scattering on the wooden floorboards. I bent to pick them up and sliced my finger.

'Shite!' Pain seared through my hand.

'Leave it, Colleen,' Sandra said, placing a hand on my shoulder. 'I'll sort it out.'

I got up, grabbed the tea towel and wrapped it round my finger. 'Did you tell him I was working here?'

'No, of course not.' She shook her head. 'I made out I didn't know what he was on about. But he must know you're here, love.'

Blood was soaking through the tea towel. 'I have to go,' I said, feeling sick. 'I can't work here, Sandra. I'm sorry.' I grabbed my hoodie and headed for the door.

'Wait! Let me look at that finger,' Sandra called. 'And I need to pay you.'

I didn't look back as I dashed out into the cool evening air. My eyes flicked around, searching passing faces, tears blurring my vision. I pulled free the tea towel, to see a large gash near the tip of my finger. It needed stitches.

I spotted a taxi rounding the corner and hailed it.

Three hours in A & E, and three stitches later, I was on my way back to the bedsit, my hood up, my head down. A constant stream of traffic roared past, but there were no taxis, and I couldn't call for one as I'd left my phone charging at the bedsit.

It was a fifteen-minute walk, and the sky was dark and clear with a sprinkling of stars. I hurried through the silent streets, looking over my shoulder every now and then. My finger throbbed, and it seemed light years ago that I'd been enjoying myself in the pub. I should have known it was too good to be true.

Out of nowhere, a creeping sense of dread came over me. I started running, certain I could feel eyes on my back, and arrived at the bedsit out of breath and hurtled up the stairs.

Seeing my front door was ajar, I froze for a moment on the landing before pushing it open with my foot. 'Hello?'

I put my hand round and felt along the wall for the light switch and flicked it down.

A pungent scent filled my nostrils, and as brightness flooded the room I saw a wreath of white lilies on my pillow. I'd only ever seen a wreath of white lilies once before – at Bryony's memorial.

I wanted to rush outside with it, hurl it into the river and watch it drift away, along with the memories it evoked. Overwhelmed with nausea, I moved slowly forward, picked up the wreath and laid it on the rickety table in the corner. Then I poured a glass of vodka and knocked it back with a shaky hand, the liquid biting the back of my throat and burning inside my chest. I poured another and scanned the room. Everything was how I'd left it: the heap of clothes spilling from my rucksack on the floor, my phone charging in the socket on the wall.

There was a card among the lilies. I plucked it out and with shaky fingers turned it over.

Rest in peace, Colleen.

There was no indication who had sent it, or who'd been in my room.

My phone pinged. Hardly breathing, I walked over and yanked it from the charger.

It was a text from Jake.

I hope you like the lilies, Colleen.

Trembling all over now, I deleted the message and threw the phone on the bed, before racing out of the apartment and down the stairs. I hammered on the landlord's door. He took his time answering, appearing in striped pyjamas that gaped at the front, and a pair of grey socks, his yellowing big toenail visible through a hole.

65

'What the hell?' he said, scratching his head. 'It's two in the morning.'

'You let someone into my room.' My hands were clenched. I wanted to punch him.

'Yeah, your husband.'

'But I'm not with him anymore.' I didn't want to share the information, but felt I had no choice. 'Don't *ever* let him in my room again.'

'He had a wreath.' The man's straggly eyebrows drew together, as if it had only just struck him as odd. 'He said you were going to a funeral tomorrow and you'd be upset if you didn't have it. What was I supposed to do? I'm not a fucking mind reader.'

'Just don't let him in again.' I was shaking so hard I could barely keep still. I would have to move on from the bedsit, but I needed to be in Sligo to meet my father.

The landlord shrugged and slammed the door, as though he couldn't care less.

Back in my room my phone was ringing. It was Jake again. I ignored it, but he was persistent. I caved in and answered on the third ring. 'Jake, please don't do this to me. I need some space,' I cried. 'I'll come home when I'm ready and we can talk.' It was a lie, but he wasn't to know that.

He didn't reply. All I could hear was the sound of his breathing.

I ended the call, turned off the phone and threw myself onto the bed, burying my head in the pillow. I couldn't fight the tears, however hard I tried, and cried myself to sleep.

When I opened my eyes it was 6 a.m. I was cold, and my finger was throbbing. The scent of lilies was overpowering. I grabbed a handful of the shattered flowers, opened the window, and threw them to the ground below. But still the stench of them was too much and I had to get out of the room.

Still wearing the clothes I'd had on the day before, I left the bedsit and ran to the internet café, my eyes darting everywhere, searching for Jake in the shadows.

The café was empty, apart from the man with the tattoos behind the counter, and I sat at a screen, praying there would be a message from my father. That he would say he was back early and wanted to see me today. I would tell him about Jake and what he was doing. If he cared about me at all, he would help.

But there was no message.

I carefully signed in to Facebook with my good hand, to see a reply from Ella and felt oddly grateful. 'My sister,' I said, trying the words out loud to see how they made me feel. But they didn't sound right. I had a sister once and I lost her. I didn't want another.

Even so, as I read Ella's message, I found myself laughing. She seemed so excited at the thought of getting to know me. Would she be so thrilled if she knew the real me – if she knew the truth?

She hadn't held back, and had opened up to me with a trust I couldn't comprehend. I had the sense that bad things didn't happen to Ella Matthews, that she wouldn't let them. Sure, her mum had died, but I felt she was the kind of woman who would cope with death, would learn and grow through the sadness.

My husband is handsome.

'Never trust a handsome man,' I said. 'That's something I can teach you, Ella Matthews.'

I continued to follow her words. She had a child. I was an auntie. *Poor kid.* Who'd want an auntie like me? 'Auntie Colleen,' I said out loud in a silly voice. This woman had everything – but she wanted me. I pressed Reply. Ella was my ticket out of the awful bedsit, and I was about to use that ticket. Ignoring her questions about the film editing, and whether I was married, I typed a reply:

Dear Ella, I'm in Sligo! Why not come over? I'm here for a while before I head home. I can't wait to meet you and your family. We could book a hotel perhaps. Maybe you could book it for us both, and I'll pay you when you arrive.

Your ever-loving sister, Colleen.

x

Chapter 11

Ella

Tuesday

Rolling thunder woke me from a dream of being chased through a dense forest by a faceless girl, the sound of her breathing heavy behind me.

I jerked upright, face damp with sweat. Maisie was crying in her bedroom, while Greg snored lightly beside me, and he barely stirred as I brought her in to bed with us.

I stroked her hair and whispered reassurances until she fell asleep, but my own eyes refused to close. I stared at the ceiling as lightning flared, listening to the rain, thoughts flitting through my head, though I couldn't have said later what they were.

A little after seven, Maisie rolled towards Greg, mumbling drowsily, and started poking him. I eased myself out of bed and went downstairs to make tea, but there was no power. 'Shit.' I kept flicking the switch on the kettle as though, like magic, it would come on, then tried the overhead light and the microwave.

Nothing.

I grabbed my phone off the worktop. The battery was dead. My only thought was, I couldn't check Facebook to see if Colleen had replied.

I switched on my laptop and my heart gave a little leap as the screen sprang to life. It still held some charge from the day before, but the broadband wasn't working.

'Morning.' Greg wandered in, his face bleary with sleep. Normally, he leapt straight into the shower, but he was in his bathrobe, a layer of stubble on his jaw.

'We've no power,' I said, slamming my laptop closed. I felt nervy and put out, as if I'd been tricked. 'There was a storm last night.'

'Sure a fuse hasn't blown?'

I hadn't thought of that and my spirits rose.

Greg went off to check, but came back seconds later shaking his head. 'Not to worry,' he said. 'We can get some coffee at work.' He moved to the window and looked at the rain-sodden garden. 'I didn't hear a thing.'

'It woke me up,' I said shortly, forcing myself into action. Maisie would be down soon, clamouring for breakfast. 'Didn't you wonder why our daughter was in our bed?'

'That's nothing unusual,' he said, turning, perhaps hearing an undercurrent in my tone. His robe had fallen open and I stared absently at his tanned chest and the soft dark hair on his belly. 'Ah.' He nodded, as the penny dropped. 'No internet connection.'

'Colleen might have left a message. My phone's flat.'

'I'm sure the power will be back on soon.' He closed the gap between us and took the carton of milk I was holding. 'You can't use that,' he said, emptying it down the sink and running the taps. 'The fridge must have been off for hours.'

'For God's sake.' I slumped against the worktop and pushed my hands through my hair. It needed washing, but I wouldn't be able to dry or style it. I couldn't even have a shower. 'Everything in the freezer will be ruined,' I said. 'And what can Maisie have for breakfast?'

'A banana, or a peanut butter sandwich.' Greg opened a cupboard and retrieved a loaf of bread. 'She's not a fussy eater.'

'I need to work on my photos from yesterday's shoot.' But that wasn't why I was fretting and Greg knew it.

'Once Maisie's at nursery, you can go to a café and use their Wi-Fi.' He was speaking in his sensible voice, as though I was the child. 'I know your password. I can check your phone messages when I get to work, if you like.'

'No,' I said, more sharply than I'd intended.

His eyebrows shot up. 'Just trying to help.'

'Sorry.' I managed an apologetic grin. 'I didn't sleep very well.'

'I'm not surprised,' he said, steering me to the table and pressing me down in a chair. 'Let me make breakfast and drop Maisie off, then you can get on with whatever you need to do.'

As he gently massaged my shoulders, he cleared his throat. 'Just don't get too excited about hearing from Colleen, that's all,' he said, and a surge of irritation rose inside me.

'Why not, Greg?' I turned from his grip. 'This is the most amazing thing that's happened to me in a very long time.'

'OK, sorry.' He stepped backwards, hands raised. 'I just don't want to see you upset, that's all.'

'I won't be,' I said. 'She sounds great. I feel as though I know her all ready, Greg. Don't ruin this for me.' I suddenly wanted him to leave. 'You were the one who told me where she lived.'

'Maybe that was a mistake,' he said quietly, turning to grab the bread from the fridge, and something about the set of his shoulders told me not to pursue it.

*

After they'd gone, I made a half-hearted attempt to empty the freezer, before abandoning it in favour of a lukewarm bath. Then I tied my hair back, pulled on a fresh pair of jeans and a clean top, grabbed my things and headed out. I wanted to find the

70

letter from the shoebox, and couldn't shake the feeling it was still at Dad's house.

Using the charger in the car, I called Dad to let him know I was coming, but as usual he didn't pick up. He was probably out walking Charlie, and never remembered to take his phone. It would be lying on the table in the hall, out of battery.

I called my agent, Jenny, to let her know I would forward the photos from the restaurant shoot later on, and to cry off a job she'd booked for me that afternoon. I wouldn't be able to concentrate. 'I've got a migraine,' I said.

'I didn't know you suffered with them.' Jenny's voice was warm and compassionate. I pictured her rosy round face and felt another twist of guilt. She'd become a good friend since I joined the agency. I felt bad for not being honest, but didn't know where to begin, or even whether I was ready to tell people about Colleen.

'It's the weather.' In the rear-view mirror, my cheeks were pink. I was hopeless at lying, even on the phone. 'There was a storm last night.'

'Oh yes, it was awful. I hate thunder,' she said, her voice clearing. 'Don't worry about this afternoon, Ella. I'll put someone else on it. You take care of yourself.'

By the time I parked outside Dad's, my temples really were throbbing.

I got out of the car, my laptop under my arm, hoping the power cut hadn't extended out here. The sun had emerged, pushing aside the clouds, and the ground was already dry.

The red-brick walls of my childhood home glowed a welcome. As I pushed through the gate, past neatly clipped hedges and billowing flowerbeds, roses scenting the air with their sweet perfume, memories lined my mind: Mum at the window, hanging curtains; sitting at her easel in the garden, her curly hair tucked under a scarf; up a ladder in baggy dungarees, clearing the gutters in autumn.

'I'm not afraid to tackle men's work,' she'd tease Dad, who was hopeless at anything resembling DIY.

In my memory her violet eyes were always smiling, but what had really been going on underneath? Had she secretly looked at the spaces around her, where her other daughter should have been? Had she regretted giving her up?

I hated that I couldn't ask her and a flicker of anger ignited then quickly died. I was certain Mum had meant me to find the contents of the shoebox and that was all that mattered.

I unlocked the door and stepped into the hallway.

'Dad?' I knew he wasn't there. His dusty old Fiat wasn't on the drive, and there was no sign of Charlie. He must have gone shopping and taken the dog with him.

The house smelt stale and had an abandoned air. I missed the soothing, homely sounds that used to accompany my visits, when Mum would greet me with a hug and homemade cake.

Despite my best efforts to keep the place clean, the hall looked shabby. The carpet was worn in places, and clusters of dog fur had gathered along the skirting boards.

A few paintings were propped against the wall in a higgledy-piggledy fashion and I stooped to pick one up. I hadn't seen it before. It was of a robin, perched in the tree in the back garden, the colours muted and dreamy. The colours were typically Mum's style and had won her some critical acclaim through the years. I could vividly recall the thrill of seeing a feature about her in a glossy magazine, and from the time she'd appeared on an arts show on BBC2, looking shy as she discussed her technique, tucking her hair behind her ear in a subconsciously nervous gesture. She hadn't sought the limelight. She'd been happiest in the studio she shared with a group of artists, or teaching students at the university where she'd met Dad.

Another picture caught my eye, of a small girl on a swing, her head tipped up to the clouds, which I suspected was me. It had been framed, but the glass was cracked, as though it had been dropped at some point, and my breathing quickened as I spotted the painting beside it. Two young girls were playing on a beach, one taller than the other, both with buckets and spades and wearing matching, orange swimming costumes patterned with white spots. They were blonde beneath their straw hats, smiling at each other against a backdrop of frothy waves and pale blue sky. It had obviously been painted with a loving hand, the colours rich yet delicate, and was intricately detailed down to every freckle, and I knew, even before I turned it over and saw the initials E&C pencilled on the back, that the girls were Colleen and me. Or, at least, how Mum had pictured us.

Tears blurred my vision as I traced a finger over their faces, trying to imagine what must have been going through Mum's mind back then. Had she hidden it in the shed away from Dad, in case it raised questions? Perhaps she'd sneak out to look at it, wondering about the child she'd given away.

I quickly put it down and looked at the remaining two paintings, but they were landscapes, the colours a little too subdued. I replaced them gently and ran upstairs to scour the bedroom, trying not to dwell on the empty wardrobe, its doors still standing open, and Mum's bedside table, cleared of her books. The bed looked unslept in and I guessed Dad was still sleeping on the sofa.

There was no sign of the letter and I wondered if it might have slipped out of my bag when I was returning to the car. If so, the rain would have turned it to pulp and there was nothing I could do.

I returned to the hallway, and after checking the electricity was working, sat on the stairs and connected to the internet, my heart kicking when I saw that Colleen had replied.

I opened her message and read it quickly, a smile spreading over my face. She was in Ireland and wanted us to go there!

For a second, my mind galloped ahead, picturing us meeting, crying and laughing and talking at the same time, but I couldn't quite bring her into focus and my smile faded as reality rushed in. Flying to Sligo with Greg and Maisie suddenly felt like too much, too soon. I had no idea whether Greg would even want to go.

I read her message again.

We could book a hotel perhaps. Maybe you could book it for us both, and I'll pay you when you arrive.

For some reason, I heard Dad's voice in my head, saying, 'If someone you've never met asks you to pay for something, don't. It's a scam.' But that had been after a news report we'd watched, about vulnerable, lonely women being conned out of their life savings by men professing their undying love.

This was my *sister*.

I noticed she hadn't responded to my questions about her film-editing career, and there was still no mention of her husband, but perhaps she'd rather wait until meeting before revealing the private details of her life.

I thought for a moment before replying, keen to get the tone right.

I'd love us to meet, Colleen. I can't wait! Would it be possible for you to come here to start with? We could meet at the airport, and go somewhere for lunch and get to know each other. Then I'll introduce you to Greg and Maisie. How does that sound? Let me know soon. I can't wait, and Maisie will be thrilled to meet her auntie! Love, Ella x

I read it twice before hitting Send, feeling brighter again, as though the sun streaming through the window by the door had reached inside me.

After logging off, I picked up Mum's paintings and took them out to the car, laying them carefully in the boot and covering them with a blanket. I would find somewhere to hang them, and maybe show Colleen.

My headache had finally receded. The sun was warm on my neck and I debated visiting Mum's grave, but although I went at least once a month to refresh the flowers, I could never quite connect with her there. I much preferred remembering her as she'd been, vibrant and full of life, not lying cold in the ground.

I realised I was fizzing with an energy I didn't know what to do with. I should go home and see if the power had returned and finish emptying the freezer. After that, I could go online to research somewhere suitable for a grand-reunion lunch with Colleen – somewhere we could talk in private.

I pulled out my phone and tapped in Greg's number. He answered on the second ring, as though he'd been waiting for my call.

'I've invited Colleen over,' I told him, excitement building once more. 'You'd better prepare to meet your sister-in-law.'

Chapter 12

Colleen

I shot up in bed, flailing my arms, hot and sweaty from a nightmare that had felt real. I'd been screaming silently as a faceless figure chased me through thorny brambles, and now my body tingled and shook as I scooped my duvet off the floor where I'd thrown it and wrapped it around myself. It was the middle of the afternoon. I'd slept away half the day, *again*.

The sun was bright through a crack in the threadbare curtains, highlighting a strip of dust particles. I leaned back, hugging my knees until my breathing settled, refusing to let a stupid dream dictate my feelings.

My gaze landed on the wilting wreath and a shudder rippled through me. The smell of lilies was still sharp and I couldn't stand it any longer. I jumped out of bed, pulled back the curtains and opened the sash window. I stuck my head out, letting fresh air fill my nostrils. The street below was empty, and on impulse I turned and grabbed the wreath and tossed it outside. It landed on a pile of builder's rubble.

'You can't scare me, you bastard,' I yelled, before slamming the window shut.

I flung myself back on the bed, feeling sick and empty in a way I hadn't since I was a child – since Bryony died.

Ten minutes later, I got up and pulled my purse from my rucksack and counted out my money. I reckoned I had enough to last me a week at the most. I needed to get out of the bedsit and hide. Could I stick it out until Reagan came back to Sligo, or Ella came to Ireland?

I ran a bath and soaked for a while, keeping my eyes wide open. I was certain no one could get into my room, as I'd wedged a chair up against the door just in case, but I wasn't taking any chances. When my flesh puckered, I hauled myself out. I found a black T-shirt in my rucksack, creased but clean, dragged on pants and jeans and returned to the bedroom.

I glanced through the window at the park opposite, where trees swayed in the wind that had sprung up. There was a figure standing by the railings in a hooded jacket. I couldn't make out his face, but felt sure he was looking at my window. *Jake?*

I drew the curtains, heart racing. When I peered back around them, the man was bending down, attaching a lead to a little black dog.

You're paranoid, Colleen.

The vodka bottle on the bedside table was almost empty, but I unscrewed the lid and took a swig.

Get a grip, girl.

I looked out again. The man was receding into the distance, the dog trotting by his side. It was quiet for mid-afternoon, and there was nobody else about. I glanced down at the pile of builder's rubble.

The wreath had gone.

*

It was early evening when I heard a knock at my door.

'Who is it?' I called, leaping off the bed after dozing on and off, unable to face leaving the room, or think about how the lilies could have vanished. I pulled away the chair and pressed my ear to the door. 'Hello?'

'It's Alfie.' There was curiosity in his voice. 'I wanted to check you're OK. There's a bit of a mess out here.'

I ripped the door open. 'For fuck's sake,' I cried, staring at the carpeted area where Alfie was standing. There were lilies strewn everywhere, like potpourri.

I picked up a handful, rushed past Alfie and ran down the stairs, hearing the soft tread of his footsteps behind me. I banged on the landlord's door until he opened up, a pathetic figure in his shabby cardigan.

'Who's been here?' I cried, showing him the crushed petals in my hands. 'Somebody left these outside my door. Did you let him in again?'

'Keep your voice down,' he said, his beady eyes darting past me to where Alfie was standing.

'Did you let him in again?' I repeated, my voice high and broken.

He pulled his gaze back to me, mouth turned down at the corners. 'Nope,' he said with a shrug.

I felt a draught on my neck. Turning, I noticed the front door was propped open. If Alfie had got in that way, *he* could have too. 'Shouldn't that be kept locked?' I said, pointing. I could sense Alfie's eyes on me. God only knew what he was thinking.

'Who are you, the bedsit Gardaí?' said the landlord. He let out a throaty laugh. 'I went out for a fag and forgot to close it. Not that I have to tell you.'

'Have you seen the state of the landing?' I thrust the petals under his nose. 'He left the wreath for me yesterday, and came back today and threw the lilies everywhere.'

'Well you'd better clear it up then.' He glared for some moments before stepping inside and slamming the door.

I stared at the peeling paint and let out an exasperated sigh. 'What's going on, Colleen?'

I turned to meet Alfie's concerned gaze. 'Nothing,' I said, dropping the petals outside the landlord's door. 'Well, something, obviously, but it's a long story.'

'You look as if you need a drink,' he said.

'Too right, I do.' I dragged my fingers through my hair. 'In fact, I need a bucketful.'

*

'Jesus, slow down,' Alfie said, as I downed a large glass of red wine while he nursed an orange juice. He'd driven to the bar, said he never touched alcohol when he was driving. It was a noisy bar, crowded with people talking over the top of each other, and my muddled head was pounding.

'Sorry,' I said, realising my hand was shaking. Was it nerves, or was I developing the DTs already? 'It's not been the best of weeks.'

'No.' He gave a wry smile. 'How's your finger?'

I held it up, staring at the grubby bandage. 'Sore. I had to have three fecking stitches.'

'Are you going to tell me what happened back at the bedsit?'

I shook my head. I didn't know where to start, and anyway, how did I know he could be trusted? I barely knew him.

'So are you coming back to work?'

I shook my head again. 'I'm looking for something else,' I lied. 'I'm moving on soon anyway, as soon as …' *As soon as what?* I couldn't tell Alfie my life was hanging on two people I hadn't even met. I took another gulp of my drink instead.

'Are you going back to your husband?'

'Jesus, what's with all the questions?'

He looked at his hands. 'Sorry, I didn't mean to—'

'It's OK,' I cut in. 'It's just I'd rather not talk about him.'

'Fine. So is there anything you do want to talk about? What music do you like?' He grinned, and the muscles in my back unclenched for the first time in days.

As the evening wore on, the drink weakened my resolve, and I found myself getting chatty. I always talked too much when I drank. 'Jake's not one of the good guys,' I said, jabbing the air in front of Alfie. 'He liked to control me. I was his Stepford Wife.'

Alfie's eyes narrowed behind his glasses. 'Bastard.'

'Is the right answer.' I banged my glass down on the table. 'You'd never control anyone, would you, Alfie?' My words were beginning to slur.

'No, I never would,' he said.

It was dark by the time we left the bar. Alfie moved closer as we walked back to the bedsit, tall and solid. I felt safe with him beside me.

'It's pointless me asking you in,' I said when we arrived. I hadn't realised what a gloomy building it was, until it loomed out of the shadows. 'I haven't got a kettle.'

'I don't mind.' He walked me inside and up the stairs. There was still a scent of lilies in the hallway, as they lay dying on the worn carpet. The smell caught in my throat, and I began to cough.

'So what's this all about?' Alfie said, taking my elbow. He seemed to have a way of prising things out of me. Or maybe it was the drink.

'It's nothing,' I said. 'Just a tiny reminder of the damage I've done in my life.'

He didn't look convinced. 'Maybe we should call the Gardaí.'

'And say what? Someone's sprinkled petals on my doormat, officer?'

A smile touched his eyes. They were nice eyes, bright and direct. 'It's pretty freaky, Colleen. Are you sure you're OK?'

'I'm fine. And you should go.' I opened the door to my room and flicked the light on.

'OK,' he said, not moving. 'I'll call you, yeah?'

'Except you haven't got my number.' I laughed. 'Come in and I'll give it to you.'

Inside, I drained the last of my vodka into a mug and we sat on the edge of the bed.

'You're fond of the drink,' he said, nudging his glasses up the bridge of his nose with his finger.

'Sure I am. It's a new thing. I'm rebelling. Jake didn't let me drink, said it would set me back.'

'Set you back?'

'It's nothing.'

'No, go on.'

I sighed. 'I was a drunken mess when he met me.' I took a gulp of my drink and picked up my phone, indicating we should key in each other's numbers.

After we'd done it, Alfie said, 'So, what brought you to Sligo?'

I shrugged.

'You don't have to tell me.'

'It's OK.' I looked at him. 'I guess it would be good to tell someone.' In the glow of the overhead light his face looked strong. It might have been the glasses, but he looked like a man I could rely on.

You thought that about Jake once.

'I've come here to meet my father,' I said, keeping my eyes on his. 'He gave me up at birth, as you do.' I heard myself sounding shakily flippant. 'I think finding out about him woke me up, somehow. Made me see my marriage was a sham. It was time to escape Jake the Controller. So, I wrote him a note, saying I was leaving and never coming back, and here I am.' I did jazz hands. 'Ta-da!'

Alfie nodded, as if nothing I'd said was shocking. 'Did you tell him where you were going?'

'No.' I looked away. 'But I told Celia.'

'Celia?'

'The woman who brought me up.' I picked up my mug, and drained it. 'I had to get away from Jake. You do see that, don't you?'

Alfie nodded, looking solemn.

'But I reckon he's found me.'

He looked startled. 'Then you really should call the Gardaí.'

'I haven't any proof. All the messages have been deleted.'

We were silent for a moment. Outside a car alarm went off, making me jump.

'He shouldn't treat you like this,' he said. 'You deserve better, Colleen.'

I wasn't sure I did. In fact, I wasn't sure how I felt. 'You don't know me, Alfie. Maybe I deserve everything I get.'

He studied me for some moments. 'So, how do the lilies fit in?'

I took a deep breath, not sure I was going to tell him until the words left my lips. 'When I was nine my sister died,' I blurted. Tears pressed against my eyes, as they always did whenever I thought about Bryony. 'She drowned, on holiday. We were on the beach, and she wanted to build a sandcastle, and …' I couldn't go on.

'That's terrible.' He put his arm around me and drew my head to his shoulder. I hadn't realised I was so close to tears, until they rolled down my cheeks. I was grateful he didn't ask me for any details.

'What's this?' he said as I finally pulled away, tracing the outline of a scar on my upper arm, where an old tattoo had been.

I shot off the bed as though he'd pinched me, and crossed to the window, standing with my back to him. My eyes felt swollen and my nose was blocked.

'Hey, I'm sorry,' he said, bedsprings creaking as he rose. 'I didn't mean to pry.'

'It's nothing,' I said.

'OK, let's just pretend I never saw it.'

I turned, and we stared at each other for a moment.

'It once said Gabriel.' I spoke more defiantly than I'd intended.

'Gabriel?'

I hesitated. I didn't want to talk about Gabriel, or remember that I'd slept with him just days ago, but barely remembered it. Or that I'd wanted his name on my arm when we were young; loved that he'd had Colleen tattooed on his shoulder. 'He was a boyfriend in a former life. First love and all that crap.'

'You must have loved him to have ...'

'I was a kid, Alfie,' I cut in. 'We all do stupid things in our teens, me more than most. When Jake wanted me to remove it, I did. At least, I tried.' I paused. 'Maybe you should leave.' I felt suddenly sober. 'I think I need to be by myself for a bit.'

He was the sort of guy who didn't need telling twice. 'I'm sorry,' he said, moving to the door, flattening his sandy hair with his hands. 'I didn't mean to make you uncomfortable.'

'It doesn't matter.'

He turned, one hand on the door handle. 'Listen, I'm going to London tomorrow for a few days,' he said. 'A company's interested in hiring me to build a website, but they want to meet me first. I'll be back on Saturday. Can we meet up then?'

'Sure.' A headache pressed against my temples.

He looked at me for a moment longer with an unreadable expression. 'Call me,' he said and left.

*

The following morning, I headed for the internet café and ordered a bacon roll. I wasn't hungry, but I needed to eat or I'd throw up.

There was no email from Reagan, but there was another message from Ella. She was clearly attempting to get out of coming to Sligo. *Shit!* As tears of anger burned behind my eyes, I realised how much I'd been relying on her to say yes – not only to escape Jake, but to save me from myself. I couldn't go to England. I had to stay in Sligo for my father.

I have to be in Sligo for a while for personal reasons, Ella, before heading back to the US. Big commitments there, I'm afraid, but I really want to meet you before I go. Please come, and bring Greg and Maisie too. I've longed so much for a family of my own, and can't wait to meet you. All my love, Colleen xx

I realised a tear was rolling down my cheek and dashed it away, unsure why I felt oddly emotional. I was either getting into the role of big sister, or Ella was starting to get under my skin.

I checked my emails one more time, and almost jumped from my seat. My father had replied: *I'm back in Sligo, Colleen. When do you want to meet? Reagan.*

Chapter 13

Colleen

I stared at his words, reading them over and over.

I pressed Reply and responded in a rush, aware my desperation to meet him flooded every word.

Let's meet as soon as possible. I can't wait to see you. We've got so much catching up to do, Reagan. Should I call you Reagan? I can meet you later if you're free. Colleen x

I added my phone number just in case and pressed Send. It was only then that it hit me: I didn't know this man. Only that he'd given me up and left me with his sister, while he went off to do God only knew what.

I banished my thoughts before anger took hold. I wanted to believe in him. I needed to believe he'd had a good reason to leave me; that he would explain everything when we met, and make it right.

His reply came through in minutes:

I'll be in Tate's Café on O'Connell Street at five today. I'll sit by the window near the door. Reagan.

'Is that it?' I said to the screen. I took several deep breaths.

Maybe in person he would be different, more affectionate. He clearly wasn't one for emails. But he'd agreed to meet me and that was all that mattered.

I left the internet café and walked back to the bedsit to let the day drift by. I locked the door and wedged a chair against it, and spent the next few hours in an agony of anticipation, alternately pacing the space around the bed, and lying on it, trying to doze.

At four o'clock, I had a bath, cleaned my teeth, and tried to do something with my hair, wondering what Reagan would think of me. Would he be disappointed? I couldn't help thinking he would be.

I finally headed out, blinking in the brightness of the late afternoon, and headed for O'Connell Street. Nerves and excitement kicked in once more, as I searched for Tate's Café. It was almost five when I spotted it, on the other side of the road, gold lettering etched on the window beneath a red awning.

Needing a moment to still my nerves, I stepped into a shop doorway. From there, I had a clear view of the café window.

He was already there, looking at his phone, sipping from a large white mug. My eyes swam with tears. He was wearing a waistcoat over a checked shirt, and his hair was too long and grey. I couldn't make out his features, but I knew, without a doubt, it was Reagan. Blinking until my vision cleared, I took a deep breath, and had just stepped out of the doorway when a text came through. It was Jake.

Have you met your daddy, yet?

I looked around, heart leaping. Another text followed:

Will he really make everything better, Colleen? I think it's too late for that.

I deleted them instantly, my hands shaking.

I looked again at my father. 'Reagan,' I whispered, and as though he'd heard he turned and seemed to look right at me. I gasped, and the years dropped away, until I was a devastated nine-year-old again, watching a man in a black leather jacket, holding a wreath of lilies.

Now, he picked up his phone, pressing it to his ear. His mouth moved as he spoke, but his eyes were still on me. I couldn't move. My whole body was shaking. Did he know I was his daughter?

As if in a trance, I crossed the pavement and stepped into the road without looking, freezing when a car braked sharply, inches away.

'Idiot!' shouted a man through his open car window, his face red and angry. 'Watch where you're going, bitch!'

'Sorry,' I said, tears of shock sliding down my face.

'Take no notice, dear.' An elderly woman took my elbow and guided me back to the pavement, while the car roared off in a cloud of exhaust fumes.

I looked back at the café. The seat where my father had been was empty. I could almost see the steam still rising from the cup he'd left behind.

'I'm fine,' I said, as the woman continued to fuss. But I wasn't. Reagan had gone.

I looked up and down the street, but there was no sign of him. Had he seen me and decided he didn't want to talk to me after all? Or maybe he'd remembered he had something better to do. My tears dried. Perhaps he was married with children and they knew nothing about me. Maybe meeting me would jeopardise his relationships.

I couldn't believe I hadn't considered it before.

I turned and ran from the old woman, who was talking about how sweet tea was good for shock.

Back in my room in the bedsit another text from Jake came through:

Shame the car didn't do a proper job, Colleen. Enjoy what's left of your life.

I collapsed onto the bed. It sounded like a death threat, and for the first time I wondered if Alfie was right. Maybe I should call the Gardaí.

Think about it, Colleen. They wouldn't listen to you. You're a mess.

I deleted the message and switched off my phone.

I'd picked up a litre bottle of vodka and a bag of Doritos from the express supermarket on the corner on my way back, and by midnight there wasn't a coherent thought in my head.

The following day, I opened the wine I'd bought, and the day disappeared in a fug of alcohol. I only got out of bed to throw up. The first time, I didn't even make it to the toilet.

Friday I woke with a thudding head, and there wasn't a part of my body that didn't ache. I cried and cried. Leaving Jake wasn't supposed to be like this. It was meant to be a fresh start.

When I couldn't cry anymore, I turned on my phone. There were three more texts from Jake, full of evil, sick words and I deleted every one. There was a message from Ella too. She'd booked a hotel in Sligo for us. Even paid for my room. And as I read, I felt a small punch of victory. She'd taken me at my word and agreed to come to Ireland. She and her family were arriving tomorrow and would meet me at The Mountain View Hotel.

But there was nothing from Reagan.

I responded to Ella, hands trembling, letting her know I would be there. If I could get out of the bedsit early the next morning, maybe Jake wouldn't see me leave and wouldn't be able to find me.

I spent most of the next twenty-four hours curled up under the duvet, avoiding the temptation to go out and buy more drink. I barely slept, my stomach churning with a mixture of alcohol and self-loathing.

At 5 a.m. I got up and packed my few belongings in my rucksack. After shoving what I owed the landlord under his door, I headed to the bus stop, where I caught a bus to the outskirts of Sligo.

I leaned my head on the bus window as it rattled along by the sea, passing clusters of cottages and fields, stopping and starting as it picked up more passengers.

The hotel looks over Benbulbin, Colleen. You'll love it, Ella had said in her text as if overcompensating for her initial refusal to visit. I wondered what made her think she knew what I might or might not love. She didn't know me at all. I didn't want her to. This was just a temporary way of escaping.

As the bus approached the hotel, I felt a twist in my stomach. Was it nerves?

I got up and rang the bell and the driver pulled over with a squeal of brakes. I was far too early. Ella wouldn't be there yet, and I doubted they'd give me the room. But it was worth a try.

'Thank you,' I said to the driver as I climbed off, hoisting my rucksack over my shoulder. The bus rolled away, revealing the hotel set back from the main road at the end of a sweeping drive. It was an old building with fancy windows and foliage over the walls. It looked stunning in the early morning sunlight, like the kind of place Jake and I used to visit when we were first married.

It was odd now, remembering our wedding – a quiet affair, with only two witnesses: colleagues of Jake's from the hospital. He'd arranged it quickly as a surprise. Probably to ensure his little project couldn't escape, though he'd organised a reception afterwards for family and friends. Not that either of us had many of either. Looking back, it felt as if it had all happened to someone else.

I crossed the road and headed into the hotel, where a smartly dressed receptionist greeted me from behind the desk, as if I didn't look like shite.

'A booking's been made for me by Ella Matthews,' I said, hitching up my rucksack, expecting her to turn me away.

'That's right,' she said, her smile fixed in place as she checked the screen in front of her. 'The room's been paid for in advance, and it's ready if you'd like to go up.'

After dumping my stuff I had a long, hot shower, trying to

cleanse away the previous days. It was difficult to keep my stitched finger dry, and I tried to recall what the hospital had told me about the dissolvable stitches.

Finally dressed in a fluffy white robe, I made myself a black coffee and circled the room. The cup was warm in my hands, and the bright and airy room made the bedsit I'd spent the last week in look like a prison cell. I felt almost safe here.

When I'd finished my coffee, I looked at my phone. There were no messages from Reagan; no reasons for him walking away. I decided to ask him what had happened. He owed me an answer, at least.

Where did you go, Reagan? I thought you wanted to meet. I realise you may have your reasons to avoid seeing me. Maybe you have a family. But I still need to know why you left me with Celia and why you've never contacted me. I think you owe me that much. Colleen.

I pressed Send, before I could change my mind, and logged off.

The bed was vast and comfortable, and I was sliding towards sleep when the sound of a child's laughter drew me to the window. A man was strolling across the immaculate lawn behind a little blonde girl who was running around the flowerbeds.

Was it Maisie? No. It was too early.

I returned to the bed and opened my rucksack, regretting that I hadn't brought at least one of the outfits Jake had always insisted I wore. I had another pair of black skinny jeans and a black T-shirt – clothes I'd bought when he wasn't with me and kept hidden at the back of my wardrobe. It was hardly the best impression to give my new-found sister.

But this was who I was now.

Chapter 14

Ella

Saturday

'Try and sit still, darling,' I encouraged Maisie, who was writhing in my lap, desperate to run up and down the aisle of the plane. We'd let her do it once, to get it out of her system, but instead of calming her down it had fired up.

Her cries for me to 'let go' descended into wails and screeches, and the passengers around us muttered their disapproval.

We'd only been on holiday twice since Maisie was born, and neither time by plane. I hadn't liked being away from Mum while she was ill.

Maisie was overexcited from the moment we boarded, completely unfazed by the take-off, which I thought would frighten her.

'Hate you!' she roared, curling her hands into fists and flailing them at me.

'I've never seen her like this,' Greg murmured, his face shiny with perspiration as we attempted to distract her with colouring books, his laptop, my phone and various food items.

'Perhaps we shouldn't have brought her,' I said, as she attempted to scale the seat in front in a bid for freedom. She flexed in my arms, bashing her head against my nose, and tears stung my eyes. 'We should have taken up your sister's offer to have her for a few days.'

'Too late now.' Greg wrestled a wriggling, protesting Maisie from me and pointed her at the window. 'Look at the clouds,' he said firmly and she was momentarily stilled. 'Anyway, I wanted us to go as a family,' he added, though I hadn't expected him to want to come at all – had been braced for a fight when he realised I'd gone as far as booking a flight and hotel. For some reason, I hadn't told him I'd paid for Colleen. 'I can see this visit's a big deal, Ella. I don't want her missing out on anything.'

I appreciated him acknowledging that meeting Colleen was important, but a sliver of doubt had crept in on the way to the airport as I recalled her message about needing to be in Sligo for personal reasons, wondering for the hundredth time what they could be. I hadn't liked to ask, worried she might back off, and had booked the hotel as soon as I'd read her message. I wondered now whether I should have insisted on coming alone. Meeting a sister was probably overwhelming enough as it was. A brother-in-law and niece might prove too much, but then again, I needed some emotional support.

Since making the arrangements a few days earlier, I'd been running on adrenalin, especially when Greg had agreed to come. He rarely took holidays so had no trouble securing time off, though he had to be back by the following Thursday for an important client meeting.

We had four days to spend with Colleen.

I'd cancelled a couple of jobs I had booked, to Jenny's surprise. Apart from my pretend migraine, I rarely took time off, and knew she could tell that something was up, but didn't like to pry. I felt bad that she probably thought I was still grieving for Mum.

I'd had my hair cut, and treated myself to a manicure and pedicure, which Greg had noted without comment. It was a distraction from counting down the minutes until I met my sister. I hadn't felt so excited since I was a child, trying to stay awake to see Santa on Christmas Eve, and I'd only distantly noted that Greg wasn't exactly brimming with enthusiasm.

I'd texted Colleen our flight and hotel details, and suggested we meet in the lounge of The Mountain View at 4.30 p.m. stressing how excited I was, but apart from a brief reply the day before, saying she was looking forward to it, we'd had no further contact.

I'd been dying to ask her more questions, but decided I would do it face to face so I could see her reactions, rather than imagining them.

To my surprise, Dad had phoned the night before, during dinner, wanting to know what we were doing at the weekend.

'Actually, we've booked a last-minute break,' I told him. 'We've been working so hard, and haven't been away for a while …' My voice broke off. He might wonder why we hadn't invited him, when I'd been trying to persuade him to go away for ages, suggesting we all fly out and visit his brother in Spain.

'Oh?' He sounded curious. 'Where are you going?'

My heart sank. For once, he was showing an interest in what I was doing and I couldn't tell him the truth. The phone had been on speaker, while I helped Maisie cut up her dinner, and Greg was shaking his head at me from the other end of the table. 'Be careful,' he mouthed.

Of course I couldn't mention Colleen, but it wouldn't do any harm to tell him we were going to Ireland. Better not to tell too many lies.

'Ireland?' he repeated, as though we were flying to Mars. 'Whereabouts in Ireland?'

'Sligo,' I said, shrugging at Greg, who was trying to communicate a warning with his eyebrows. It wasn't as if the place had any meaning for Dad. I suspected he'd forget our conversation the second he hung up.

'What's in Sligo?' *My sister,* I longed to say. *The sister Mum gave away and didn't tell us about.* 'Why there, of all places?'

Greg had his eyes closed, miming a stabbing motion at the table, thumb and forefinger pinched together as though—

'We stuck a pin in a map,' I said, cottoning on. 'We didn't want to spend too much time travelling, so picked somewhere close. It looks really nice.' I tried to remember what I'd read online. 'Nice beaches and a heritage centre. Plenty for Maisie to see. As I say, it's just for a few days. We'll be back next week, because Greg has an important meeting at work and—'

'I'd better go,' Dad interrupted. 'My programme will be on in a minute.'

For a second, tears had threatened. It was an obvious excuse to get me off the phone, even though he was the one who'd called me.

'Have a nice time,' he added, as if sensing I was upset. 'You deserve a break.'

As the plane began its bumpy descent onto the runway at Dublin Airport, Maisie finally drifted off to sleep, at last strapped into her seat.

'Typical,' said Greg, stroking her hair, and we exchanged proud parent smiles, his tension seemingly forgotten. 'Her sense of timing needs work,' he added.

Once we'd collected our bags, and Greg had picked up the hire car and we'd settled a still-sleepy Maisie in the back, my nerves ratcheted up.

'I can't believe this is happening,' I said, as Greg typed the hotel address into the satnav and directed the car towards the motorway.

'Neither can I.' He reached over and gave my knee an absent squeeze. It was early afternoon and the sun was blazing down from a cloudless sky. He wound the window down a couple of inches, letting in a stream of warm air. 'I just hope you're not going to be let down.'

'Oh Greg, give it a rest.' My doubts had slipped away and I couldn't stop smiling. 'Just be excited for me.'

As we picked up speed, I pulled down the visor and checked my reflection in the mirror. My eyes were sparkling, my cheeks pink, and my hair was extra glossy. I looked lit up, all my feelings on display.

I tried to imagine what Colleen was feeling. She was bound to be nervous.

My own stomach started to churn. I'd been drinking coffee all morning and hadn't eaten much breakfast. I tended to lose my appetite in times of high emotion, and wondered if Colleen was the same. Or perhaps she took comfort from food.

'I wonder if she's fat or thin,' I said to Greg, glancing at his profile, distracted by how sexy he looked in his open-necked shirt and navy jeans with a couple of days' growth on his chin and upper lip. He was trying to grow a beard. 'You can't tell much from a Facebook photo.'

'Would it matter either way?' Greg gave me a sideways look.

'Of course not,' I said, tucking my hair behind my ears. 'I just don't know what to expect.'

'I'm surprised there weren't any other pictures on Facebook, to be honest,' he said, winding up the window so I could hear him properly over the noise of the traffic. 'With all the travelling she's done, you'd have thought she'd have loads of photos on there.'

'I'm not actually her friend on Facebook. We've just been exchanging messages,' I said, sounding defensive. 'She could have hundreds of pictures for all I know.'

Maisie woke with a noisy yawn and rubbed her eyes with her fists. 'Where are we?' She blinked as she took in her surroundings. 'Hungry,' she said.

By the time I'd rummaged out the food I'd packed, and supervised a rather messy, impromptu late lunch, we'd arrived at The Mountain View and Greg was pulling the car into the circular driveway.

'Well. I guess this is it,' he said, switching off the engine and staring at the building as if worried it might burst into flames.

In the ensuing silence, broken only by the sound of Maisie slurping orange juice through a straw, I stared at the old stone exterior, its lattice windows reflecting the pale blue sky. The walls were draped with wisteria, and two giant fern-filled urns flanked the wide front porch.

'Bird!' cried Maisie, pointing to a stone peacock on a plinth in the well-kept garden. She clapped her hands, eyes shining. 'Can I stroke it?'

'Not just now, darling.' I darted my gaze back to the upstairs windows. Was Colleen here already, watching out for us? Or maybe she hadn't arrived yet, preferring to leave it until the last minute. At least I had time to try and settle my nerves, though there didn't seem much chance of that happening.

My palms were clammy as we booked in. I kept swallowing, and found myself hoping I wouldn't run into Colleen unprepared. Maisie – revived by her sleep – was charging along the hardwood floor in the oak-panelled foyer, pausing only to gape in wonder at a series of rustic paintings lining the dark green walls.

I needed a shower, and to think. I turned to Greg. 'I still don't know what I'm going to say to her,' I said. 'I've thought about it so many times, and it always plays out differently. Maybe I should have made notes.'

'You don't need notes,' he said with a touch of impatience. 'She might not even turn up.'

'She will, I know she will.' I couldn't seem to stand still. 'Anyway, it's better to be spontaneous and let things take their course.'

'Calm down,' Greg said, and I stiffened when he gave me a hug.

'Can you stay with Maisie for half an hour, give us time to introduce ourselves?'

His brow furrowed. 'I don't think—'

'*Please*, Greg.'

He looked about to argue, then relented. 'Fine. Half an hour.'

Our room was a blend of old and new, with a four-poster bed and arched, floor-to-ceiling windows overlooking a lawn beside the car park, dotted with quirky sculptures. Beyond was a view of the mountains that had presumably given the hotel its name.

'Mine!' shrieked Maisie, belting into the adjoining room and flinging herself onto a single bed piled high with patchwork cushions. She began to bounce up and down and Greg followed her through and hoisted her into his arms.

'What are we going to do with you, young lady?' he said, throwing her up and catching her. Watching them, I was flooded with affection. Greg was just worried about me – that was all. As part of his job, he was used to weighing up situations from every angle, but this time, I just wanted him to act like a husband.

'I think I'll take madam for a walk in the garden, and see if we can burn off some of this energy,' he said. Maisie beamed her approval at this plan. 'We'll see you later.'

I blew them both a kiss as they headed out, Maisie clutching her old teddy. Once they'd gone, I took a shower and tried to regulate my breathing. I wanted to appear cool and collected, not a sweaty nervous wreck.

Wrapped in a complimentary bathrobe, I called room service. I hoped I'd feel better if I lined my stomach, but couldn't manage more than a half a cup of coffee and a couple of bites of the salmon sandwich delivered by a smiling waiter.

I washed my hands again before picking out an emerald green sleeveless top. I teamed it with a pair of cream skinny jeans and slid my feet into a pair of jewelled flip-flops. Smart, but casual. Was I trying too hard?

I crossed to the window, but couldn't see any sign of Greg or Maisie in the sun-soaked garden. Twisting and turning in front of the full-length mirror, I pictured Colleen doing the same. *Oh God!* She could be in the room next door! I glanced at my watch. She would be here by now, somewhere in this hotel.

I smoothed on some make-up, my hand shaking. It was worse than getting ready for a first date.

Oh, Mum. Why aren't you here with me? Why didn't this happen a long time ago?

Finally, it was four twenty-five.

My breathing was still too shallow as I left the room and made my way down the thickly carpeted stairs, gripping the wooden banister for support.

What if she doesn't like me?

A feeling of nausea rose and the bitter taste of coffee filled my mouth.

My foot slipped on the bottom stair and I crashed into a man coming up, his gaze fixed firmly on the phone in his hand.

'Sorry,' I said, when he flashed me a look of intense annoyance. He had the most vivid blue eyes I'd ever seen, but they held no trace of warmth.

'Watch where you're going,' he muttered, pushing past.

Charming.

I crossed to the lounge, feeling shaky, suddenly longing for Greg and Maisie to appear and defuse the tension. A murmur of chatter floated out, accompanied by teaspoons clinking against china and a ripple of piano music.

I hesitated on the threshold, eyes sweeping over the guests: a lookalike mother and daughter on a leather sofa; an elderly couple at a table by the window; a red-faced man with a timid-looking woman, eating crustless sandwiches.

I checked my watch again. Maybe Colleen was running late. Perhaps I should sit down, facing the door, so I would see her come in. At least that way I would have the advantage.

As I edged inside, clutching my purse, a breathless voice behind me spoke my name. 'Ella?'

My flesh rose in shivering goose bumps. I spun around and stared at the figure in front of me, taking mental snapshots. Dark cropped hair, elfin face, and pale freckled skin. Wide, green eyes, thickly lashed. Her clothes were thin, cheap, a bit trampy-looking. She was shorter than me, and maybe it was her boyish build and the haircut, but she looked much younger than her thirty-three years.

I took a step back. 'Colleen?'

'Yes.' Her voice was low, unmistakably Irish. 'Your half-sister,' she added, uncertainly.

I realised I wasn't hiding my surprise, but she looked so different to how I'd imagined. I quickly pulled myself round. 'I know who you are,' I said, in a voice that didn't sound like mine.

Her amazing eyes drank me in. *Mum's mouth*. And her scent ... I couldn't pin it down.

There were tears on my face and I was aware that people were staring. 'Come here,' I said, and opened my arms.

Chapter 15

Ella

Colleen moved into my embrace, as though obeying some deep instinct, and my arms closed around her. She was thin, her bones close to the surface, and I could feel her ribs through her flimsy T-shirt, and the rapid flutter of her heartbeat.

Breathing in her musky scent I was overwhelmed with emotion. *My sister.* If I'd had any doubts we were related, they dissolved the second I held her. There was no denying she looked like Mum, and like Maisie too. And her freckles – they were mine. *Ours.*

'Colleen,' I murmured into her feather-soft hair, trying to convey how I felt, without understanding it myself. How could I have missed someone I'd never known? But I had.

Seeing her, holding her, was like a piece of me slotting into place. 'I'm so happy to meet you. I can't believe you're here, that you actually exist.'

She was still for a second then wrenched away, putting some distance between us. She wrapped her narrow arms around herself, eyes darting around the hotel lounge as if seeing it for the first time, and sounds rushed back, reminding me we were in a public place.

I pulled a tissue out of my purse and dabbed my eyes, laughing a little, embarrassed. 'Sorry about that,' I said. 'I don't normally cry.'

I wanted her to say something, to tell me it was understandable under the circumstances, that she was emotional too, but she remained silent. She turned her astonishing eyes on me, and as she raised a hand to rub the back of her neck, a shiver of unease passed through me. She looked pale and tired, as though she hadn't slept. Her full lips were pressed together, and a deep groove cut between her eyebrows, making her seem stern. She looked like someone who'd suffered, rather than the happy adventurer I'd been expecting. *Maybe it's the shock of finding out about me and Mum.* 'Shall we sit down?' I said when the silence grew awkward. 'You must have so many questions.'

She lifted a shoulder. 'Sure,' she said, as if she wasn't bothered. 'Whatever you like.'

Her words were like a slap. Wrong-footed, I turned, stumbling a little, and led the way to a table with a view of the terrace, where I pulled out a chair. 'It's beautiful here, isn't it?' I sounded too chirpy, as if I was dealing with a client at work.

'It's certainly that.' She dropped on the chair opposite and propped an elbow on the table, looking almost sleepy as she rested her chin in her hand.

I picked up the menu and put it down again. 'Shall we have coffee?' My voice was too prissy. 'Or tea, if you prefer.'

Colleen raised her eyebrows. 'Sure.'

Is that the only word she knows? It felt like an effort to drag a smile across my face. 'Can you believe I've never been to Ireland before?'

'Lots of people haven't.' Her tone was sardonic and I instantly felt stupid. This wasn't how I'd imagined things going at all.

'You've travelled a lot, by the sound of it,' I persisted, lifting a hand to attract the waiter's attention. I saw her track the movement and wondered if she was judging me. I was probably coming across as an air-headed, middle-class housewife. I couldn't tell what she was thinking, but I was certain my emotions were written all over my face.

'I've been around,' she said shortly. She fiddled with a thin gold chain, linked to a letter 'B', that hung around her neck, her gaze drifting past me to the view outside. She opened her mouth as if to say more then closed it again.

I released a shaky breath and ordered a pot of tea, accepting the waiter's suggestion that we try the hotel's homemade lemon cake. I looked at Colleen for approval, but she was absently tracing circles on the table with her finger and didn't notice. 'So, how was America?'

For a moment, she seemed startled, as though it wasn't the question she'd expected me to ask.

'Big. And hot,' she said after a pause.

'Were you working on a film?'

'Holiday,' she said shortly.

I could have kicked myself. I was making small talk instead of getting to the point. And she was probably jet-lagged, if she hadn't been back in the country long.

'I'm surprised you're not more tanned,' I blurted.

She looked blankly at her arms, then rubbed them with a self-conscious grimace. 'I burn easily,' she said, as though she'd never given it much thought. 'I tend to cover up, or wear suntan lotion. Factor 50.'

'Oh, me too.' I clutched at this common thread, extending my own lightly tanned arm. 'I have to build up gradually. And my hair gets lighter in the summer.' *What the hell is wrong with me?*

Colleen didn't respond to that little gem. 'So, you had no idea I existed until last week?' she said. At last her eyes met mine, and I could see that her beauty was unusual; not obvious. It came and went, depending on her posture and the tilt of her chin. She definitely had the sort of looks that turned heads. In fact, at that moment, in the doorway, the man I'd bumped into earlier on the stairs paused to give her a second look.

'No idea at all.' I returned my gaze to Colleen and haltingly told her about clearing Mum's room and finding the box in her wardrobe, containing the photo and the letter. 'It was a total shock, but a good one,' I said, on firmer ground as I opened my purse and retrieved the picture. 'I think I was ready for something good to happen after Mum … after she passed away.'

I paused as the waiter approached with the tea and cake, and waited until he'd set them down before handing the photo to Colleen.

She leaned over it, narrow shoulders hunched, her eyes flicking back and forth. She turned it over and read her name on the back. 'It's so weird,' she said, and it was the first time I'd heard real feeling in her voice.

'It must have come as a shock.' I laid my hand over hers and felt her stiffen.

She pulled away, leaving the picture lying between us on the table. 'I saw her once.'

My stomach leapt into my throat. 'What do you mean?'

'She came to the house in Cork when I was a child, where I lived with Celia, my mother. The woman who brought me up. I think she was looking for me.'

I felt as if the blood had drained from my body. 'My God,' I said, pressing a hand to my mouth. 'Are you sure it was her?'

Colleen nodded. 'Positive.' She poured herself some tea without milk, and picked up the cup in both hands, blowing away steam. 'I didn't know who she was,' she went on. 'Celia wouldn't let her in.'

I sagged in my chair, feeling winded. I thought of all the trips to York that Mum had taken, to visit Aunt Tess. Had she really been there, or was she in Ireland, trying to reclaim her daughter? I suddenly recalled the receipt I'd found in her coat pocket, from Annie's Tea Room. 'Did you ever see her again?'

Colleen shook her head. 'We moved to Waterford not long after that.'

'Did you ask Celia about her?'

Her shoulders bounced. 'Why would I?' she said. 'I was only five.'

'But you remembered her.'

Her eyebrows lifted as she swallowed a mouthful of tea. 'I suppose. But only because Celia was upset.'

She seemed calm – uncaring, almost – whereas I felt as if someone had let off a box of fireworks in my stomach. 'So, you knew that you were adopted?'

'Not back then I didn't, no. Celia only told me recently.' This seemed vague, but I sensed I mustn't press her. 'She also told me my father cleared off after I was born.' She lifted her chin, and once again I was struck by her likeness to Mum. *What would Mum say if she could see us now? Is this what she would have wanted?* 'Celia's his sister.'

'What?' I sat forward, trying to absorb what she'd said. 'So … Celia, your adopted mother … she's really your *aunt*?'

Her eyebrows shot up again. 'I suppose so,' she said, as routinely as if we were discussing the weather. 'I thought of her as my mum back then, though. She was good to me for a while.'

For a while? Questions flooded in, falling over each other. 'And you weren't curious about your real mother, when you found out?' I managed. 'Didn't you want to know her?'

Colleen's cup clattered back onto its saucer. 'She didn't want me.' Her voice was hard. 'Why on earth would I want to know *her*?'

Oh, God. This wasn't going well. By now, we were supposed to be exchanging life stories, discovering we had tons in common, before moving on to making arrangements to visit each other's homes to get to know one another better. Instead she was studying me, like a wild animal scared to get close, and I was confused and jittery. Moisture had gathered in my armpits, between my breasts and dampened my hairline.

I felt tricked somehow. From the tone of her emails, I'd expected someone nicer. A sporty daredevil, like she'd described; someone fun and lively, curious and interesting.

She'd sounded so excited to meet me. But then again, why shouldn't she be furious, now she'd had time to dwell on things? In her eyes, I was the chosen one – the child Mum kept. If the boot was on the other foot, wouldn't I feel bitter? But it wasn't even that. She just didn't seem that bothered about me, *or* Mum. I was struggling to make sense of it all – of her.

'I'm sorry,' she said suddenly, fluttering a hand between us, as though sensing my confusion. 'It's been a very strange few weeks. You've no idea. Finding out about you and us sharing a mother.' She released a heavy sigh. 'Let's just say, it wasn't as much of a shock as you might think.'

I tried to imagine her circumstances and what she meant, but it was beyond me, and something warned me not to pry. At least she was here. That was what mattered.

'Ask me anything you like,' I said, striving to stay on track as I took back the photo and returned it to my purse. 'I'll do my best to answer.'

I was expecting questions about Mum, or my upbringing, or whether Mum had ever hinted at having another child. Maybe she'd want to know about my father, my schooling, my marriage and career. My mind raced ahead, trying to decide how to frame my replies. I wouldn't play up that I'd been a happy and much-loved child – by Mum at least – and that I'd gone to good schools and been financially supported through university, because that might make her feel worse and I wanted more than anything for us to get on.

It was becoming clearer by the minute that it wasn't going to be easy. 'Colleen?' I nodded for her to speak.

'You said there was a letter,' she said, crumbling her portion of cake with her fingers and scattering them across her plate.

'Yes.' I felt a blush creeping up my neck. 'There is one, but

'I'm afraid I've lost it,' I said, picking up my napkin and dabbing my face. *Where was Greg?* It was so hot. I wished I'd suggesting sitting outside now. The room was stifling and the tinkling piano music was getting on my nerves.

'You lost it?' Colleen's eyes widened and she let out a bark of laughter. 'Feck's sake, Ella.'

The familiar way she said my name softened the shock of her swearing. 'I'm sorry,' I said. 'I'm sure it'll turn up. There wasn't much in it,' I added. 'Someone called Reagan was letting Mum know Celia's address, in case she wanted to stay in touch. He said they'd done the right thing, so I assumed he must be your father.'

'My father.' A light came into her eyes and when her whole face softened, disappointment sliced through me. Clearly her father, despite abandoning her, was a more powerful force than a sister she'd never met.

'Do you have a relationship with him?' *Was I jealous?* How ridiculous. I didn't even know Colleen and had no claim on her.

'Not yet,' she said, her lips curving into a secret smile, and I wondered whether he was the 'personal reason' she'd given for being in Sligo.

Before I could ask what she meant, there was a commotion at the door, and I looked over to see Greg and Maisie entering the lounge. Relief washed through me. I hadn't realised just how tense I was.

'What is it?' Colleen said, turning in her chair.

'My husband and daughter.' I couldn't help the note of pride in my voice, watching them approach. Heads turned at the sight of Maisie in her pink-and-white gingham dress, and the matching hairband that tamed her wayward curls, spontaneous smile unfurling, and Greg looked attractive too, his hair still damp from the shower.

I rose as they reached our table and picked up Maisie, who was peeping shyly at Colleen through her eyelashes. 'I've missed you, darling,' I said, kissing her neck.

'Missed you too, Mummy.'

I smiled at Greg, trying to somehow communicate my tangled feelings, but his eyes were on Colleen, and for the first time I noticed her breasts were naked beneath her T-shirt, and the way her tight, black jeans outlined her slender thighs.

'This is Greg,' I said to her, resting a hand on his forearm.

'My daddy,' Maisie said, formally.

'Good to meet you.' Colleen stood to shake Greg's hand. She looked tiny next to him, her small hand disappearing inside his. There was an awkward moment as he leaned down to kiss her cheek, and she turned her head so that his lips grazed the corner of her mouth.

'Sorry,' he said, unruffled, releasing her hand and turning to smile at me. 'You don't look that alike,' he observed carefully, pulling a chair from an empty table and sitting down. 'Any tea left?'

Colleen's face turned pink. She seemed flustered and switched her attention to Maisie. 'Look at you,' she said, her face folding into the first genuine smile I'd seen. *A smile I'd failed to inspire.* She held out her arms, and to my surprise, Maisie wiggled away from me, into Colleen's embrace.

'Like your hair,' she announced, pushing her pudgy hand through Colleen's short layers with an enviable lack of self-consciousness. 'I've got curlies.'

'They're beautiful,' Colleen admired, jigging her up and down, and I saw a softer person – someone who'd be a good auntie to my daughter.

'You talk funny,' said Maisie.

'That's because I'm Oirish,' Colleen countered, exaggerating the word so that Maisie giggled and tried to copy her.

'She's adorable.' Colleen gave me a look I couldn't decipher, still smiling broadly. 'I once knew a little girl who looked a lot like you,' she said to Maisie.

'Who was that?' I rested a hand on Greg's shoulder, needing to feel its warmth. He was eating the slice of cake I'd ignored, but I knew he was watching every word and gesture, taking it all in.

For a moment, I thought Colleen wasn't going to answer. She was singing something to Maisie and didn't take her eyes off her when she finally spoke. 'It was a girl I knew a long time ago,' she said softly. 'She died.'

Shock rippled through me. Was she referring to her own child?

'It sounds like you two still have a lot of catching up to do,' Greg said, into the sudden lull. He was studying Colleen and I wondered what he was thinking. 'Would you like me to go away again?'

'No.' Colleen, Maisie and I all spoke at once.

Greg gave a controlled laugh. 'Well, it's nice to be in demand,' he said. 'How about we go for a walk and then on somewhere for dinner?'

'Good idea,' Colleen said, not looking at me as she tucked a maverick curl beneath Maisie's hairband. 'Let's get this party started.'

Chapter 16

Colleen

Greg rose, finishing the last of the cake, and wiped his fingers on a linen napkin. He took Maisie from me and she writhed, rubbing her eyes.

'You're tired, missy,' he said, and she squirmed some more.

He headed towards the door. He looked fit, as though he worked out, moving with confident strides. I rose to follow, but heard a clatter behind me. Ella had knocked the table, and her cup lay smashed on the floor. She bent to pick up the pieces, her face flushed. I glanced at my bandaged finger, remembering the glass I'd dropped in the pub.

'Careful,' I said, crouching beside her. 'Don't cut yourself.' I held up my hand. 'I'm living proof it hurts.'

She didn't smile, and I saw the confusion in her eyes. It was hardly surprising. How could she know what was going on in my head, when I barely knew myself? How could she know that I'd met her here mainly to escape Jake and meet my father?

A waiter appeared. 'Don't worry,' he said. 'I'll get that.'

Greg was waiting in reception, trying to restrain Maisie who was tugging on his hand when we approached. 'Perhaps we could eat here later on,' he said, nodding towards the restaurant area. I looked over and glimpsed large windows framed with floral curtains, and a set of French doors opening onto the grounds.

'Or, we could have a McDonald's,' I said, with an urge to ruffle his feathers. 'I'm easy.'

Greg laughed, showing his perfect white teeth. 'Seriously?'

'Sure. Don't you just love a Big Mac and fries?'

His smile faded. 'Well yes, but …'

'Don't be silly,' Ella said, her eyes signalling some sort of warning to Greg.

'Happy Meal,' Maisie cried, clapping her hands.

'No,' Ella persisted, her tone agitated. 'Please, Greg, let's just book a table here for eight o'clock. We don't like Maisie eating too many takeaways, remember?' She picked up her daughter, who'd started crying. 'Just book it, please, Greg. Maisie can have a nap in her stroller, so she'll be OK for later.'

'Fine,' he said, raising his hands, as though in surrender, but his voice was gentle. I wondered if he was furious deep down, that there was something lurking under his calm exterior. What were his demons? There had to be something. Affairs? Drink? Drugs? Was he a workaholic? When he wasn't smiling, he looked stern. Maybe he was just like Jake.

As he headed to the restaurant to make the booking, Ella flashed me an apologetic smile. 'I need to get her stroller from the car.' She tensed as Maisie flung herself about, her cries growing in volume.

'Hey,' I said, trying to meet Maisie's eyes. I pulled a silly face and poked out my tongue. She stopped crying.

'Wow. You have the magic touch,' Ella said, a smile crossing her lips.

I held out my arms. 'Here, let me take her while you go and get her buggy.'

Ella tightened her grasp. 'I don't know …'

'I'm not going to steal her,' I said, hurt that she didn't trust me. But then, I'd given her no reason to.

'Of course you're not. Sorry.' But she still didn't pass Maisie over.

'Ella, for God's sake, I know how to look after a child.' The words felt all wrong and Bryony flashed into my mind. I was the last person on earth who should be responsible for a child.

'Of course, sorry.' She finally handed Maisie over. 'Stay with Colleen,' she told her, pulling a tissue from the pocket of her jeans and dabbing her daughter's face. 'I won't be long.'

As Ella hurried through the double doors, blonde hair shining, I sat on one of the leather sofas with Maisie on my lap. The weight of her was reassuring, but made my throat tighten. Bryony used to sit on my lap while I read her favourite Dr Seuss books.

'Collie,' said Maisie, smiling up at me, her face still blotchy and damp. My heart clenched. Bryony had called me Collie. Collie wouldn't do.

'I'm Colleen,' I corrected softly. 'Auntie Colleen.' It sounded good, and tears threatened as I breathed her in, burying my face in her thick hair.

'Where's Ella?' I jumped. Greg was standing over us.

'She's gone to get the buggy,' I said, rising. 'Won't be a minute.' I felt uncomfortable around him. He gave the impression he could see right through me and knew what I was thinking.

'Daddy.' Maisie held out her arms, and when he took her, the space she left felt cold.

'Let's meet Ella outside, shall we?' he said, turning away from me.

By the car, Ella strapped Maisie into her buggy and handed her a teddy bear, uncannily like the one I'd played with as a child, and she snuggled into it and closed her eyes.

We walked out of the hotel grounds, the sun hot on my neck. It still felt strange not having long hair.

Greg took the buggy from Ella, letting us walk ahead. It was obvious he was giving us some time alone together, but my mind had gone blank.

'The mountains look grand, don't they?' I managed at last. I nodded towards Benbulbin, silhouetted against the sky.

'An unusual shape,' Ella said, but I could tell she didn't want to talk about the landscape.

'They were formed in the ice age, so they tell me.'

She smiled. 'Would you climb them?'

'Christ no, I'm not a fool.'

'But, I thought ...'

I realised what she was about to say, recalling the lies I'd rattled off in my emails. 'I like to jump rather than climb. Doesn't everybody?'

'I can't say I'm keen on either,' she said with an awkward laugh. 'I like walking, and I do yoga when I have the time. I find it hard to relax, if I'm honest. Greg goes running every morning; he says it keeps him sane. He's much fitter than I am ...' Her voice petered out, and there was a flush of red high on her cheekbones. I wondered if it was the mention of yoga. Wasn't it the type of thing that posh mums with too much time on their hands did? The kind of thing I might have done if Jake had let me.

We walked on towards Rosses Point, making occasional small talk. Ella was much less talkative than she'd been initially. It was my fault. I'd found it so hard seeing her all perfect, with her happy little family.

There was no doubting things between us seemed tense. I'd painted myself into a corner with the lies I'd told; given her a picture of myself that I wasn't even trying to live up to.

We walked for about twenty minutes before reaching a huge statue of a woman, holding her hands out towards the sea.

Maisie woke and looked up at the monument. 'Big lady,' she said, pointing her chubby finger and kicking her legs. 'Daddy, look, big, big lady.'

'Waiting on the shore,' I read from the plaque, sounding like a tour guide. I certainly didn't feel like part of their happy family. I was a stranger, and not a very sociable one at that.

The walk back was even more stilted. Ella clearly had no more idea what to say than I did, and resorted to chatting to Maisie. Greg didn't speak at all, but I felt him watching me, his face inscrutable.

I was sweating when we arrived back at the hotel, and glad of a chance to escape.

'We'll see you in reception at eight,' said Ella with a smile that seemed forced, and I thought again how disappointed she must be.

We all got out of the lift on the second floor. Maisie had fallen asleep on Greg's shoulder, and Ella's hand was in his. They looked like a family from a lifestyle magazine, and a surge of envy rose inside me.

I didn't look back as I walked down the corridor and slipped my key-card into the door of my room. Inside, I plugged in my mobile to charge, grabbed a handful of bottles from the mini bar, and flopped on the bed.

I picked up my phone and my heart flipped when I saw Reagan had replied to my email.

Colleen, I'm sorry I didn't get to see you on Wednesday. Something came up. Are you free tomorrow? Reagan

I pressed Reply.

I'll meet you at midday – same place.

I sent my email, and returned to his message, running my fingers over his words, before finally throwing my phone to the floor with a thud.

I was confused, unsure now whether he or anyone else could ever sort out the mess in my head.

Three mini bottles of vodka later, my eyes grew heavy. I curled on my side, pulling my knees to my chest, my eyelids closing over my eyes, longing for sleep.

'Colleen?'

It was Ella, knocking on the door. I jumped from the bed, disorientated.

'Colleen. It's quarter past eight.'

I opened the door. 'Christ,' I said, running my fingers through my hair. She was dressed in a pale blue dress, studded with little white flowers, and strappy high heels. Her hair was plaited into a bun and she smelt of something expensive. 'I fell asleep.'

'That's OK,' she said without smiling. 'We'll see you down there in a bit.'

'No, I'll come now.'

She paused, and looked me up and down. 'You're not changing?'

'No.' I stepped out and closed the door behind me. I didn't want to tell her I had nothing else to wear. That I'd left anything that might have been suitable in Waterford; that I no longer wanted to dress the way that she did. 'This is fine,' I said, knowing I sounded abrasive, and saw her face tighten.

Downstairs in the restaurant, Maisie was in a highchair, playing peek-a-boo with Greg, her plump legs swinging.

'Collie,' she said with a giggle, pointing at me with a moist finger.

My heart turned over. 'Colleen, yes, hello, little cutie.' I kissed the top of her head.

Ella smiled a rather tense smile as I sat down.

'Shall we have a drink?' I said, grabbing the wine list before the food menu. I would need to be hammered to get through this evening.

'I wouldn't mind one,' Greg said, glancing at Ella.

'Are you sure?' She sounded anxious.

'We're celebrating, aren't we? One won't hurt. Go on, have one.'

'No, not for me.' She raised her hand, and the huge diamond ring flashed on her wedding finger, catching the last of the evening sunshine slanting through the window.

I wondered if Ella had noticed I wasn't wearing one. I'd left my emerald engagement ring and gold wedding band in Waterford, on the kitchen table with my note.

We ordered wine, and orange juice for Ella and Maisie. Greg smiled at me. 'So, Colleen, this must be exciting for you.' I wondered if Ella had asked him to make an effort. 'I know Ella's been looking forward to meeting you.'

I looked at her. She seemed shy, cheeks flushing a delicate pink.

'Well, it's different, that's for sure,' I said, shrugging. 'I certainly had no idea I had a half-sister.'

'Me neither,' said Ella, her eyes brightening as we landed on the one topic she clearly wanted to discuss. 'I still can't believe Mum never told me about you.'

The wine arrived, and the waiter began to pour it.

'Maybe I will have just one.' Ella pushed her glass forward in a rather desperate gesture.

'Well, here's to us,' I said, picking up my glass once the waiter had gone.

'To us.' Ella clinked glasses with me, breaking into a smile that hid the shadows beneath her eyes. She was attractive in a glowing, fresh-faced way. Most people would be glad to discover a sister like her, but it was obvious we had absolutely nothing in common.

'Cheers,' said Maisie, picking up her trainer cup, and we laughed.

'So, you're from Waterford, Colleen.' Greg took a sip of his wine. 'Are you married?'

Ella gave him a look that suggested he was being too forward. I wondered if they'd already found out about me, and knew about Jake.

'Yes, I'm from Waterford, though I lived in Cork until I was five,' I said, and drained my wine glass. Greg picked up the bottle and splashed in more. 'And yes, I'm married. His name's Jake.' I pondered what to tell them. *I've left him, and now he's following*

115

me and sending me death threats. 'We're very happy.' The words almost stuck in my throat.

'He doesn't mind you jetting off?' Ella looked puzzled and, for a moment, I couldn't work out what she meant.

'Oh. America.' I shook my head. 'No, he's happy for me to see a bit of the world, and knows my job takes me everywhere. Obviously, he can't always take time off work to come with me. He's a surgeon, you see, and very much in demand.' I leaned back in my chair and gulped my wine. 'So, what do you do for a living?' I said quickly to divert her from asking any questions about my so-called job.

'I'm a food photographer,' said Ella. That explained the raspberries on her Facebook page. I knew she was expecting a response, but I wasn't used to making this sort of small talk.

'And you?' I turned my attention to Greg.

'He's a media lawyer, and a good one,' said Ella, flashing him a small smile. 'He protects high-powered people and senior executives from unwanted media attention, don't you, Greg?' I had no idea what she was talking about. 'He's hoping to be made a partner next year,' she went on, 'but he works too hard. I do too – we've both got a really strong work ethic, which isn't a bad thing, but …' She stopped suddenly, a flush spreading across her cheeks, as if realising she was talking too much and I could view it as boasting.

Greg took over, fingers steepled beneath his chin. 'Have you always worked as a film editor?' He sounded sceptical, as if he knew I'd made it up.

'Pretty much,' I said, and felt a stab of shame. I'd never even had a proper job. I'd filled my days cleaning, mostly – keeping the house nice and shiny for Jake – and my evenings accompanying him to functions, playing the trophy wife. If I suggested looking for a job, he would remind me that I wasn't qualified for anything. If I became too friendly with anyone, he made sure it didn't last. I overheard him once, telling a neighbour I'd

116

suffered a breakdown a long time ago. 'She's fragile,' he'd said, in that charming way he had. 'Needs taking care of.' It made him feel good to be seen as my saviour.

'Have you worked on any films we might have heard of?'

I sat for a moment, sipping my wine, my brain refusing to conjure something up as they both stared. 'I doubt it,' I said finally. 'Mostly boring commercials.'

'No children of your own then?' Greg asked.

Christ, he's persistent. 'Not yet.' I was pissed off by the intrusive question. 'What is this? The fucking third degree?'

'Greg!' Ella said, and shot me a look as if to warn me not to swear in front of Maisie.

An awkward silence fell.

Only Maisie was oblivious, banging her cup on her tray with cheerful abandon.

The pianist was playing a tune I couldn't quite place, something that pulled at my heart, and I wished I were a million miles away from this place. Alone.

I went to pour more wine and noticed the bottle was empty. We hadn't even eaten. I thumped the bottle down and Greg raised his hand to order another.

'So, you're happy?' Ella's mouth struggled to form a smile. 'I mean, you've had a good life?'

'Feeling guilty, Ella?' I said, too loudly. 'I was abandoned by my birth mother, who kept her next baby. Clearly a better version of me. What's not to be happy about?' I laughed as though I was joking, but the light went from Ella's face and I hated myself. I wasn't even sure how I felt about Anna, or the fact that she'd left me, and none of it was Ella's fault.

Before I could communicate any of this, Maisie let out a scream. She'd somehow bitten her finger. Her eyes squeezed together and her face turned red, tears rolling down her cheeks. 'Mummy,' she cried, holding out both arms.

Ella jumped to her feet and whipped her out of her highchair, onto her knee. 'She's tired,' she said to Greg, dropping kisses on Maisie's finger. 'It's been a long day.'

People turned to stare as Maisie continued to cry, and Ella's cheeks coloured.

'I said we should have had a Maccy D, didn't I?' I said, leaning back in my chair.

Ella's face crumpled. She looked as though she was about to burst into tears too.

'Do you want me to take her up?' Greg said, pushing his chair back.

'No, it's OK. I'll take her.' Ella was obviously desperate to escape. 'You two have a nice meal. I've lost my appetite.'

'That's silly.' Greg was avoiding looking at me. 'You're here to be with your sister, not me.'

'Tell you what,' I said, rising, my body shaking. It was unreasonable, but I was hurt that neither of them wanted to be around me. 'Let's call it a night, shall we?'

'No really, Greg, you stay.' As Ella got up, I caught a shimmer of tears in her eyes. 'Goodnight, Colleen,' she said, busying herself with Maisie. 'Let's meet for breakfast at nine tomorrow, and do something together afterwards.'

'Sure,' I said. The waiter was heading over with a second bottle of wine. 'Sounds good.'

Ella left with a crying Maisie in her arms, leaving behind a trace of her perfume, and more than a hint of disappointment.

There was an awkward moment as Greg filled our glasses. He looked tired, his eyes straying to the door, as though longing to follow his wife.

We ordered our food, and when it arrived we ate in virtual silence. Or rather, Greg ate his fish, while I pushed a slab of bloody steak around my plate. I didn't even like steak.

'How long have you been married?' I said finally, when we'd laid down our knives and forks.

'Four years.' His voice was polite but distant.

'You and Ella seem very happy.'

'We are,' he said, putting his hand over his glass as I tried to refill it with wine, and some sploshed onto the tablecloth.

'Quite the perfect couple,' I continued, not sure where this was going.

'Hardly,' he said. 'But I do love her very much.'

'You're lucky.' It came out like an accusation.

'I believe you make your own luck in this world.' Greg leaned back, folding his napkin into a small square.

'Well, that's total crap,' I said. 'Other people affect your luck and happiness all the time.' I drank more wine, knowing I shouldn't. It was making me sound bitter.

'You're not at all what I expected.' He narrowed his hazel eyes, becoming animated. 'In fact, I can't quite work you out.' He leaned forward and, in an unsettling tone, added, 'Ella's had a lot to deal with lately. Don't make her unhappy.'

'Now, why the devil would I do that?'

'I don't know, Colleen.' He lifted his eyebrows. 'You tell me.'

I poured the last of the wine and drank it in one big swallow, noticing the waiter approaching with the dessert menu. 'I won't have pudding, thank you very much, sir,' I said, in my best ladylike voice. 'I don't know about you, but I've had enough for today.' I rose and staggered from the table. 'Time for bed, said sleepy head.' I threw a dirty look at an elderly couple who were clearly disgusted by me.

Greg caught up with me in the foyer. He took my elbow and steered me into the lift.

I smirked. 'Quite the gentleman, aren't we?'

As the doors slid together, I slumped against the wall.

'You're pissed,' he said.

'Thank you for noticing.' I tried to curtsey and toppled towards him, giggling.

He caught me, his hands gripping my shoulders.

'You're a mess. It doesn't take a genius to work that out.'

I shuffled closer and pressed my hand to his cheek.

He eased away, his hazel gaze steady. 'Don't,' he said.

Never trust a handsome man, Ella. Better you know that sooner rather than later.

I stood on tiptoe, lifted my face and pressed my lips to his.

He pushed me away. 'What the hell do you think you're doing?' he said, as the lift shuddered to a stop.

Through the alcohol fog in my brain, I registered a pinch of hurt at being rebuffed. I lunged at him again, just as the lift doors opened, and my gaze slammed into Ella.

'Ooh, hello,' I said, lurching against Greg's arm as he swung away from me. 'Thought you'd gone to bed.'

Ella's eyes were wide and confused. 'She wouldn't settle without a goodnight kiss from her dad,' she said, a pyjama-clad Maisie nestled against her shoulder. 'What's going on?'

'Nothing,' Greg said tightly.

'Nothing,' I mimicked, then gave a hiccupping laugh. 'Oops! Pardon me.'

Ella's gaze whipped between us and suspicion darkened her eyes. 'Take her back,' she said in a voice I hadn't heard her use before, thrusting Maisie at Greg.

As his arms shot out to take her, he looked at me over her head and his expression made me freeze. 'I knew Ella should have kept away from you.' He turned to his wife. 'Ella—' he began, but she pushed past him into the lift.

'Put her to bed, Greg, it's getting late.'

He made a frustrated sound, but Maisie was starting to stir, murmuring and rubbing her eyes, and the lift doors closed as he strode away without a backwards glance.

'Someone's grumpy,' I said, in an effort to bring back Ella's sunny smile. I didn't like the look on her face – the sort of look Jake used to give me, as if I was the worst person he'd ever met.

'And you've had too much to drink.' She wanted to say more, I could tell, but was holding back.

I felt an urge to goad her. 'You're not what I was expecting,' I said, moving closer. Her breath smelt of tea and toothpaste. 'You're both a bit boring, actually.'

'And you're drunk.' There was a bite in her voice that told me my jibe had hit home. 'And you're nothing like *I* was expecting, either.'

'What *were* you expecting, darlin' sister?' I tried to make it sound sing-song, but it came out slurred. 'Someone prissy and perfect like you, with your cute little job and your shiny hair, and clothes from those places for women who like spending their husband's money?' She flinched as the words left my lips and I wanted to take them back.

'You don't know anything about me.' Her voice shook. 'I thought that was why we were here, to get to know each other, but you're acting like you don't even care.'

'Maybe I don't.'

She hauled in a breath, eyes glittering. 'In that case, maybe it's best if we don't see each other again.' She paused. 'I don't think you're the sort of person I want in my life.'

That hurt. *A lot.* 'S'fine by me,' I lied, twirling my hand. 'Run along to your *perfect* husband and *perfect* daughter, and carry on with your *perfect* life, why don't you?'

She shook her head, her lip curling. 'You're unbelievable.'

'You don't know how true that is, my dear.' I gave a deep bow that made my head swim, and when I looked up, she'd opened the lift doors and was hurrying away, a hand pressed to her face.

A lump lodged in my throat. *Now look what you've done.*

I pushed the button for the ground floor and the lift shot back down. I stumbled through reception and staggered outside, where it was dark and cool. Everything was spinning like a fairground ride, and I was violently sick in a bush. I cried as I lurched down the road that had led us to Rosses Point, earlier that day.

'What's wrong with you, Colleen?' I shouted at the sky. It was as though I had a self-destruct button. Ella and Maisie were the first good things to enter my life, and this was how I treated them.

I wasn't sure how long I'd been walking when I dropped on a bench, trying to work out where I was. It was dark, not even a street lamp or a house light to pierce the blackness. The silence was oppressive.

I closed my eyes, tears squeezing through my lashes.

I didn't hear the car pull up in front of me.

Chapter 17

Ella

Sunday

What were you expecting? Someone prissy and perfect like you?

I'd fallen asleep with Colleen's cruel words rolling like bullets in my brain, the image of her scornful face pressed behind my eyelids, but woke filled with remorse.

I shouldn't have confronted her like that. It was obvious she'd had too much to drink, probably because she was nervous, and I'd made everything worse by saying I didn't want her in my life.

You're both a bit boring, actually.

Was that what she really thought of us? *Of me?*

I couldn't deny that it hurt.

Maybe I needed to be patient and draw her out of herself slowly; give her time to adjust and feel comfortable with me. I hadn't expected us to be so different but, with hindsight, I'd been led by emotion, rather than logic. I hadn't factored in meeting a real person, with complicated feelings and – as it turned out – a spiky personality. She probably hadn't anticipated how meeting me would affect her either. Whatever had made her lash out like that, I couldn't believe she didn't want to know me, and I wasn't going to give up without giving us another chance to talk – this time while she was sober.

I turned over in the vast, comfortable bed, wanting to talk to Greg, but he was asleep with his back to me and I couldn't face disturbing him. When I got back to our room last night, heart racing, wiping tears from my face, he'd been in with Maisie, saying she wanted him to stay with her, and it hadn't seemed appropriate to tell him what had happened, or ask him why he'd had his hands on Colleen when the lift doors opened. He'd been so good to stay, when I'd fled the restaurant with Maisie, desperate to escape Colleen's increasingly random behaviour, and was probably just steadying her on her feet. It had been obvious she was drunk.

Instead, I'd pulled the curtains across the window, noticing Colleen, weaving out of the hotel grounds, head bowed, and after crying into a towel in the bathroom, horribly aware that Mum wasn't around to answer all the questions circling my brain, I'd crawled under the duvet exhausted, and into a dreamless sleep.

Now, I slid out of bed, and went to take a shower, and by the time I'd finished, Greg was awake, propped against the pillows with his hair standing out at odd angles. Maisie was rolling on top of the duvet, singing, 'Twinkle, Twinkle, Little Star'.

'It's a beautiful day,' I said, dragging the curtains open and retrieving a scattering of toys that Maisie had arranged on the rug at the end of the bed. Streaks of sunlight beamed through the windows and slanted across the thick, cream carpet.

'Bootiful,' Maisie agreed.

I pulled on clean clothes, wondering if Colleen had slept well and was feeling more positive this morning and regretted what she'd said last night – if she could even remember it. 'I'm starving,' I said.

'Me starving,' Maisie echoed, lifting her pyjama top and patting her tummy. 'Can I have Weetabix?'

'We'll see. Go and find some clothes,' I urged.

She clambered obediently off the bed and scurried into the other room. I watched, smiling, as she upended her pink rucksack all over the floor and held up a pair of lilac leggings for approval.

'Lovely.' I gave her a thumbs-up and looked at Greg, surprised he hadn't spoken. 'Are you OK?'

'I'm fine.'

'You look tired.'

'I didn't sleep that well.' He swung his legs out of bed and sat facing away from me, tension radiating from him.

'Greg?' I paused. 'I'm sorry for leaving you to it last night. How was the meal?'

He rubbed his face with both hands before lifting his head. 'You know how it ended,' he said, not looking round. 'What did she say to you after I'd gone?'

'A lot of stuff I'm sure she didn't mean.' I tried to keep the hurt out of my voice. 'We're boring, apparently.'

'Ha,' he said, but it was a mirthless sound. 'I'd rather be boring, than a drunk.'

'Greg, it was one night,' I said. 'We were meant to be celebrating, you said so yourself. I'm sure she doesn't normally drink that much.'

'Did she say anything else?' There was a twist in his voice I didn't understand.

'Like what?' I walked round the bed and stooped to kiss him, the bristle of his cheek scratching my skin. 'Greg?'

When he didn't react, anxiety snaked through me. 'What is it?'

He looked past me into Maisie's room. 'I think she's trouble.'

My hand dropped from his shoulder. 'What do you mean?'

'I think coming here was a mistake.' My heart made a painful somersault when I realised he was deadly serious, even though

I'd had the same thought myself. 'She's not the sort of person we need in our lives.'

It was another echo of my own doubts, and Greg's first instincts about people were usually right, honed by years of 'cutting through bullshit' at work. 'We just need a bit more time,' I said, injecting my voice with a dose of optimism I didn't quite feel. 'I know she came across defensive and a bit hostile, but you can hardly blame her.'

'It was more than that.'

I glanced round, checking Maisie was out of earshot. 'What are you talking about?' He was gripping the edge of the bed, his knuckles white. My heart revved up. 'Greg?'

He rose abruptly and walked to the wardrobe, and began rifling through the clothes I'd hung there. 'She made a pass at me, OK?'

I thought of his hands on her arms when the lift doors opened, and felt a dropping sensation. 'What do you mean?'

He wheeled around, a pale blue shirt dangling from one hand. 'She tried to kiss me, Ella. Twice.'

For a moment I felt as if all my circuits had been cut.

'I know what you're thinking.' He flung the shirt on the bed and came over to grasp my shoulders. 'But she really did try to kiss me.'

I reeled away from him, unpleasant memories resurfacing. When Maisie was a baby, Greg had got drunk at a company event and slept with a colleague. Sonya, she was called. I'd met her once, when she called at our house with some work documents. She was small and curvy, with glossy black hair in a high ponytail, and it was immediately obvious how much she'd fancied Greg. She called me afterwards and told me in exaggerated detail what she and Greg had done in bed together.

He didn't deny it, swore it only happened once and that he could barely remember it. She'd been flirting with him for weeks, he told me, grey with anguish.

'I know it's not an excuse,' he'd said, eyes glassy with tears.

'I'm a shit and I don't deserve you, but I promise it will never happen again. I'll stop drinking.'

I'd let it go. Worn out by Mum's illness and Maisie – who was teething at the time and not sleeping – I hadn't the energy to deal with it. If I'd sometimes burst into tears at odd moments afterwards, I didn't dwell on the reasons why. I'd believed Greg when he said it wouldn't happen again. He confronted Sonya, told her to leave us alone, and she eventually left the company.

Greg was as good as his word and stopped drinking. Even as a teenager, he hadn't been able to hold his drink. Alcohol brought out a side of him he didn't like, he said. He didn't want to risk losing me.

He was drinking last night. I stared at him through a blur of tears, seeing his hands on Colleen's arms.

'I only had two glasses,' he said, holding up a hand is if warding off my thoughts. 'Colleen was the one knocking back the booze, Ella. You saw what she was like.'

'But you don't usually drink.' I sounded accusing. 'Why last night?'

'Ella, please, don't do this.' Greg extended his hand, a plea in his eyes. 'Why would I have told you she tried to kiss me, if it wasn't true?'

'To get your side of the story in first.'

'Surely if she was going to tell her side of the story, she'd have told it last night.' He looked as if I'd slapped him. 'Christ, Ella, I can't believe you think so little of me.'

'Why?' I made a sound between a yelp and a sob. 'Because you've never lied to me before?'

He looked crushed. 'Ella—'

'You know how much meeting Colleen matters to me,' I said, tears falling. 'Why are you doing this?'

'Doing what?' His eyebrows pulled together. 'I haven't done anything!'

'You're spoiling it all,' I cried.

'I think Colleen's doing a good job of that herself.' His voice iced over. 'You just said, she told you she thinks we're boring. Probably because I rejected her.'

'I can't believe she would go that far, not when we've just met.'

'You don't want to see it,' he said, adding, after a pause, 'Except, you did see it, didn't you? You left the restaurant because she wasn't what you wanted.'

I rushed forward and pushed him hard in the chest.

Taken by surprise, he stumbled backwards, shooting his hands out to stop himself falling into the open wardrobe.

'What you doing, Daddy?' Maisie ran over, her face bright with delight. 'Is it hide-and-seek?'

'Not right now, sweetheart.' I wiped my face with the back of my hands before she could spot my tears. She was wearing a mismatching red T-shirt with her leggings, but I hadn't the heart to insist she changed. 'Pop your shoes on and we'll go and have some breakfast.'

'But Daddy's not got clothes.'

'I won't be long,' he said, giving me a hard look as he headed to the bathroom. 'You two go ahead.'

There was no sign of Colleen in the dining room. I wondered if I should have given her a knock to wake her up, to let her know I hadn't meant what I said about not wanting her in my life, but if Greg was right and she'd drunk too much, she might be sleeping off a hangover.

The waiter from the day before showed us to our table and made a fuss of Maisie. I didn't want to think about what Greg had told me, but his words spiralled in my head, digging deeper and deeper. If Colleen *had* tried to kiss him, it really was the end of the road. If I couldn't trust her around my husband, then what was the point of being here?

But maybe he'd got it wrong. Greg had been drinking too and might have misinterpreted an innocent goodnight peck from Colleen. I tried to recall their expressions when the lift doors had slid open – guilt, anger? Something had been off, and I should have pursued it then. There was no point going off the deep end now – not before hearing Colleen's version. Then I would talk to Greg and apologise. We might even laugh about it later.

In an effort to avoid glancing at the doorway, I focused on helping Maisie choose some cereal from the breakfast bar. I could see she was charming the guests and staff with her smiles and stream of chatter.

'What lovely manners,' said an elderly lady with cropped white hair, giving me an approving smile. 'You're clearly doing something right, dear.'

I wondered what she would have said if she'd seen Maisie on the plane, and was glad my daughter appeared to be on her best behaviour.

'Thank you,' I said with a smile, filling a bowl with fresh fruit and yoghurt for myself.

Maisie insisted she wanted to sit on a proper chair. She knelt beside me, spooning her Weetabix into her mouth, a napkin tucked in the neck of her top. 'Where's Collie?' she said when she'd finished, head cocked like a bird.

'I don't know.' I pushed aside my plate of half-eaten fruit. My earlier appetite had fled. *Where was she?* Had she taken me at my word and was refusing to come down? 'I think she's still sleeping.'

I poured a second coffee, eyes searching the dining room, then flitting to the sliver of reception area visible from our table and the gardens outside.

Greg appeared as I sipped my drink, his hair slicked back. He looked calm and composed, but his face was pale above his newly grown beard, and he didn't meet my eyes as he pulled out a chair and sat down.

'Greg, I'm sorry—' I started to say.

'She's not here then?' There was a challenge in his voice.

Irritation rose. 'I'll go and fetch her.'

'I don't think we should discuss what happened in front of Maisie,' he said, as if that was what I'd planned to do.

'We don't know that there's anything to discuss yet.' I was shocked by how cold I sounded. I kissed Maisie's cheek. 'Stay with Daddy,' I said and walked away, pretending I hadn't heard Greg call my name.

I paused outside Colleen's room. Today would be better, I decided, resting a hand on the dark wood door. She and I would go somewhere together, the two of us, and talk properly – honestly and openly. Everything would be fine.

I knocked sharply, heart pumping. I had a smile ready, but it slipped as the door remained closed. I pressed my ear to it, but heard nothing inside.

I started as a couple passed by, their footsteps silent in the thickly carpeted corridor.

I knocked again. No answer.

A vision popped up of her lying face down on her bed in a puddle of vomit, unable to get to her phone, and I ran downstairs. 'Do you know if the occupant of room eighty-nine has checked out?' I asked the receptionist, every muscle in my body tensing for her reply. 'Colleen Brody.'

She smiled politely. 'We can't give out personal information.'

'Please,' I said. 'It's urgent.'

'Everything OK?'

'I'm not sure,' I said. 'She's my sister, we were supposed to meet for breakfast. I've knocked on the door, but there's no reply.'

'Oh.' The receptionist seemed taken aback. She looked very young, with wide blue eyes like a doll's. 'Let me see,' she said, tapping her computer keyboard. 'No. She hasn't checked out,' she said, eyes sweeping my face.

'Do you have a key-card for the room, so I can check on her?' My heart was beating so fast I felt faint.

'I'm not sure.' She looked round as if seeking help, but a

130

large group of people was being checked in and her colleague was busy.

'She's booked in under my husband's name. Greg Matthews,' I said, gnawing my thumbnail.

She checked her screen again, then plucked a key-card from under the desk and handed it over. 'I hope your sister's all right.' Her pale eyebrows pulled together. 'It's funny, because someone else was asking about her.'

'Oh?' About to dash back upstairs, I paused. 'Who?'

'A man?' she said with an inflection, turning it into a question. 'He seemed concerned about her too.'

Greg? Who else would know she was here? 'Thank you,' I said, rushing towards the stairs. 'I'm sure she's fine.'

I returned to Colleen's room, the receptionist's words reverberating in my ears. Was that why Greg had wanted Maisie and me to go down to breakfast first? So he could check on Colleen and get their stories straight?

But that would be so unlike him. We didn't have secrets … not anymore. Or so I'd thought.

I knocked once more on Colleen's door and when she didn't answer, let myself in.

It was gloomy, the curtains half-pulled across, but I knew at once she wasn't there. There was no sense of her presence: no rumpled bed, no clothes strewn about – just a small indent in the pillow and a couple of empty bottles from the mini bar on the bedside table.

Perhaps she'd left without checking out. Fled in the night, unable to face me. Was it because of Greg, or what I'd said about not wanting her in my life? Had she upped and left, without checking out?

My stomach turned over. I stalked to the window and yanked the curtains back, blinking as bright light flooded in. I turned back to the room, hoping I might have been wrong and she would emerge from the adjoining bathroom. A phone was face down on the floor, and I picked it up and laid it on the bed. *Why would she leave her phone?* Her rucksack was in a heap by the wardrobe, and next to it a pair of black knickers.

My mind raced back to last night. Unlike me, Colleen hadn't brought anything down to dinner apart from her key-card, which she'd placed by her plate on the table.

She couldn't have left the hotel if her things were here.

Hope bubbled up like champagne. She must have gone for a walk. Why hadn't I thought of that? The simplest explanations were usually the right ones.

Feeling slightly furtive, I perched on the edge of the bed and switched on the phone. There was no password and the screen sprang to life, and an email from Reagan appeared. She'd arranged to meet him yesterday and he hadn't turned up. I remembered her smile when I'd mentioned his name, and let out a noise of frustration. There were so many things I needed to ask her. Why would she have gone out without her phone?

Dread curled around my spine.

Holding the phone like a hand grenade, I rushed back down to the dining room, almost colliding with Greg in the doorway. He was carrying Maisie, chatting to the elderly, crop-haired woman who'd spoken to me earlier.

'Colleen's not here,' I said, interrupting their conversation, managing to keep my voice low enough so that only Greg could hear. 'I think something's wrong.'

Chapter 18

Colleen

I woke, my eyes gritty and sore, my head pounding. I quickly realised something was over my head, making my breathing erratic. I snatched it off and a shaft of sunlight from a narrow, rectangular window close to the high ceiling almost blinded me.

I was curled up on the floor, and the piece of carpet beneath me stank of something unpleasant. 'What the *fuck*?' I jolted upright, shivering, though it wasn't cold, and a lancing pain shot down my arm.

Horrible details rushed back: the bag being thrust over my head; me fighting, useless and pathetic in my drunken state; him seizing my arm, dragging me like a doll, something popping in my shoulder. He'd yanked me up and slung me over his back like a bag of tools. I'd screamed, but it was weak, barely audible and made no impression. He threw me in the boot of a car, and pain had shot through me as my head cracked on metal. I must have passed out. I had no idea how far we'd travelled, or where I was.

My eyes crawled round, adjusting to the light. The room was

small and square, with roughly plastered walls and a concrete floor, the ceiling stained with damp.

What had happened? I'd got horribly drunk and kissed Greg. *Oh God!* The memory made me shudder. And I'd run off into the night like a teenager and made myself into a pathetic victim, like I had once before. Jake's victim.

'Don't push me,' he used to say, if I suggested meeting up with a friend from my old life, or getting a job. 'You don't know what I'm capable of.'

I blinked back frightened tears. I hadn't thought him capable of this.

The room was filthy, hazy sunlight picking out clusters of dust and cobwebs in the corners. I struggled to move my throbbing head. An ironing board was propped in one corner, and there was a mop, a bucket and a broom near a sink. In the opposite corner were three wooden boxes of varying sizes, all padlocked.

I tried to think through my pain and fear. If I stacked the boxes, I could probably reach the window. It was unlikely from the size, but I could try to ease myself through it.

I strained my ears, but all I could hear was faint birdsong outside.

'Jake,' I yelled, staggering to my feet. Agony exploded in my shoulder and head, and the floor tilted towards me. I stumbled towards the heavy wooden door and turned the dull brass knob, but it wouldn't open. 'Jake, please!' I called, banging the wood with my fist. 'Let me out.'

Nothing.

I turned and slid down to the floor, holding my injured arm across my stomach. Slowly, the pain in my head dulled to a throb, but my mouth was parched and I desperately needed to pee.

Reality hit me with the force of a punch. *I was his prisoner.*

I let out a whimper as I turned my palm upwards. Blood had seeped through the bandage round my finger and it stung as it had the day I cut it in the pub.

I closed my eyes, thinking of Ella – my only hope. Would she have expected me to join her for breakfast? Raised the alarm when I didn't turn up? In spite of what she'd said last night, I didn't want to believe she would turn her back on the hope of a sister. I'd seen the desperation in her eyes. Tears stung as I remembered the awful things I'd said to her – the way I'd thrown myself at Greg. If she *had* packed her bags and headed back to England, I wouldn't have blamed her.

But no one would know I was missing.

Alfie's face floated into my head – lovely Alfie with his geeky glasses and cute smile. He'd be back from London soon. Would he try to call me, and worry if I didn't get back to him? I knew it wasn't likely. And even if it was, he didn't know about my meeting with Ella.

I tried not to think about Reagan.

I turned and banged on the door again. 'Jake! Let me out, now … please.' It came out as a pathetic whine. 'We can go back to Waterford,' I went on, sniffing back my tears. He'd never liked me crying. 'Everything can go back to the way it was, I promise. I'll never leave again.' The thought of being trapped with Jake, spending even another day with him, made my stomach heave. But it had to be better than this. Once home, I would plan my next escape more carefully.

The sound of a car approaching made the hairs on my neck stand on end. I rose as a door slammed, and I heard the clunk of a central locking system.

'Jake?' I looked up at the window, wishing it wasn't so high – or so narrow. My heart leapt as a pair of man's legs moved past. I was in a basement. 'Let me out!' I yelled.

He didn't stop, and silence descended again.

A sudden determination rolled through me. Using my good arm, I dragged the two biggest wooden boxes – one looked just like a chest Celia used to keep Bryony's toys in – and positioned them on top of each other under the window, wincing as my arm protested. I clambered onto them, and reaching up with my good arm, managed to flick the rusty catch free and push the window open a fraction.

'Help!' I shouted, hoping a passer-by might hear. 'Help me, please. I'm locked in.'

Footsteps sounded behind the locked door, descending the steps. I jumped from the boxes and grabbed the broom. Keeping my back to the wall, I felt my way along until I was beside the door and waited for it to open, hearing the blood roaring in my ears.

There was a scrabbling noise, and a key slid under the gap at the bottom, with a label attached. I stared at it for a moment, then threw down the broom and stooped to pick up the key. Was he letting me out?

'Jake?' I called, pressing my ear to the door. I could hear him breathing and a chill ran through me. If I opened the door, would he attack me? Kill me? *Enjoy what's left of your life, Colleen.* That's what his text had said.

Footsteps sounded, heavy and fast on the stairs, and when it was clear he'd gone, I pushed the key in the keyhole and attempted to turn it. I wiggled it, heart pounding, but it wouldn't budge.

'It doesn't fit,' I shouted, thumping the door. 'Jake! The key doesn't fit the door.'

I rushed towards the boxes and clambered up again. 'Wait!' I called, hearing the clunk of the car unlocking, followed by the engine revving. 'Come back!'

But the car pulled away, quickly gathering speed, and then there was silence again.

'Shit!' I screamed and jumped down. I stood, swaying for a moment, my heart clattering. I'd only felt this helpless once before, when Bryony … I turned my mind away. No point going down that road.

I made a horrible noise that scared me. I wanted to cry. Punch something – someone.

I still had the key in my hand and there was something printed on the label. I held it up to the sunlight, feeling dizzy and faint, my legs like rubber, and read the words:

Colleen. Open box number 1

Chapter 19

Ella

'How long does it take to get a doll from the car?' I said, as Maisie ran up to her dad and grabbed her favourite Barbie. I'd been pacing around our room for what felt like ages, chewing my thumbnail, trying to shake the feeling of dread that had descended.

'I got talking to a couple who'd been for a walk up Knocknarea Mountain.' Greg sounded unconcerned, as if I hadn't blurted out that something must have happened to Colleen. Either that, or he didn't care. 'They've been to see Yeats's grave as well,' he went on, throwing his keys on the bed. 'I couldn't help thinking that's what we should be doing.'

I rolled my eyes. 'We can't go hiking up mountains with a three-year-old,' I said. 'And how can you think about that when I don't know where Colleen is?'

'I still don't get why you're so worried.' Frustration sharpened Greg's tone. 'After all the trouble she's caused.'

'She's left her phone behind,' I said, in case he'd forgotten that part.

A frown touched his brow. 'Don't you think you're being a bit dramatic?' He was making an effort to keep his voice light for Maisie's benefit. 'She's probably just gone for a walk.'

Had she gone because of what I'd said? Another thought sprang up before I could stop it: maybe Greg had responded to her kiss and she'd felt so guilty she couldn't face me again. Pushing the suspicion down, I said, 'I'm sure I saw her last night, staggering away from the hotel.'

Greg's expression hardened. 'Maybe it's a good thing if she's done a runner,' he said. 'I don't want to see her again.'

'Greg, don't be like that.'

I picked Maisie's pyjamas up off the floor and folded them. 'Go and find your toothbrush, sweetheart.' She smiled, and tottered into the bathroom, brandishing Barbie like a sword.

I turned to Greg. 'She's only got a rucksack with her and hardly any clothes,' I said, keeping my voice low. 'That's why she didn't get changed for dinner last night. It's as if she wasn't prepared for meeting us at all.'

'For God's sake, Ella, she's been abroad, hasn't she?' Greg pointed out. 'She's probably used to travelling light.'

'Surely that would mean she'd have more luggage,' I persisted, wishing I'd asked more questions. 'And don't you think it's odd that she barely mentioned her trip?' I recalled her pale-as-milk skin. She hadn't looked like someone who'd been travelling.

'I've told you what I think of her, Ella.' Greg looked at me with a tired expression. 'Just because you're related, it doesn't mean you're automatically going to bond. Or even like each other.' He paused, and I could see him weighing up whether or not to continue. 'You should quit now, before you get in any deeper.'

His words sliced through me, sharp and painful. 'Would that suit you better?' I'd said it before I could stop myself, and he spun away from me, pushing his hands through his hair.

When he faced me again, his expression was full of pain. 'You still don't believe me, do you?'

I couldn't hold his gaze. 'Greg, I—'

Cutting me off, he moved over and grabbed my hands. 'Do you realise what's happening?' His voice was strained. 'You're choosing to listen to someone you don't even know, over someone you've been living with for years. Someone you love.'

'Well, they do say love is blind.' It was a desperate attempt to alleviate the tension, but I regretted the words the instant they flew out.

Greg stepped back, his expression closing. 'If that's how you feel, there's no point me even being here.'

'Oh, Greg, don't be silly ...' My words trailed off as Maisie appeared, waving her toothbrush in the bathroom doorway.

'Got it, Mummy.'

'Good girl,' I said. 'I'll come and help in a minute.'

Greg's phone began to ring and he shook his head, moving into the other room to take the call. My mind spun as I watched him go. Nothing was happening the way it was supposed to. I wanted to turn back time, meet Colleen again, but this time I wouldn't leave the restaurant. I would ask her to tell me what was troubling her, because it was clear to me now that something was.

Tears threatened as I helped Maisie brush her teeth and gather her curls into bunches.

I sat on the bed and let her put lip gloss on me, struggling to find the words to make things right with Greg. If only Colleen would come back. Maybe once I saw her everything would fall into place.

'That's enough, darling,' I said, taking the lip gloss from Maisie before she could dab it on her eyelids.

I became aware of Greg's voice growing louder.

'There's a crisis at work,' he said, coming back in with a distracted air. 'A major client is thinking of jumping ship. I'm sorry, but I need to go back.'

Panic hissed in my ears. Was this a ploy to escape a confrontation with Colleen? I scoured his face, my mind flashing back to his broad hands circling her arms in the lift.

'Sounds bad,' I said, trying to relax my face muscles. In a way, it would be easier to deal with Colleen on my own, but Greg was my husband—

'You're coming too, aren't you?' His voice cut through my thoughts, and I was shocked. Not just by his ability to know what I was thinking, but that I hadn't even considered going home with him. 'I'll book a flight for this evening.'

'Greg … I …' I cleared my throat. 'I want to stay.'

His head jerked round. 'Are you being serious?'

'Just until I know where she is.'

He studied me for a long moment. I tried to read his thoughts, but his face was blank, and I looked away first. 'I'm taking Maisie,' he said. 'Libby will be thrilled to have her until you get back.'

'Yay! Auntie Libby!' Maisie cried, with the easy adaptability of the very young. Or maybe, like Greg, she couldn't wait to get away from me.

'I don't want her to go back,' I protested, getting off the bed. 'This was supposed to be a holiday.' But even as I spoke, I was trying not to think about how much of what was happening Maisie might be absorbing. I'd stayed strong and cheerful since Mum died, as much for my own sake as hers, but my emotions had become slippery lately. She'd be better off with Greg's sister and her happy-go-lucky brood.

As Greg called the airport, I reasoned it would only be for a couple more days. Make or break. If I clashed again with Colleen, once I'd found her, that would be the end of it.

'Not much of a holiday,' Greg said, after he'd rung off. 'We shouldn't have tagged along in the first place.'

'Why did you then?'

His eyes widened at my tone. 'I wanted us to spend some time together,' he said, bleakly, shaking his head. 'Clearly my mistake.'

'Oh, Greg. Don't say that.'

141

'Want to go to the beach,' Maisie said, as if she'd just remembered us talking about it before we came. As her lower lip jutted out, Greg pulled his gaze from mine and transformed his face into a smile.

'We can still go,' he said, lifting her off the bed with such care my heart contracted. 'The flight's not until six so we've plenty of time.' He flashed me a wary glance. 'Might as well make the most of it.'

I was gripped with panic again. 'What if Colleen comes back and we're not here?'

'Tough.' Greg's eyes cooled. 'If you're so concerned, leave a message for her at reception. Unless you'd rather stay here.'

His tone was confrontational, but although part of me longed to stay, I wanted to spend a few more precious hours with Maisie. And I didn't want to part on bad terms with Greg. 'Let's go then,' I said, forcing a brightness I didn't feel, and was rewarded by Maisie reaching out to give me a kiss, her eyes radiant with excitement.

'Clever Mummy,' she said, solemnly patting my overheated cheeks with her hot little hands. 'I love you very much.'

Tears threatened. 'I love you too, sweetie.'

After filling a beach bag, I suggested we take the car to Rosses Point Beach. Greg drove the short distance, along a winding road that dipped and rose, revealing the unspoilt countryside and a stretch of glittering sea against a low backdrop of mountains.

'Lovely, isn't it?' he said neutrally, and I nodded in agreement. The heavy silence that fell between us was punctuated by cheerful questions from Maisie, but all the time, my eyes were scouring the landscape, seeking Colleen.

If she'd been as drunk as I suspected when she left the hotel, she could have passed out. Or fallen and broken her ankle and be lying in agony somewhere. Perhaps I should check the local hospital or call the police.

Despite what Greg had said, I wasn't convinced she'd returned to the hotel at all the night before, let alone gone for a walk that morning. I doubted she was the early morning type, especially if she had a hangover.

I knew if I voiced my concerns to Greg, he'd ask how I thought I knew so much about her in such a short space of time. But it was as if our argument last night and her absence this morning had allowed my initial impressions of her to settle and expand. Her body language, the way her eyes had darted round, her fingers restlessly crumbling the slice of cake, and the snippets of conversation we'd had, flooded back.

She was a woman with secrets.

But I couldn't say any of it to Greg. He had his own views of Colleen, shaped by whatever had happened after I'd left them alone together, and I knew for now we were on opposite sides of an unbridgeable chasm. He couldn't understand why I was still drawn to Colleen, when she'd been so cruel to me. I barely understood it myself.

The scenery outside the car window blurred in a haze of tears.

'Here we are!' Greg adopted a determinedly cheerful air as he parked a short walk from the pale gold beach, which was bustling with visitors making the most of the sunshine, erecting windbreaks and laying out brightly coloured towels.

Out in the bay, a couple of windsurfers were attempting to ride the barely existent waves, their shouts and laughter drifting on the salty air.

I'd never liked the beach very much as a child, the gritty way the sand invaded my body and clothes, but Maisie was enthralled, wriggling impatiently as I rubbed sun cream into her fair skin.

'Build sandcastle, Daddy,' she ordered when I'd finished, pulling buckets and spades out of my bag.

Greg, in baggy combat shorts, removed his canvas shoes and T-shirt. His shoulders glowed brown, where mine were pasty apart from a scattering of freckles.

'Shall I?' I held up the sun cream.

'I can do it myself,' he said, taking the bottle from me.

Stung, I sat down and wrapped my arms around my knees. The sun was hot, but didn't seem to be penetrating my skin. I felt chilled in my strapless sundress and whipped out a towel, draping it around me. The sun glanced off the sea to dazzling effect and my temples began to throb.

Watching Greg and Maisie, their heads close together as they dug into the sand and filled their buckets, I felt a pang of something I couldn't decipher. Dad had never hunkered down with me like that. He'd rarely involved himself in anything I was doing, unless Mum prompted him: 'Aren't you going to help Ella with her homework, Andrew? You're the history genius around here!'

I wondered whether Colleen had grown up with a father figure in her life. My instinct was that she hadn't. I thought of the message from Reagan and remembered she was supposed to be meeting him today. My heart skipped. Maybe she'd already arranged something and was heading there now. Perhaps once they'd met, she would return to the hotel, keen to share the experience. She might tell him about me and ask about Mum, and come back with some answers for us.

Spirits lifting, I admired Maisie's sandcastle, which Greg had furnished with elaborate turrets. 'Fancy a paddle?' I said, rising. I slipped off my flip-flops and wriggled my toes into the sand, determined to focus on my daughter. But even as I led the dash to the water's edge, I couldn't stop imagining how Colleen would be feeling about reuniting with her father. It must be overwhelming for her after all these years, meeting us both within twenty-four hours.

When Maisie had finally had enough of paddling, and of Greg and I swinging her through the frothy waves, we made our way back up the beach to where we'd left our belongings.

'I'll go and get us an ice cream,' Greg offered, to ecstatic hand-claps from Maisie. He still hadn't spoken directly to me, but I sensed a thaw in his attitude and there was a softening around his mouth and eyes.

'Here,' I said, pulling my purse from a secret pocket in my bag and passing him a handful of euros. 'I'll have a '99 please.'

'Me have a '99 too,' chirped Maisie, beaming, and Greg and I laughed, knowing she had no idea what it was.

'Such faith that we'll come up with exactly what she wants.'

I examined Greg's words as he strode to the vintage ice-cream kiosk, but couldn't detect any sarcasm. Hating that I was scrutinising everything he said, I bent to put away my purse, and heard a small vibration from Colleen's phone, which I'd tucked into my bag.

Checking Maisie was occupied, happily spinning in circles like a Dalek, I slid it out.

A red light was flashing, indicating a text. Stifling a stab of guilt, I opened it.

I'm here, where are you?

It was from Reagan. My heartbeat quickened as another text arrived.

I get it. I didn't wait on Wednesday, and now you're punishing me. I don't blame you. I'll be here again tomorrow, same time. Please come x

Relieved her phone didn't have a password, I impulsively typed a reply.

Something came up, I'm sorry. I'll be there tomorrow. Where is it, again?

He responded right away.

Tate's Cafe, O'Connell Street.

I didn't reply. My hands were shaking. There was no way Colleen wouldn't have gone to meet him today, as arranged. I'd seen how desperate she was.

'Greg,' I called as he approached, holding three cones, which were starting to drip in the heat.

'What is it?' His expression grew blank, as if readying himself to receive whatever nonsense I was about to spout, and I felt a pinch of anger.

'They're melting,' I said, reaching for the ice creams. I couldn't tell him. He'd be angry and probably accuse me of being over-dramatic again, and the realisation I had neither the strength nor inclination to deal with it sent a shockwave through me. I bit my lip to stop it trembling and made a performance of looking for tissues in my bag to wrap around our cones.

'I really enjoyed that,' Greg said later, as we drove back to the hotel. 'I wish we *were* here on holiday and that I could stay.' His voice was laced with regret as he rested a hand on my thigh.

'Me too,' I said, but my voice lacked conviction. 'Eyes on the road,' I added with a laugh, feeling the heat of his gaze, and didn't know whether to be glad or sorry when he didn't respond.

Back at the hotel, I asked at reception whether Colleen had returned.

'She hasn't come back,' I told Greg, back in our room.

'Maybe she got cold feet and took off somewhere for the day.'

'She was planning to meet her father,' I said, not mentioning the text I'd read and replied to.

'Here?' His eyebrows drew together. 'In Sligo?'

I nodded.

He gave a short laugh. 'Killing two birds with one stone,' he said, in a way that suggested he wasn't remotely surprised.

'Greg.'

He relented. 'Look, she's probably having fun with him and lost track of the time. Sorry,' he finished, misunderstanding my expression. 'I know it must hurt that she's with him instead of you, but she's obviously got problems, Ella.' He stuffed his clothes into his suitcase while Maisie sprawled on the duvet, cuddling her bunny, her thumb jammed in her mouth.

'Give her another chance,' I said, irritation making me snappy. If it hadn't been for the incident in the lift the night before, I wouldn't be feeling as if I had to keep things from him. 'Are you sure you don't want me to drive you to the airport?'

He shook his head. 'I'll get a taxi, save you getting lost on the way back here.' He threw me a look. 'Sure you don't want to come with us?'

I looked at Maisie, already missing her. 'I can't, Greg.' I let out a sigh. 'Please try to understand.'

'I am trying, Ella, believe me.' He zipped his suitcase with unnecessary force. 'I'm worried you'll end up disappointed.'

This time I held his gaze. 'Me too.'

We hardly spoke again before he left. We had a snack sent up to our room, but I barely ate as I tried to console a fractious Maisie, who was flushed and overtired.

'She's going to be awful on the plane.' I was close to tears myself. 'Remember the journey over?'

'She'll probably sleep,' Greg said, a nerve twitching in his jaw. 'Don't worry, we'll be fine.'

'Call when you get home.'

'Of course.'

We'd been reduced to exchanging platitudes, like casual acquaintances.

I waved them off outside the hotel, choking back tears as their faces dissolved in the glare of late afternoon sun, and my breath caught in my throat when I turned and came face to face with the blue-eyed man I'd bumped into on the stairs the day before. He was film-star handsome in a rather clichéd way: chiselled jaw, glossy dark hair and over six-feet tall.

'Can I ask you something?' he said. He was softly spoken, his Irish accent muted.

'What is it?'

'I was wondering whether you'd seen Colleen today?'

'Colleen?' My stomach flipped. I remembered him pausing to look at her on his way past the restaurant the day before.

'I saw you talking to her,' he said.

'You know Colleen?'

'Of course.' He gave a tight-lipped smile that didn't touch his eyes. 'I don't suppose she told you I was here?'

I glanced back at the road, but the taxi carrying my family away had gone. 'Who are you?' My gaze swivelled back to the man, but with a leap of intuition I knew what he was going to say.

'I'm Colleen's husband, Jake.' His voice was somehow resigned. 'I think my wife has disappeared.'

Chapter 20

Ella

Why hadn't Colleen told me Jake was coming? was my first thought. I could have booked a double room. She'd been at pains to mention her happy marriage, so why not tell me then?

Because she'd been drinking, I reminded myself. It must have slipped her mind.

After a long pause, I said, 'She didn't say you were here.'

'I thought not.' He gestured inside. 'Shall we go and sit down?'

My heart raced as I followed him through the foyer and sat on a bottle-green Chesterfield sofa in reception.

Glancing around, he beckoned a passing waitress. 'Could we please have a pot of tea?' he said, bestowing the girl with a charming smile.

She nodded and flushed scarlet before hurrying away.

'I hope you don't mind,' he said to me, sitting so close I could smell his aftershave – something expensive and rather overpowering. Close up, his skin had an unhealthy pallor, and the whites of his eyes were bloodshot, and I remembered he was a surgeon and probably worked long hours. 'I've been so worried about Colleen.' He rubbed his brow. 'I haven't eaten or drunk a thing all day.'

'That's fine,' I said, shifting away a fraction. Things felt surreal without Greg and Maisie to anchor me, as though I was dreaming. 'I still don't understand why she didn't mention you were coming.'

His jaw tightened. 'I'll come straight to the point,' he said. 'We had an argument before she went away.' He tipped his gaze to the ceiling, and it took me a moment to realise he was holding back tears.

'To America?'

'America?' His gaze dropped back to mine. 'She didn't go to America,' he said, with a mirthless laugh. 'I'm afraid my wife's something of a fantasist.' He shook his head, as if he couldn't bear the truth of his own words. 'When she can't face reality, she makes things up,' he continued. 'Things she'd *like* to be true. It's her way of coping.'

I was surprised he'd come out with it so baldly to a complete stranger, but somehow, I wasn't surprised by his words. He'd confirmed what I'd begun to suspect already: that Colleen hadn't been honest with me. It hurt, but she must have been unhappy to have invented things to impress me. Perhaps it was linked to her childhood, to Mum abandoning her. 'You knew she was meeting me here?'

'No.' Jake lowered his eyes, smoothing his hands over his knees. They were nice hands, broad with long fingers. *Surgeon's hands.* His trousers were dark and expensively cut, and his crisp white shirt box-fresh, but his tie was clumsily knotted and there was a patch of dried blood on his chin where he'd cut himself shaving.

'I knew something was going on with her,' he said, his expression collapsing into sadness. 'I was worried, because she's not good at handling stress, but she wouldn't talk about it. I thought it was to do with meeting her father.'

'Reagan.'

'She told you?'

I nodded, stomach tipping as I recalled the text I'd sent him. 'Anyway, I followed her here, but we argued again,' said Jake.

I wondered when this had happened; why Colleen hadn't said anything. *Because she was trying to give the illusion she was happy, like Greg and me.*

'She told me to leave, said she had things going on that were none of my business and didn't want me anywhere near her.' Jake's smile was taut. 'I booked myself into another room, but told her I wasn't going anywhere until we'd sorted things out.'

No wonder she'd been edgy last night, fleeing from the hotel after dinner. And what about her supposed kiss in the lift with Greg? Was she so confused she didn't know what she was doing? Or had Greg taken advantage of her vulnerable state?

Confusion swirled through me. I stared at Jake's feet, in their dusty brown leather shoes. First one foot jigged, then the other, as if they longed to race him out of the hotel to search for his wife.

'I saw her talking to you in the dining room,' he said. My head jerked up, but I didn't say anything. 'I didn't want to interrupt,' he went on. 'I was worried she'd cause a scene. I saw her again later having dinner and thought I'd wait and talk to her.' He paused, seeming lost in thought for a moment. 'I knocked on her door about eleven, but she wasn't here. Or at least she didn't answer her door.' He dropped his head and raked his hands through his hair. 'I couldn't find her this morning, and you weren't here either.'

It wasn't an accusation, but guilt twisted inside me. 'I couldn't find her,' I admitted, my voice trailing off as the waitress returned with our tea.

Jake poured from the silver pot, adding a drop of milk to each cup. I was thirsty, but didn't trust myself not to spill hot liquid everywhere. I couldn't stop trembling, despite the mild air drifting through the hotel doors.

'So, who are you?' He held his cup in both hands and studied its contents. 'A friend?'

'I'm Ella. Her …' I hesitated, not sure whether it was my

place to explain in case Colleen hadn't told him. Then again, it sounded as if Colleen wasn't sure what she wanted, and it would be good to have someone on my side who cared about her. If she returned. *When*, not if. People didn't discover they had a family, arrange to meet them and then just disappear. I might not have been to her taste, but she'd been so excited about meeting Reagan.

'Her …?' Jake lifted an enquiring eyebrow. His pupils flared, making his eyes look almost black.

'We're very happy.' Colleen's words bounced into my head. Her face hadn't softened when she'd said it, the way Dad's did when he talked about Mum, or the way Greg's did whenever my name came up.

'I'm an old friend from way back,' I said on a whim. 'We lost touch years ago. I tracked her down on Facebook and suggested we meet up. I was coming to Ireland anyway, on a holiday and business trip.' I couldn't believe how easily the lie had tripped off my tongue and hoped he didn't have access to her Facebook account.

Jake nodded, seeming to accept my explanation with something like relief. It was preferable to her meeting another man, if that's what he'd suspected. *Did she often go around kissing men who weren't her husband?*

'I'd advise you to go home, Ella,' Jake said. He drank his tea in two gulps and replaced his cup on the glass-topped table in front of us.

'Sorry?' I stared, wondering if I'd heard right.

'Was that your family I saw you waving off?' He looked over to where a young couple were arriving, laden with bags, their faces flushed and happy. 'You should have gone with them,' he said darkly.

'But … something might have happened to Colleen.' It was an echo of my words to Greg that morning, which seemed like days ago. 'Don't you think we should check the hospitals?'

He barked out a short, sharp laugh. 'You really don't know her, do you?' he said. 'This is what she does, Ella.'

'What?'

He leaned forward, arms hanging loosely between his knees, his hair falling forward. 'She takes off without notice,' he said, not looking at me. 'Goes walkabout. Gets everyone worked up and calling the guards, then she walks back in as though nothing's happened.' He sounded matter of fact now, as if he already knew deep down that this was what had happened. 'She was gone for six months, once. Sent me a couple of postcards telling me not to worry. I never got to the bottom of why. Something about finding herself.'

'But you're still married.'

He shifted position, flexing his shoulders. 'I love her,' he said, and I was instantly ashamed of the flash of annoyance I'd felt, that he was sitting here talking about his wife instead of trying to find her. He'd probably been searching all day, hoping history wasn't repeating itself, only to come to the conclusion it probably was.

He fished something out of his back pocket. A worn, folded photograph. 'We used to be happy before she ...' He left the words hanging.

I craned my neck and saw a younger Colleen, looking every inch a rock chick, in a baggy mohair sweater, ripped jeans and chunky books, her smile relaxed and open. She was leaning against a motorbike, a man's hands – Jake's presumably – on the handlebars.

My heart turned over. Her hair was fair like mine, but tousled. It suited her. I instinctively reached for the photo, to take a closer look, but Jake thrust it back in his pocket as though he regretted showing me. He was biting his lower lip, and I had the impression he was stemming a surge of emotion.

'I'm sorry,' I said, my hand hovering somewhere near his. It struck me afresh how little I knew about Colleen, and I considered telling Jake who I really was. But what was the point? If she'd run away, she clearly wanted nothing to do with me.

For the first time, I allowed myself to believe she really had kissed Greg the night before. Perhaps it had been her way of ruining any chance of a relationship between us. If so, she'd at least had the decency to leave and not take it further.

'She told me she's a film editor,' I said. 'Is that true?'

He briefly closed his eyes. 'She doesn't work.'

'Right.' Hurt slid through me. No wonder she hadn't elaborated about her job. 'And does she normally leave without taking her things?'

His gaze sharpened. 'How do you know she didn't?'

'We'd arranged to meet for breakfast and I was worried when she didn't come down,' I said. 'I asked to be let into her room and saw her rucksack with some clothes in it.'

He seemed to deflate. 'That's typical, I'm afraid.'

'Will she have any money?'

'She'll have her credit card.' He massaged his temple. 'She's very good at spending her husband's cash.' He sounded bitter. Maybe she was in the habit of emptying their bank account. 'She'll probably get a job in a bar,' he added. 'She likes pretending she's independent.'

Pity for him rose. It couldn't be easy, having to explain that your wife kept running away like a troubled teen. I thought of her mobile in my bag, knowing I should give it to him – not sure why I hadn't. Wouldn't her contacts be on there? He might want to ring round, but I reasoned he probably already had. All the same …

I was on the verge of handing it over, but remembered it would mean admitting I'd taken it in the first place. Some instinct told me Jake wouldn't like that; not when he thought I was just a casual acquaintance.

The moment passed.

'So, you really think she won't be back?' I picked up my cup at last, aware my hands were trembling. The tea was cold, but I drank it anyway, overwhelmed with thirst.

'I'll give her until morning then I'll return home.' Jake sounded as weary as I felt. 'She might even be there when I get back.' The sun coming through the window was low in the sky, placing shadows beneath his eyes, making him look older. Not that I looked much better. I was still in my flip-flops and my strappy sundress was patterned with ice-cream stains. My scalp was itchy too, as sand had got into my hair, and I desperately needed a shower.

I wished I could talk to Greg. He would be on the plane by now. I hoped that Maisie was sleeping. 'Good luck,' I said, rising, my head full of conflicting thoughts. I felt as if there was more I should be asking, but what? Jake was tormented enough, and he'd told me more than I deserved, considering I hadn't been honest with him. 'I think I'll head up to my room.' I stuck out my hand, aware it was sticky and hot. 'Thank you for talking to me.'

He shot to his feet and shook my hand. His grip was cool and dry, his expression neutral, and I wondered if he was disappointed that I couldn't tell him where his wife had gone. *His wife.* Sometime during our conversation, I'd stopped thinking of Colleen as my sister. He'd fleshed her out into someone I didn't know – maybe didn't want to know. Perhaps Greg's instinct – and mine, last night – had been right and she wasn't the sort of person I needed in my life.

'I hope she comes back soon,' I said, turning to pick up my bag so he couldn't see the tears swelling in my eyes. 'Tell her she can call me when she does. If she wants to.'

'I will.'

A dense silence fell, pierced by the sound of cutlery clattering in the restaurant. For a second, I thought Jake might say something else; ask what Colleen had been like when I knew her, and my muscles tensed in readiness. I wasn't sure I was up to inventing something, just to make him feel better.

But he didn't speak, and when I looked up he was moving

through the hotel doors with even strides, fading out into the evening like a ghost. Or, a man who'd grown too used to searching for his wife.

I walked back to my room feeling sluggish and syrupy, my feet dragging, my stomach knotted with tension and hunger. After my shower, I would call room service and have them send up some food, and then I would book a flight home.

But, almost without realising, I'd come to another decision.

Before I left Ireland, I was going to meet Colleen's father.

Chapter 21

Colleen

My eyes were closed, and my mind whirred with random memories. The gold watch lying on my dressing table back in Waterford and the expensive trinkets Jake had bought me over the years. I'd never been one for expensive jewellery or designer dresses. In fact, Jake hated that I always wore Bryony's cheap necklace. I refused to take it off – one of my rare acts of rebellion – but aside from that, I always wore what he asked me to wear.

I opened my eyes, realising I must have passed out. From the little I could see outside the window, the sun was now low in the sky, but I had no idea what time it was. I raised my hand to my aching head, and felt a bump and dried blood. My arm was agony, and my tongue was coated with a fur-like scum. I pulled myself up from the floor, staggered to the sink and threw up.

'Somebody help me,' I spluttered through coughs and gasps.

I turned on the tap. A whoosh of clear water spurted out and I splashed my face and drank from my cupped hands. After running a finger over my teeth and smoothing my hair, I wiped my face on my arm.

'I'm sorry!' I shouted, as I turned off the tap. 'I'm sorry for being me, Jake. Is that what you want me to say?'

I didn't even know if he was there. I doubted he was.

The key, with the label I'd read before passing out, was on the floor by the door. I picked it up and looked again round the room. There were padlocks on the wooden boxes I'd stacked beneath the window. The key must fit one of them.

I padded over and looked more closely. I hadn't noticed when I dragged them there, that there was writing carved into the wood. On the biggest box were the words *Colleen Box 1*.

My blood chilled as I took in that the smaller one was marked *Box 2*, and the third, no bigger than a shoebox, was marked *Box 3*. My name was scratched into all of them.

My stomach churned as I fingered the padlock on the first one.

What if there was an airborne poison inside? But, I rationalised, if Jake was going to kill me, he would save it until box 3, once he'd had his fun.

I sat down on the floor, turning the key over and over in my hands, inspecting it, my heart racing. The silence, apart from the drip-drip-drip of the tap, made me want to scream.

I clenched my fist around the key's jagged edges. I had to get out of here. A surge of adrenalin shot me to my feet. I clambered onto the boxes once more, and craned my neck. I could just see through the window. There was a rough patch of flattened ground where the car had been earlier. So, Jake *had* gone.

It was hard to see much from ground level. I could only make out a thicket of trees in one direction, and no other buildings, but something about the layout seemed familiar. I tried to heave myself up further, feeling sure I could slither through the window if only my arm didn't hurt. I tried again, but the pain was intolerable. I let out a yelp and crashed to the ground, the key falling from my hand and bouncing across the concrete floor.

I scrambled against the wall, fighting sick. *Keep calm, Colleen, you're going to be OK.* But I was far from calm. My heart hammered against my ribs, and every part of me shook. 'God help me,' I said. Not that I believed in God. I wasn't religious, despite Celia's efforts to convince me.

I'd never liked boxes either, now I thought about it. My step-father, Terry, had bought Bryony a jack-in-the-box for her third birthday, and she'd laughed and laughed whenever Jack's garish face popped up. But I'd hated its painted-on features, and the way it shot out had made me jump to the point of tears.

I leaned over and grabbed the key. There was only one way to find out what was in the box, even if it meant playing Jake's stupid little game. I lifted myself onto my knees, inserted the key into padlock number one, and turned it. When it sprang open, I fumbled it out of the way and lifted the lid.

There were several items inside, shrouded in white tissue paper.

I pulled them out one by one, hands trembling as I unwrapped them: a tin of beans, a pair of yellow rubber gloves, a floral apron, a tube of pale pink lip gloss, a pair of sheer hold-ups, a blue-and-white checked dress and a pair of black, high-heeled shoes in my size. At the bottom, a shoulder-length blonde wig lay like a dead animal.

I plucked out a sheet of paper, printed in large black letters.

If you want to get out of here alive, you will do as I say. Put on the clothes, shoes and the wig. I always preferred you blonde, Colleen. Then clean the room for me. I know how much you like cleaning. The beans will keep your strength up. I'll be watching you.

I looked up, and for the first time noticed a small camera positioned high on the wall in the corner, moving slowly, a red light flashing.

'Bastard!' Tears of fury rose as I imagined him watching, laughing in that supercilious way of his. 'You should be at work,' I yelled. 'Saving lives, not tormenting mine. Why the hell are you doing this?'

I lunged for the broom and attempted to knock the camera down, but couldn't quite reach. Panting, I sagged against the wall.

Sweat lay on my forehead, and my arm felt like it was on fire. I was trapped. I had no choice but to follow his instructions. God only knew what he would do if I didn't.

'Bastard!' I grabbed the wig and jammed it on my head. It was cheap nylon – nothing like my real hair, apart from the colour – the same shade of blonde as Ella's.

Turning my back on the camera, I struggled out of my T-shirt and jeans. Sobbing in pain, I pulled on the stockings and stepped into the dress. I couldn't manage the zip. I dragged the lip gloss across my mouth, tied the apron round my waist and stuffed my feet in the shoes. 'Happy now?' I cried up at the camera. This was a whole new level of cruel, even for him.

Jake had called me his pretty little puppet. I'd hated the way he'd smiled as he said it, as though he could control me. Truth was, he could – at first. He'd been so handsome and charming – still was – and I'd fallen into his arms, wondering how I got so lucky.

I ignored the beans, which I'd never liked anyway – another of his sick jokes – and moved towards the sink and opened the cupboard door. There were so many cleaning products inside, my heart sank.

I filled the sink with water and cleaning fluid, then took the broom and began sweeping. A cloud of dust rose and I coughed, but refused to cry.

It took a long time with my injured arm and cut finger, but I scrubbed and cleaned the floor, the walls, the sink and the cupboards. Finally, the basement smelt fresh and every surface sparkled.

I sank onto the edge of the biggest box, sweating beneath the wig and stockings, and surveyed the room. Looking back at the camera, I wiped my damp forehead on the back of my hand. The lens stared at me blankly.

I stood up and pulled off the apron, throwing it to the floor, then ran the water once more and rinsed my face, glimpsing my tiny reflection in the tap. I looked a bit like Ella: the same pattern

160

of freckles, the blonde wig. My anger drained away as I thought of her. I should have told her everything from the off, instead of being mean and judgemental. I couldn't believe now I'd tried to kiss her husband, just to prove that all men were as awful as Jake. I hated myself for being so cruel. It wasn't her fault my life was a mess. Maybe Anna and Reagan had set the ball rolling, but everything since was my fault – my fault I'd ended up in this concrete basement, alone and scared for my life.

Trembling with pain and exhaustion, I sat back on the box, eased off the shoes and rubbed my sore heels. I removed the bandage from my finger and examined the tip. It was pink and puckered, but no longer bleeding. It would be OK. Which was more than I could say for anything else.

Fear expanded, white and hot inside me. 'Please find me, Ella,' I whispered, tears sliding down my cheeks. If she found me, I would tell her I was sorry. That I would be the sister she dreamed of, just as I became the wife Jake wanted me to be.

As darkness fell, I flicked the light switch up and down. There was no bulb. Still wearing the dress, and using my hoodie as a makeshift blanket, I curled into a tight ball on the floor, a low moan of despair escaping, echoing around the basement.

Eventually I drifted off to sleep, slipping in and out of a nightmarish doze for hours, imagining Bryony was beside me, that I was holding her close, and sometime in the early hours, imagined I heard her whisper, 'It's your fault I drowned, Collie. It's all your fault.'

Chapter 22

Colleen

Monday

Tears slid down my cheek and into my hair, jolting me awake. I pulled myself up, gritting my teeth as my aching body protested, though I was relieved my arm didn't feel as painful.

I headed across the room and peed in the mop bucket, trying not to think too hard about the camera, and what I'd been reduced to.

I rose, emptied the bucket into the sink and glanced up at the window. The sky was a candyfloss pink and I tracked a pair of birds circling a single cloud. I could tell it was early. The air hadn't warmed up yet. The wig was lying on the floor like roadkill, and with a surge of anger I kicked it across the room.

As I let out a scream, a car pulled up outside, and as heavy footfalls descended the stairs, loud and fast, I realised, for the second time in my life, I was afraid.

'Jake.' My voice was a small, useless thing. I crossed the floor, shivering as the cold concrete struck the soles of my feet.

He slid something under the door. Another key.

'Jake, for Christ's sake! This has gone on long enough.' I pressed my mouth to the edge of the door. 'Whatever it is, we can talk about it. Please, let me out.'

I was pathetic. He was probably loving it. 'Jake!' I thumped the door. 'Jake?' I could hear him breathing. 'Say something, for fuck's sake.'

Silence.

I slammed both palms on the wood, and let out a cry as pain shot up my arm. Seconds later, his footsteps retreated.

'*Shit!*' I rubbed my throbbing shoulder, biting down on my tears.

I looked up at the window, but there was no point attempting to clamber out again. Even if I didn't hurt all over, he was watching. He would know I was trying to escape.

Ignoring the key, I crossed to the cupboard and grabbed the tin of beans. I felt faint with hunger and knew I should probably eat to keep my strength up. Though for what, I wasn't sure. Maybe it would be quicker if I starved to death.

All the same, I pulled off the lid with the ring pull, then rummaged through the big box for a spoon or fork, but found neither. The drawer above the cupboard was empty too. He wanted me incapable.

Standing by the sink, back to the camera, I scooped out the beans with my fingers and shovelled them into my mouth. Tears pricked my eyes as I swallowed, trying not to gag.

'And you wonder why I left you,' I said, once I'd finished.

I rinsed my fingers under the tap and wiped them on the apron. 'If you think I'm going to fall apart, you're mistaken,' I muttered. 'I'm stronger than you think.'

I paced, thinking about the limited view from the window – the flattened ground and the dense trees in the distance. And then it hit me. It reminded me of the view from the holiday cottage, where we'd stayed the week Bryony died. *Oh God.* Was this another perverted attempt to torture me?

Before I could wrench them back, memories of that holiday began unfolding in my mind. Playing hide-and-seek on the beach at Aughris Head, Bryony's little legs carrying her off.

'Come and find me, Collie.'

I cover my eyes and count, 'One, two, three …'

My teeth began to chatter, and with an enormous effort, I pulled my mind away from that torturous time.

Outside the window, the sun slipped behind a cloud, reducing the light in the room to a dull grey. The day yawned ahead of me, vast and unknown, and I took a deep breath, continuing to fight tears.

I looked at the key, still lying on the floor with a label attached. About to give in and pick it up, I caught my breath as a sheet of paper came sliding under the door.

'Jake?' My heart skidded against my ribcage. I hadn't heard him come back. 'Please let me out, Jake. Please!' But the silence was total.

Crossing the floor, I bent and snatched up the piece of white A4 and read the large bold print:

Open the box, Colleen. You don't want to know what will happen if you don't.

I pressed my ear against the door, trying to work out if he'd gone, but there was nothing – not even the sound of breathing.

The key was labelled *Box 2*. On the reverse of the label were the words: *You've let me down, Colleen.*

'I've let *you* down?' I gave a bitter laugh. 'You just don't get it, do you, Jake?'

I picked up the box marked 2. What else could I do? I placed the key in the padlock and turned it. Inside were two more tissue-wrapped items. I knew what they were by their shape, and fresh tears sprang to my eyes.

Ripping off the paper, I stared at a blue bucket and spade. Such small things, but they represented the moment my life changed. *How could Jake use that against me? Hadn't I punished myself enough?*

I turned to the winking camera, imagining him grinning.

'Let me out,' I pleaded, my resolve not to cry dissolving. I felt sure he'd loved me once. Maybe he still did, in his own warped way. 'I'll come back home with you,' I added, the urge to get out of this room, at any cost, growing stronger. 'I'll be good, Jake. I promise. Just give me another chance to prove it.' I dropped the bucket and spade and spun away from them, pressing the heels of my hands into my eyes, my face wet with tears.

But it was no good.

He'd triggered the memory of that awful day my little sister drowned.

Chapter 23

Colleen

'Build sandcastles, Collie?'

I gasped, fighting back tears. The past was playing out before my eyes, like an old cine film – Bryony so vivid in my mind, her thick dark hair pushed back into a ponytail, her green eyes wide and bright. And I thought I could hear her laughing somewhere, my imagination running wild.

We'd found a deserted beach that summer's day.

'Isn't this lovely?' Celia had said, our picnic lunch in a big checked bag over her shoulder, her hand in Bryony's while I skipped down the sandy path behind them, happy to be on holiday.

The cove was separate from the tourist area, but accessible from the main beach.

'Our secret place,' Celia said, smiling as she spread out stripy towels and erected the windbreak. It was warm and sunny, but a breeze was blowing off the sea, ruffling the waves. 'It's quite a find. We'll come here every day, I promise.' She'd scooped her dark hair into a ponytail that matched Bryony's, and she looked pretty in a red striped dress, her legs tanned.

'Collie, build sandcastles?'

Bryony hadn't been able to pronounce Colleen, and I would tease her, saying, 'A collie is a dog that looks after sheep, not a big sister.'

She'd tugged at my arm, then held out her blue bucket and spade in her chubby hands. '*Please*, Collie.'

'No,' I said, sprawling on one of the towels, my heart-shaped sunglasses pushed on top of my head as if I were a film star, not a nine-year-old. 'I'm reading. Now go away.'

'Don't be mean, Colleen,' Celia said, glancing up from her crossword puzzle to give me a reproachful look. But I was never mean to Bryony. I loved her.

'I'll play soon,' I said, rolling onto my stomach to read the book I'd brought, wriggling my toes into the sand, the sun warm on my back.

After a lunch of egg sandwiches and blackcurrant the breeze picked up, blowing over the windbreak, scattering sand.

'Well, that didn't do its job very well,' Celia said, laughing. Strands of hair had escaped her ponytail and were whipping around her face. Shielding her eyes, she looked out to sea, where waves crashed on a rocky outcrop, thick and frothy like the foam on one of Terry's pints of Guinness.

He wasn't with us that day. He'd gone to the pub, according to Celia, who didn't seem to care, and I certainly didn't. Celia was more relaxed when he wasn't around.

The wind grew stronger, sending dark clouds across the sun, leaving a chill in its wake. Celia shivered, her eyes darting over the horizon. 'It's so wild out there,' she said, almost to herself. 'I think we should pack up and head back to the cottage. I'll make us some hot chocolate.'

We'd groaned, and pleaded to stay a bit longer.

'But I have goose pimples on my goose pimples,' Celia said with a laugh. She rose and gathered our things together, stuffing the remains of lunch into her bag. 'Come on, girls,' she said. 'You'll catch your deaths, down here.'

Bryony balled her hands into fists and stamped her foot. 'I don't *want* to go,' she said, robust in her frilly swimsuit. 'Want to go and paddle with Collie.'

'No, not today.'

Celia had wanted her to wear her water wings, even though Bryony had learned to swim in the swimming pool near where we lived, because she said 'the sea was a different animal' but I knew Bryony had hidden them somewhere, always determined to swim without them.

'We can come back tomorrow, sweetheart.'

'Don't *want* to go.'

I didn't want to leave either. I wanted to play, now that I'd finished my book. I didn't want to go back to the cottage and see Terry.

'Can we stay a bit longer?' I said. 'The sun will come out again soon.'

'Please, Ma.' Bryony jumped up and down, clapping her hands, eyes pleading. 'Please, please, please.'

Celia caved in. She could never resist Bryony for long.

'Fine,' she said, smiling and shaking her head. 'I'll go back to the car and get our cardigans,' she went on, heading towards the path. 'I won't be long.' She looked at me over her shoulder. 'Look after your sister, Colleen.'

Bryony wanted to play hide-and-seek, though there weren't many places to hide.

'Come and find me, Collie,' she cried, rushing away.

I covered my eyes and counted. 'One, two, three …'

Squeals of excitement streamed behind her.

I got up, peering through my fingers, and followed her tiny footprints through the sand. 'I'm coming to get you!'

It all happened so fast.

'Collie, look at me.' Her voice was far away. I dropped my hand and realised I was close to the water's edge. The waves had grown bigger, crashing against the shore, and Bryony was a long way out, her dark hair, so like Celia's, plastered to her head as she bobbed up and down, drifting closer to the rocks.

'Bryony!' I yelled, running into the sea and wading out, hands slashing through the water. I dragged myself through the waves, eyes fixed on her face. She was laughing and waving her arms, unaware of the danger. 'Hold on, I'm coming!'

I was in waist deep when her head hit one of the rocks looming out of the water.

'Bryony!' I screamed, as she disappeared. I thrust forward, swimming towards her, but a strong undercurrent pushed me back. Water shot up my nose, and I beat back panic-stricken tears as I choked on salty water.

I stopped and doggie-paddled, trying to see Bryony through streaming eyes, but she'd gone. Terrified, I scanned the bobbing horizon. I couldn't see her anywhere, and with horror realised I wasn't strong enough to get myself back to the beach. I could feel the force of the water, the undertow like a rope, pulling me backwards.

'Bryony!' I shouted, through a lungful of water. 'Bryony, where are you?' My voice was small, snatched away by the wind.

'Colleen!' I flipped round to see Celia on the beach. She dropped the cardigans and raced into the water, tripping and stumbling, her mouth gaping in terror.

It wasn't long before our screams attracted people from the main beach, and they rushed into view like toy figures, some ploughing through the waves towards us.

Strong arms grabbed hold of me and pulled me back to the beach, Celia's screams ringing in my ears, mingling with the mournful cry of seagulls overhead.

I was inconsolable, screaming that I had to go back in to find my sister, though I knew it was pointless.

Bryony's body was never found.

Celia had been a good mother before that day.

I never had looked like her in the way Bryony had, and I used to wonder why. I told myself I must look like my father – not Terry, I knew he wasn't my biological father – but the man I'd called Da in Cork, the man in the pinstriped suit. I'd been convinced he was my real father, and Celia had never told me otherwise – until recently. I supposed I'd dreamed he might come back one day.

I'd envied the bond Celia had with Bryony, but I still loved my sister with all my heart. No one seemed to care how her loss affected me. How I felt broken inside, as though all the air had been squeezed out of my lungs and I couldn't breathe – how my stomach ached all the time, but I couldn't eat.

I wished and wished I could turn back time, that I'd thrown down my book and played with Bryony when she first asked. Maybe if I had, she'd have been tired, and happy to leave the beach when Celia suggested it.

Celia didn't say Bryony's death was my fault. Worse, she refused to believe she was dead and became convinced I was mistaken, that I hadn't seen her head hit the rock and watched her disappear.

'She'll be back, you'll see,' she said over and over.

I gave up saying, 'Ma, I saw her go under the water.'

During the months following Bryony's death, Celia would wait by the window for her to come home. She grew thinner. It was as though I didn't exist anymore. She cooked meals when she remembered, and was never cruel, but it was as if part of her had disappeared that day on the beach. She no longer held me, looked at me, or talked to me in the same way.

Terry got drunk at every given opportunity, mourning a daughter he'd rarely spent any time with. 'I can't live like this, Celia,' he kept saying, maudlin with drink. 'We need to say goodbye to Bryony, let her go.'

'She's not dead, Terry,' Celia would yell back, the tears that came so easily distorting her voice.

'A service, that's all,' he said. 'A way of keeping the door ajar. We need something, Celia, a way to move on.' I guessed, looking back, he was trying to be kind, and in the end Celia had agreed.

The service at the church was small, and the priest spoke of Bryony in a way that suggested she wasn't gone forever. I sat, feeling sick, wanting to shout that I'd seen her go under the water. That she was dead. I didn't want her to be, with every fibre of my being, but she was. But I knew they wouldn't listen, so I stayed silent, my heart a small, tight ball of grief.

The saddest sight that day was a wreath of lilies placed outside the church by a man I didn't recognise at the time. *'For Bryony,'* the card read. *'Forever in our hearts.'*

Celia went crazy when she saw them. 'She's not dead!' she cried, tossing the wreath aside, tears streaming down her face. 'My baby isn't dead.'

I knew now that the man who left them was Reagan. My father.

Terry left a year later and we never saw him again. He'd been a useless pile of shite, so I was glad to see the back of him, and Celia barely noticed his absence.

She didn't notice me either. Not then, and not when I started failing at school and skipping classes. She was oblivious when I got in with a bad crowd, didn't care when I moved to Dublin at seventeen and found a job in a pub, renting a room above it. I met Gabriel there. My first boyfriend. He was a bit older, but there was instant chemistry. When I found out he was a drug dealer it made him more attractive somehow, not less, and when he got me hooked it was almost a relief. I liked the way drugs took me away from everything, from the guilt that constantly gnawed at my insides.

A noise outside the door brought me back to the basement. The dark sky outside had given way to heavy rain splattering the window. I wiped my face on the backs of my hands and pushed myself up.

The doorknob began to turn. Heart thudding, I stood motionless, listening. 'Hello?'

Was he coming in? I spun into action, stacking the boxes again, not caring if he knew what I was doing. My arm pounded with pain, but I gritted my teeth. I had to climb up, climb out and get away.

The knob turned once more and I froze.

'Jake?'

Another piece of paper slipped under the door, and I could see the words clearly from where I was.

Do you want to build a sandcastle, Collie?

Heart thumping, and every limb shaking, I scrambled up onto the boxes.

I heard his footsteps heading up the stairs as I strained to see out of the window. I couldn't make out much in the lashing rain, apart from soaking wet grass. Just out of eyeshot a car door slammed and an engine started. Seconds later it pulled away, brakes squealing.

I reached to open the window, which had fallen back on its latch, but it was no good. I hadn't got the strength to even do that, let alone climb out. With a cry of despair, I let myself fall to the floor, where I lay in a heap, arms wrapped around myself.

I was going to die.

I might as well get used to the idea.

Chapter 24

Ella

I rose early, after a mostly sleepless night spent crossing from the bed to the window, in the hope of catching Colleen returning to the hotel.

Greg had texted me a picture of Maisie around midnight, with the caption, *Sleeping at my sister's house*. I'd called him, but he sounded tired and our conversation had been stilted.

'You need to come home,' he said, when I told him Colleen wasn't back. 'It's obvious she's unstable.'

'Not unstable.' Some instinct to defend her had reared up. 'Troubled, maybe.'

'What I told you, about her kissing me—'

'I'm still not ready to give up on her,' I said at the same time, and an awkward silence followed.

He exhaled a sigh. 'But hasn't she given up on you?' As if regretting being so blunt, he quickly added, 'Maybe when she's had time to digest everything, she'll be in touch.' His words had a steely undercurrent. It was obvious he wanted Colleen out of our lives. Doubt reared up once more. First, he'd seemed keen to come to Ireland with me, taking time off work when things were frantic, and then he couldn't wait to leave.

And why had Colleen really run away? Was she worried her husband would find out she'd kissed – or been kissed by – another man?

I knew I should tell Greg about Jake, and that I was planning to meet Reagan, but some instinct had warned me not to. I'd rung off, pleading a headache.

Now, I rolled out of bed, took a quick shower and dressed. After knocking on Colleen's door and getting no reply – not that I'd really expected to – I hurried down to the dining room. Maybe, by some miracle, she would be there.

Five minutes later, I toyed with a plate of scrambled eggs, eyes fixed on the entrance, waiting – hoping – either Colleen, or Jake would appear.

I pushed my plate aside and fished Colleen's mobile from my bag, wondering if there might be some clues to her state of mind in her other texts. Feeling shifty, I opened her messages folder. There was nothing – from Jake, or anyone else.

Strange. Surely Jake would have contacted her to at least check she was OK. Greg and I texted regularly, even if it was just 'hello'.

Outside, clouds had rolled across the sky and a chill stole over my skin. With a shiver, I got out my own phone and texted Greg *good morning*, adding a smiley face for reassurance. I tried to picture him, sweet-talking his important client into staying with the company, but the image felt unreal.

Guilt pushed at me. I still hadn't booked an earlier flight back to England. I would do it later, I decided, and try to make up with Greg once I was home.

I rubbed a tight knot in the back of my neck and sighed. The elderly woman, who'd been so taken with Maisie yesterday, was giving me odd looks from a table by the window, perhaps wondering why I was alone.

I threw her a smile as I rose and said, 'Beautiful morning,

isn't it?' just as heavy rain began to pelt the windows. My face burned with colour and I left before she could reply, returning to my room to grab a jacket before heading out.

As I crossed to the foyer the receptionist called out. 'Mrs Matthews?'

My heart gave a thud. 'Yes?'

'A gentleman asked me to give you this, before he checked out this morning.' She held out a folded note with a knowing smile, as if she suspected I was having an affair.

'Thank you.' Aware of her curious scrutiny, I moved out to the porch, where a family were daring each other to run through the rain to their car.

'Bring it round the front, I don't want to get my hair wet,' the woman instructed her husband, patting her highlighted bob. She saw me looking and grinned. 'Not exactly holiday weather, is it?'

I agreed it wasn't, before turning my back and unfolding the sheet of paper, which bore the hotel's logo.

Dear Ellen, I'm sorry I unburdened myself, yesterday. Thank you for listening. I hope you understand and can make allowances for my wife's behaviour. Have a safe trip home. Best wishes, J.

I was touched that Jake had taken the trouble to leave a note, even if he'd got my name wrong. Maybe I should have told him the full story. If he'd known Colleen had arranged to meet Reagan, he might have wanted to come with me.

I resolved that if she showed up, I'd insist on her calling Jake right away.

Pushing the note in my bag, I headed for my car and by the time I'd driven into town the rain had stopped and the sun was out again. I found a space in a bustling car park on Wine Street, glad I had some euros in my purse for the ticket machine. It was a short walk from there to O'Connell Street, which was a pleasant mix of old and new buildings that housed shops, pubs, cafés and restaurants.

Despite the rain the air was thick with humidity, and rich with food smells. I felt oddly nervous as I zigzagged along the busy pavement. I was so used to working every day, I could barely remember the last time I'd been alone in a strange place that didn't involve meeting a client.

I spotted the gold lettering of Tate's Café beneath a scarlet awning and, keeping my head down, crossed the road. I was early and needed to gather myself before going in, and work out what to say.

Stopping outside a nearby chemist's, I took a deep breath and checked my reflection in the window. It was hard to make out among the notices and advertisements, but my hair, which I hadn't dried properly after my shower, looked fuzzy. I smoothed it down, feeling wired up and flushed, too hot in my cream suede jacket. I took it off, but noticed my sleeveless top was creased and pulled it back on again.

I hung my leather shoulder bag across my body, then pulled out my phone to check for messages, but the screen was empty.

Glancing up and down the street, I remembered the way Colleen's face had lit up when she'd mentioned Reagan, and I felt a blast of guilt that I was the one going to meet him instead of her.

I looked at my watch again, my heartbeat speeding up. *This is it.*

I squared my shoulders and adjusted my jacket again, told myself not to be silly. *Pretend it's work.* But I couldn't fool myself and my hand shook as I crossed the road and pushed open the door of the café. It was steamy inside, with a comforting, sugary-rich smell that reminded me of childhood visits to my grandparents' house in Hampshire.

I caught the eye of a dark-haired man in the queue at the counter and my heart gave a lurch. He looked me up and down and winked, before turning back to the newspaper he was holding. My face flamed. He was too young to be Reagan.

The importance of what I was doing began to press down. Meeting Reagan would change everything. I felt sure this was the man my mother had loved before Dad – had perhaps loved all her life. A man she'd loved enough to have a child with. A child she'd never spoken about. *A child she'd abandoned.*

Oh God. What if I didn't like what he had to say? Maybe he'd be angry that I wasn't Colleen and refuse to speak to me. What if he wasn't even here?

I shouldn't have come. I should leave—

'Colleen?' A male voice interrupted my chaotic thoughts. 'Colleen, is that you?'

I spun around. A man was rising from a table by the window and I realised he must have been there all along, looking out for her. I tried to fix his image in my mind, but the light was behind him, making a silhouette of his shape.

'Reagan?' I moved forward, knocking someone with my bag and bashing my hip on a chair, adrenalin pumping through me. He was standing, hands outstretched, and I could see he was medium height and build, with a slight slope to his shoulders.

As he came into view, I took in his greying fair hair, worn a little too long at the back and receding at the front. He had green eyes, blazing from a broad, tanned face, the edges etched with laughter lines. There was something of the rock star about him – faded blue jeans, a battered leather jacket over a T-shirt and biker-style boots. First impressions: nice, but ordinary.

What had Mum seen in him?

'You're not what I was expecting.' There was a trace of puzzle-ment in his voice, which was soft and deep with a strong Irish accent. His eyes had narrowed, as if sensing something was off-kilter, and in a distant part of my brain I was glad he wasn't fooled.

'I'm not Colleen.' My voice was too small, like Maisie's.

He lowered his hands and rested them on the table, bringing his face closer to mine. He smelt of sun-dried leather and the sea, underlaid with something minty. 'Who are you then?' Lines creased the freckled skin of his forehead. 'Has Colleen sent you?'

177

I couldn't take my eyes off him. 'I'm Anna's other daughter,' I said at last, and this time my voice was clear. 'I'm Ella.'

His smile, when it came, was slow and wide with lots of white teeth, transforming him into someone younger and better-looking.

'Of course you are.' He nodded, as if it made perfect sense. 'Different colouring, but same-shaped jaw, same nose.' He sketched an outline with his fingers. 'From what I remember of Anna, anyway.'

I grabbed a chair and flopped down, feeling as if my bones were melting.

'Can I get you a drink?' he said, seeming unfazed while my heart skittered like a runaway pony.

'Tea, please.' I forced a smile to hide my confusion and put my bag on the table.

He made his way to the counter, still smiling, nodding at people as he pulled a handful of coins from his jacket pocket. I tried to see him through Mum's eyes, but it was impossible.

I could only picture her with Dad.

Reagan returned with the tea and a plate of flapjacks and I wondered, slightly hysterically, if I was destined to spend my time in Ireland being bought refreshments by men connected to Colleen.

'How come you're here instead of your half-sister?' he said casually, settling himself down and tipping two sachets of sugar into his mug. 'Bottled out, did she?' A shadow passed over his face. 'Can't say I blame the girl. It's been far too long.'

'It's complicated,' I said, searching his face for a resemblance to Colleen. The eyes were the exact same shade and her ears were like his – small and neat – and something about his hand movements reminded me of her. I fidgeted forward. 'I only found out about Colleen myself a week or so ago.'

His eyebrows rose. 'Anna never told you about her?'

'Nothing at all.' My stomach rumbled and I picked up a buttery

178

flapjack and took a bite. 'I found some stuff among my mother's things,' I said when I'd swallowed. I had an urge to ruffle his calm. 'After she died.'

Reagan leaned back and passed a hand over his face. 'Ah, I'm sorry to hear that,' he said, sounding sincere. 'I hadn't seen Anna for so long. I'm afraid we lost touch after—'

'After she abandoned your baby.' The words rushed out of me. 'I know that you dumped her as soon as you found out she was pregnant with Colleen.'

He winced. 'Not quite,' he said, hunching forward to resume stirring his tea. 'We were young, had a fling.' He chuckled, as if the memory had just come back to him. 'She was in Ireland on holiday with a couple of friends. The parents of one of them had a house near the beach. It was her first time away without her family.' I couldn't remember Mum ever mentioning a trip to Ireland. *But then, she wouldn't have, would she?* 'We weren't as careful as we should have been,' Reagan went on, still stirring his tea, his eyes steady on mine. 'She didn't want a baby, Ella. Neither of us did. She had plans for a career – she was a brilliant artist – and my music meant everything to me. My sister, Celia, was desperate for a child. She's ten years older than me, and at the time had been trying for a while. It made sense she should take the baby.'

'Just like that?' I slammed my mug down, slopping tea on the table. 'If she didn't want a baby, why not have an abortion?'

Reagan's gaze didn't waver. 'She didn't believe in that and it was up to her.'

'But what about her family? How did they …?' My words trailed off.

'When she found out, she told everyone she'd fallen in love with Ireland and wanted to come back for a while, that the scenery had inspired her painting. She said she'd get a job to support herself. She was eighteen, they couldn't exactly stop her.' Reagan gave a shrug. 'We stayed with Celia until the baby was born, and then went our separate ways. Anna returned to England, told her family some story and picked up where she'd left off, as far as I know.'

Anger rose, hot and thick. 'You didn't give a toss about her or your child.'

Unperturbed, he pushed the plate with the remaining flapjack towards me. 'Like I said, we were young.' He shrugged again. 'I never planned to settle down; Anna knew that. She was ambitious. She didn't want to be tied down with a baby any more than I did. We were happy for Celia to raise Colleen. We knew she'd be in good hands.'

'It wasn't just a temporary arrangement?'

Reagan shook his head. 'Anna signed some papers. It was permanent.'

My face stung as though he'd slapped me. 'I can't believe that Mum would have given her up without a fight, unless she had to.'

Reagan lifted an eyebrow. 'With respect, you didn't know your mother back then.'

'But … you were madly in love. I—'

'Who says we were madly in love?' His gaze was quizzical, but not unkind. 'I can't believe she would have told you that.'

I felt winded. Mum *hadn't* told me, or even indicated she'd loved anyone before Dad. My fevered imagination had conjured up the scenario, straight from a movie script. Maybe it had made the whole thing easier to bear.

'It was purely physical between us,' Reagan went on, laying down his teaspoon at last. 'We'd had too much to drink that particular night. It was nice, and we enjoyed spending time together, but neither of us was in love, Ella.' He said it gently, as if he knew how I was feeling – though I wasn't sure I knew myself. 'We made the decision together and that was that. There was no agonising. If anything, your mother was glad to have made my sister so happy.'

'But she came to Ireland to see Colleen when I was little,' I said. 'Celia wouldn't let her in.'

Reagan lifted his mug, then put it down and released a heavy sigh. 'I know. She mentioned it. Maybe things had changed for Anna after she had you.' He gave a half-shrug. 'Maybe it made her think.' He paused. 'Celia ended up having a child of her own later on, a daughter called Bryony, but she drowned. I went to the funeral.' He cast his eyes at the table. 'Or, as Celia called it: "a celebration of her daughter's life".'

'That's awful,' I said, shocked. So, Colleen had already lost a sister. I tried to imagine how life-changing that must have been.

'That was the last time I saw Colleen, though she didn't know who I was,' Reagan went on. 'I admit it was hard; it was a devastating time for everyone. Celia wasn't the same afterwards.'

'You didn't fancy hanging around and being there for Colleen?'

Reagan raised his eyes. 'I was into my music big time by then, doing well abroad. Especially in Japan, weirdly.'

'You should have stayed for her.'

A slight flush rose on his cheekbones. 'I do feel bad,' he said, looking at his hands. 'But at the time, I didn't want the responsibility. I wasn't reliable. And she had her stepfather, Terry.'

At least he was being honest. I had the feeling Reagan wasn't capable of lying, though I couldn't have said why. I stayed quiet for a moment, trying to absorb his words.

So, there'd been no big love affair between him and Mum, no lifetime of yearning for a lost love. Just a business-like arrangement, so they could get on with their separate lives. *Was I sorry or sad?*

It meant that Mum had loved Dad: had *chosen* him. He wasn't second best, as I'd suspected. I realised my overwhelming feeling was one of relief, that I didn't have to slot a completely new version of my mother over the old one. Even if she'd had some regrets about leaving Colleen, trying and failing to see her at Celia's, she'd somehow put it behind her and committed to her life with Dad and me.

But where had that left Colleen?

Tears pricked my eyes. 'So, why make contact now?'

'It's something I've wanted for a while, but Celia had made me promise not to tell Colleen who I was. When Celia finally gave her my email address, and Colleen got in touch, I couldn't wait to meet her.'

I recalled the message I'd read. 'You didn't show up.'

'I'm trying to line up some work, either here or in London,' he said. 'I had a call I'd been waiting for, a meeting I couldn't turn down. I've some money put aside, but not enough to last long. I need the work.'

'Hardly puts you in line for father of the year.'

'Touché.' He gave a little salute. 'Maybe, for all of us, it's to do with getting older,' he said. 'Putting things right, in Celia's case, by finally telling Colleen the truth about her parents, and for me …' He thought for a second. 'I wanted some continuity in my life.'

'So, it's all about you?'

'Ouch!' His smile was tinged with sadness. 'I suppose I walked into that one,' he said. 'It's not all about me, Ella. Believe it or not, I want to have a relationship with Colleen before it's too late.'

'Do you think you deserve one?' I wasn't sure why I was being so rude. He seemed like a nice man; a man anyone would be glad to have as a father, if only he'd done it sooner.

'That's for Colleen to decide,' Reagan said, a gentle rebuke in his voice.

A flush crept up my neck. Thinking back, there hadn't been a trace of judgement in Colleen's expression when she spoke about meeting her father. Whatever his failings, I knew she'd forgiven him, whether he deserved it or not.

'I can't understand why she ran off,' I said, deciding there was no point playing devil's advocate. Reagan was right. Whatever their history, it was up to Colleen to decide what she wanted to do. 'She was so keen to see you.'

'She was?' His smile dropped. 'What do you mean, ran off?'

'She left the hotel the night before last and didn't come back.' Saying it aloud brought back the sense that something was wrong.

'I was the one who sent you the text message, yesterday. I didn't want you to think she'd forgotten your arrangement.' I picked up my mug and put it down again. 'I thought she'd gone for a walk to think things through, but she left her phone behind and hasn't returned.'

When Reagan's expression darkened, my feeling of unease increased.

'So, in the space of a couple of days, she met a half-sister she'd no idea existed, and was planning to meet a father she'd not seen since childhood?' His gaze intensified. 'That's a hell of a lot to take in.'

'It's awful,' I said, feeling the truth of my words. It *was* awful. The strongest person could crack under that kind of information, and I had a horrible feeling Colleen wasn't that strong. 'Her husband Jake told me that this is something she often does. That she runs away a lot.'

'You've met her husband?'

'Yes.' Something in his voice made me look at him sharply. 'He was here yesterday, worried about her.'

'Really?' Reagan's forehead furrowed. 'Celia mentioned Colleen had left him,' he said. 'She was under the impression things hadn't been good between them, though Colleen didn't confide in her.'

'That's not what she told me.' I was fighting a growing confusion. 'But like I said, it's something she's done before.' I recalled Jake's pallor and anxious eyes. 'He was worried sick about her.'

'I'm sure he was.'

'He said they'd argued before she left Waterford, and then again in the hotel, but she told me their marriage was good.'

Reagan's expression was sober. 'Why do you think she lied?'

'I think she was trying to impress me.' My heart gave an uncomfortable flip. 'I don't know what to do.'

He shifted on his seat, hands gripping his mug. 'You say she hasn't got her phone?'

I nodded.

'Well, I could try emailing her again. Maybe she'll pick up her messages somewhere and reply.' He shook his head. 'I don't know what else we can do either, if I'm honest, Ella. Like you, I don't really know her.'

We looked at each other, silently acknowledging how sad those words were.

'Would she contact Celia?'

'I doubt it.' He sat back and glanced through the window, before returning his gaze to me. 'I'm staying at the Strandhill Hostel on Shore Road for a while. If Colleen contacts you, let me know, and I'll do the same for you. If she doesn't …' He let the words hang.

'Actually, I'm leaving later today,' I told him, pushing my chair back and standing up. 'I have a husband and a daughter in England—'

'Of course,' he interrupted, becoming brisk. He rose and held out a hand. 'It's been a pleasure to meet you, Ella. You're a credit to your mother.' He enfolded my fingers in his. 'I really am sorry things haven't worked out for us with Colleen,' he added. 'Though I probably deserve it.' His smile looked forced. 'Anyway, you know where I am, so call if … well, if there's anything I can do.'

'I will.' I felt dangerously close to tears all of a sudden. 'Thanks for the tea.'

'You're welcome.'

As I picked up my things and turned to leave, I felt a sharp sense of panic, as if there was something else I should be doing. 'Goodbye,' I said, after a pause.

'Goodbye, Ella.'

On the way back to The Mountain View, my head spun with all the new information. As I pulled into the car park, Colleen's mobile pinged and after parking clumsily, I took it out of my bag.

Colleen, I hope all's going well with your da! I'd hoped to be back on Saturday, but got caught up in London. I should be back soon though, if you're still there. I'd love to see you again. Alfie x

I felt a dart of surprise. She hadn't mentioned anyone called Alfie. He sounded nice, but … My heart gave a leap. Were they having an affair?

My thoughts began to collide. I remembered Colleen's smile, her bright expression when she mentioned Reagan; how even though meeting me hadn't gone well, she'd at least made the effort to turn up. And now someone called Alfie was arranging to visit, clearly keen to see her.

Why would she run away?

I couldn't go home yet. I had to find out where she was, even if it meant getting the police involved, or the Gardaí, as they were called over here. I quickly texted a reply to Alfie, letting him know the name of the hotel – but not who I was. Maybe he could help shed some light on the situation.

I slipped Colleen's phone in my bag, got mine out and called Greg. It went straight to voicemail.

'Listen, Greg, I can't come back today. I think Colleen might be having a fling with someone called Alfie. I just got a text message from him. On Colleen's phone.' I felt myself blushing. 'I kept hold of it yesterday,' I said. 'I have to find her and talk to her, and make sure she's OK.' It sounded theatrical, and it wasn't even the full story. The truth was, I wanted to find Colleen for me. I didn't want to believe it was over, that she cared so little about me she'd run away. 'Tell Maisie I love her and that I'll be home very soon,' I went on. 'Oh, and can you call Dad, let him know I'm OK? Love you.'

As I rang off, I was stunned to see Jake striding across the car park with a large black holdall in his hand. I leapt out, slamming the car door behind me. 'Jake!'

He didn't respond. He was holding out his key fob, pressing the remote to unlock his car – a dusty, silver four-wheel drive with smoky windows.

'Jake, wait!' I rushed towards him.

'Ellen?' He turned and tracked my approach with something like horror. 'I thought you'd left.'

'It's Ella, and I thought you'd left too!' I laughed, but it sounded brittle. He looked more unkempt than I remembered, his jaw shaded with stubble, his hair rather lank. He probably hadn't slept any better than I had the night before.

'Just leaving,' he said, deep grooves bracketing a thin-lipped smile. 'What about you?'

'I was thinking of calling the police,' I said, scooping a strand of hair behind my ear. 'Something's not right.' I was trying to frame how to tell him I'd met Colleen's father, and about the message from Alfie, but realised he was shaking his head.

'Colleen texted me earlier,' he said flatly. 'She's fine, but she's not coming back. Said to tell you she's sorry.' His voice was detached, as if he'd already moved on. 'So, that's that.' A sudden breeze lifted his hair and he flattened it with a look of irritation. 'I'm sorry, Ella.'

I bit my thumbnail. Nothing felt right, but I didn't know why.

A moment or two passed. The sun went in and spots of rain began to fall. 'I'll go and get her things for you,' I said, the first thing that came into my head.

Jake looked as if he wanted to say no, then changed his mind. 'OK,' he said. 'Don't be long.'

I hurried inside and up the stairs, fumbling her key-card out of my bag. Once in her room, I scooped her things off the floor, thought about writing her a note, realised I didn't have time, struggled with the broken zip, then shot downstairs, hoisting my own bag over my shoulder.

Jake was standing by his car, foot tapping. Perhaps he was keen to get back to his patients now. As I reached him, Colleen's bag slipped out of my grasp and the contents shot over the tarmac as the rain grew heavier, lashing the ground.

'Sorry,' I mumbled, bending to retrieve Colleen's few items of clothing before they got soaked, pushing them back in her bag. I wondered if I could slip her mobile back in without Jake noticing, but felt oddly reluctant to relinquish it.

At the thought of her phone, my breath caught in my throat. Colleen didn't have it with her. How could she have texted Jake?

He was on his haunches beside me, hair flattened by the rain, reaching for a credit card that had slipped out of my grasp.

'Look, Jake,' I said, straightening. 'I'm really worried about her.'

'I just told you, she's fine.' He stood, thrusting a hand through his soaking hair. 'Let's talk in the car,' he said, throwing the rucksack in the boot, before moving round and opening the passenger door. 'We're getting drenched.'

I glanced around. The car park was empty, rain bouncing off the ground.

'Get in, please, Ella.'

I couldn't think of a reason not to, so clambered in, feeling shaky and sick.

Jake eased into the driver's seat. The shoulders of his shirt were sodden, outlining his shoulders, and his eyelashes glistened with raindrops. I heard a clunk. He'd locked the doors.

'What are you doing?'

'I'm afraid I lied.'

A bolt of alarm shot through me. 'What do you mean, lied?'

He turned, his eyes penetrating mine. 'The thing is, Ella, I know where Colleen is.'

Chapter 25

Ella

Shock reverberated through me. 'Have you known all along?'

'Not when we spoke yesterday, no.' There was an air of suppressed anger about Jake, as if he was annoyed at being caught out. 'I was here in my car, around midnight, when she came back. I'd been driving around, looking for her, again.' He paused. 'She wouldn't say where she'd been and we argued.'

'I don't understand.' I smoothed my damp hair back. 'Why didn't you tell me this before? You knew how worried I was.'

A nerve twitched in his jaw. 'Look, Ella, she didn't want you to know,' he said. 'And I thought you were leaving today, so it didn't matter.'

'Of course it matters.' My chest felt tight, as if someone was squeezing it. After the stress of the last couple of days, I wanted an explanation. 'You couldn't get her to stay here for one more day?'

'I tried, but she wouldn't listen.' His fingers tapped the steering wheel. 'I had to promise her I wouldn't tell you she was here.' It struck me that she couldn't have told him who I really was, or he'd have mentioned it. 'The truth is, Ella, she was relieved to hear you were going.' His mouth twisted in what might have been an apology. 'She wanted to run off again, but I persuaded her to come to the farmhouse with me instead, so we could talk.'

'Farmhouse?'

'An old place I own that belonged to my grandfather. It's a bit run-down, but we stayed there before we got married. When we were happy.' He pushed his hair back off his forehead.

'So, what happened?' I said with difficulty. I still couldn't believe she hadn't stayed long enough to say goodbye.

'When we got there, I told her she needed professional help, that I know a good psychiatrist, and she totally lost it. Tried to scratch my eyes out.' His mouth tightened. 'She smashed the place up and locked herself in the bedroom.'

'Oh, God.' It took a moment for his words to sink in. 'I didn't realise things were that bad,' I said at last.

'I'm used to it, Ella.' He bowed his head and a trickle of water dripped from his hair to his lap.

A moment passed. Rain drummed on the roof of the car like angry fingers. 'So, how come you're back here?' I peered through the window. The rain had reduced to a blur.

'We left in such a hurry I forgot to check out properly.' He half-smiled. 'Plus, I needed to give her some space.'

'Why didn't she take her things?'

He shifted position and rubbed his eyes. He looked tired, his eyes sunk in his face. 'It took all my powers of persuasion to get her into the car,' he said. 'I completely forgot about her stuff, and she didn't mention it.'

'What about her father?'

'What about him?' He gave me a piercing look. 'She doesn't want anything to do with that loser.'

I fell silent for a moment, mind whirring. She'd obviously had second thoughts about Reagan, just as she had about me. 'Is there anything I can do?' I didn't know what else to say.

'Like I said, she didn't want to see you.'

I chewed my lip, recalling all the things Jake and Reagan had told me about Colleen that she hadn't wanted me to know. It hurt, yet something was holding me there. I needed answers. *Mum wouldn't want me to give up.*

'I'm not her friend, I'm her sister,' I blurted out. If he was being truthful, I needed to be, too.

Jake's mouth fell open. 'What?' He looked like he'd been punched, his face the colour of porridge. 'Colleen's sister died a long time ago.'

Shaken by his expression, I said, 'I'm her half-sister. We have the same mother.' I wondered if I was making things worse by telling him. 'She died earlier this year.' I swallowed a hard ball of grief. 'I only found out about Colleen a few weeks ago,' I went on. 'We exchanged messages and arranged to meet when she came back from America, only she wasn't in America, and ...' Jake's eyes strayed past me, and I felt a leap of alarm as he started the engine without warning and reversed the car into the road. 'What are you doing?' I said, scrabbling for my seatbelt and plugging it in.

'You can talk to her.' His voice was tight with repressed emotion. 'If you are who you say you are, she might listen to you.'

'But you said she didn't want to see me.'

'That's before I knew who you really were.' His tone grew pleading. 'It's got to be worth a try, Ella.'

'She hardly knows me,' I said, but a flicker of hope ignited inside me.

'Well, now's the time to change all that, don't you think?' He changed gears with a crunch, as though now he'd made up his mind, he couldn't wait to get there. 'Maybe seeing you is what sent her running,' he said. 'You owe it to me to at least try.'

Hot guilt welled up inside me. He was right. Colleen had probably run away because meeting me and my family had been too much for her, on top of Reagan not turning up and whatever had happened with Greg. And now Jake had found out she'd kept our meeting a secret, and that I'd lied to him too.

'OK,' I said, voice shaking. 'I'll give it a try.'

His blue gaze flickered over me, radiating disapproval. 'I wish you'd told me the truth to start with.'

My stomach tightened with misery.

The rain had finally stopped and Jake wound down his window as we merged with traffic on a dual carriageway. Warm salty air rushed in and I inhaled a wobbly sigh. My clothes had trapped hot air against my skin, and I longed to rip off my jacket.

'Jake, I'm so sorry ...' I began.

'Please, Ella.' His tone was clipped. 'I don't want to hear any more.'

I slumped back in my seat, feeling wretched. I didn't know Jake or Colleen and hadn't the slightest clue about the workings of their relationship. For all I knew, I was contributing to the break-up of their marriage. I longed for Greg, and for the velvet softness of Maisie's cheek against mine. I wanted to call Greg, but I'd dropped my bag in the footwell and now that Jake was watching the road, his face fixed and intent, I was reluctant to draw attention to myself again.

To break the difficult silence, I considered asking him whether he and Colleen had ever wanted children, or whether she'd ever had counselling in the past, but a glance at his grim expression warned me he wasn't in the mood for small talk.

Pale sunshine washed through the windscreen and over his face. In profile he looked a little hawkish, his nose slightly hooked at the end – no longer as attractive, though it could have been the stress. One hand repeatedly scraped his drying hair off his forehead.

He caught my gaze and I looked away, catching sight of a road sign to somewhere called Drumcliff. The streets and beaches of Sligo had given way to an empty stretch of road, surrounded by hills and fields. In the distance, I caught a glimpse of sea through a bank of trees, but it was clear we'd moved inland. The landscape was rural; dry-stone walls, sheep and outbuildings.

'Where is this farmhouse?' I said with a brightness I was far from feeling. My conversation with Reagan seemed aeons ago, and my sleepless night was catching up with me.

'Almost there,' Jake said suddenly, almost jovial now. When he threw me a grateful smile, I felt a layer of anxiety peel away. It was going to be fine. Between us, Colleen and I could explain to Jake about my mother. Perhaps in less formal surroundings I'd be able to reach Colleen. I could tell her about seeing Reagan, and how he was longing to get to know her properly – that he wanted her in his life.

My spirits lifted further as Jake indicated and followed an overgrown road downhill, eventually reaching a narrow winding lane. At the end was a five-bar gate at the mouth of an overgrown field. Beyond it, I could just make out a two-storey, grey-stone building partially hidden by trees.

Jake stopped the car, jumped out and opened the gate.

'It's very secluded,' I said when he got back in and bumped the car over the long grass, onto a flattened patch of ground in front of the house. 'What's it called?'

'It doesn't have a name, it's just an old farmhouse.' His flash of good humour had vanished. His lips were a tight line, his eyes flinty, and a shiver of apprehension rolled through me.

Close up, the house was in a dilapidated state: slates missing from the roof, the brickwork crumbling and broken panes of glass in rotting wooden window frames. There was a neglected pond nearby, obscured by rushes, and a derelict paddock at the side of the house. 'Looks like it needs a bit of work,' I said, getting out of the car.

'It's fallen into disrepair over the last ten years. It used to be a nice place.' Jake slammed the driver's door and locked the car, before striding towards the house. 'This way.'

I hesitated. 'Shouldn't you let her know I'm here, first?'

He stopped and turned, shielding his eyes with his hand. 'I think it's better this way.'

'I've forgotten my bag,' I said, pointing at the car. 'I'll need to call my husband.'

'Barely any signal out here.' His tone was measured, but I felt a whisper of fear. 'There's a landline,' he added. 'You can ring from inside.'

Thank God. There was something about the place that was getting to me – an air of neglect, as if no one had lived in it for centuries. But my sister was here right now, and that was what mattered.

I blew out a breath and followed Jake round the side of the house, to a weather-beaten blue door set into the wall. 'Through here,' he said, yanking it open on creaking hinges and standing aside to let me through.

It was dark after the brightness outside. I blinked a few times, letting my eyes adjust. We were in what might have been a kitchen once, but clearly hadn't been inhabited for a while. The walls were rough plaster, and cracked wooden worktops ran around two of the walls. There was a makeshift table made of wooden pallets, and a rusted sink beneath a broken window, but otherwise the room was empty.

'Colleen's very quiet,' I said, almost slamming into Jake as I turned.

'Probably asleep.' He moved swiftly past, ducking through a low door, and I followed him down a narrow passageway that smelt of damp and rotting apples, waiting while he opened a cupboard on the wall and fumbled out a key beside a smaller one labelled *Box 3.*

'I thought you said she'd locked herself in her bedroom.' My voice sounded shockingly loud. It was too quiet. The sort of quiet where you hear your own heartbeat pounding in your ears.

'Did I?' Jake's tone was combative. 'I meant the basement.'

'What?'

'It's for her own good,' he said. 'You'll see.' He jumped down a set of stone steps, leading to a dimly lit area with a narrow door.

At the bottom, he turned and held out his hand. 'Come on.' He curled his fingers. 'I'll catch you.'

I felt slow-witted, as if I was missing something crucial. Why had he locked her in and lied about it? Then I remembered him saying she'd tried to scratch his eyes out. What if she attacked me?

'I'm not sure about this,' I said. My teeth were chattering. It was cold in the house, as though the sun hadn't penetrated the walls for years. 'Maybe I should wait in the car.'

'Oh, Ella. You're such an innocent.' Shockingly, he reached up and grabbed my hand and yanked me down the stairs.

'Ow!' I wrenched my ankle at the bottom and stumbled against him, an excruciating pain shooting up my leg. 'What are you doing?' I attempted to wriggle free, but his grip was too strong. In the half-light filtering down the passageway from the kitchen, his face looked cruel. 'Jake, please let go of me.' He pressed me against the door, so the knob dug into my hip, his breath moist on my face, and I twisted my head away. 'What are you doing?'

'You should have gone home, Ella.'

Panic bolted through me as understanding dawned. It wasn't Colleen I needed to be afraid of. It was her husband. 'Jake, please let go. You're frightening me.'

'Good,' he said quietly, releasing his grip as a scrabbling started on the other side of the door. He looked at me and pressed a finger to his lips. 'Sounds like my wife is awake,' he whispered.

'Colleen, is that you?' My voice quavered. Maybe Jake was lying and he'd brought me here for some other purpose. The thought pushed tears to my eyes. 'Colleen?'

'Ella?'

At the sound of her voice I leapt back, pain flaring in my ankle. I tried to speak, but the urge to pass out was too strong.

'Jake, is that Ella?' Colleen's voice was disbelieving. 'Why have you brought her here, you sick fuck?' The door rattled. 'Ella, get out of here. He's crazy,' she said on a sob.

Fear clawed at my throat. 'What does she mean?'

Now behind me, Jake chuckled softly, and the sound froze my blood. He leaned over my shoulder and thrust the key into the lock and turned it, then brought his lips to my ear. 'In you go,' he whispered. 'Time for your family reunion.' He opened the door a fraction and shoved me hard in the back. I fell inside, onto a concrete floor as the door slammed swiftly shut, the key turning in the lock.

'You arsehole!' There was a flurry of movement around me, followed by the sound of fists pummelling the door. 'You coward! You can't do this, Jake. You won't get away with it.'

His footsteps retreated until there was only the sound of desperate weeping. It took a moment to realise it was coming from me.

'What the hell's going on, Ella? How in Christ's name do you know Jake?'

Suddenly, Colleen was squatting beside me, her arm going around my shoulders. She hugged me and stroked my hair, all the while muttering profanities aimed at Jake, but I couldn't stop crying. I knew he would come back. And when he did, he was going to kill us.

Chapter 26

Colleen

'Enough of the tears, Ella.' I'd been hugging her for so long, my T-shirt was damp. 'You'll flood the place.'

She jolted away as I rose to my feet, her watery eyes skittering to the window.

'We have to get out of here.'

'Don't you think I've tried?' I followed her gaze. 'It's too small.'

'If I give you a leg-up, you could wriggle out.'

'The window won't open wide enough.'

'We could at least try.' Her voice was strangled by panic. 'We can't just wait for him to come back.'

In spite of myself, I felt a sliver of hope. 'Go on then.'

The next few minutes were a blur of panic-fuelled movement, as Ella – clearly in pain from the way she cried out as she hobbled towards the boxes – braced herself so that when I climbed up she could support my wobbling weight on her shoulders, but it was obvious straight away that the window wasn't wide enough to squeeze through, even if I could have pushed the frame out.

'Let me try.' Ella sounded desperate, but as well as a rapidly swelling ankle that made her wince when she moved, she was curvier than me. It was obvious that neither of us was going anywhere.

'No point,' I said, collapsing back on the floor. 'We're screwed.'

Ella retreated to the wall and sat down, arms curled around her knees. She'd lost a flip-flop in the kerfuffle, and her hair was all over the place. She looked childlike and vulnerable and the protective surge I felt towards her scared me.

She's here because of me.

'How the hell do you know Jake?' I asked again, crossing to kneel in front of her, conscious of how awful I must look in the weird dress he'd made me wear. I didn't smell too great either, especially after the latest burst of activity.

'He said he was bringing me here to talk to you.' Her words were fast and breathless as she gulped back tears. 'He … he said you'd locked yourself in a bedroom and wouldn't come out, and the least I could do was try and get through to you.'

'Oh my God.' I rubbed my forehead. 'You should have ignored him, Ella. Jake is crazy. I can't believe you were so gullible and fecking stupid.'

Her head jerked up, and with a flash of spirit she said, 'You told me you were happily married, Colleen. How was I to know I was dealing with a twisted psychopath? Why did you lie?'

I studied my fingers. 'I …'

'If you hadn't lied, neither of us would be here now.' She was shaking, her voice trembling, her eyes enormous pools of hurt. 'Why didn't you tell me the truth, Colleen?'

I looked at her, in her fancy suede jacket, with her pearly, mani-cured nails, and anger flared, hot and unreasonable. I shrugged, blasé. 'Why tell the truth when a lie will do.'

'You're pathetic.'

'Listen, nobody forced you to come to Ireland,' I spat. 'I didn't ask you to invade my life.'

'What the hell did you think *would* happen when you asked

me to book the hotel? When I turned up?' She scrabbled up, holding one foot aloft, steadying herself against the wall with her hands. 'You said you wanted to meet me, that you were *happy* about meeting me.' She was shouting, her face flushed and tear stained. 'If you'd only told me you'd left your husband again …'

'Again? I've never left him before,' I shouted back.

She looked confused, as if she was translating my words in her head. 'He said it wasn't the first time you'd run away.'

'Oh, and you're going to believe every word a crazed, kidnapping arsehole has to say?'

'How could I have known what he was really like?' Her face was incredulous. 'I only spoke to him over a pot of tea, and—'

'To be honest,' I cut in, feeling worse with every word that came out of my mouth, 'what mine and Jake's relationship is – was – had nothing to do with you. I didn't tell you at the hotel because it was the first time I'd met you. You were a stranger.' My voice was hard, but I couldn't help it. She should have gone home and forgotten about me. 'You still are.'

Tears flooded her eyes once more, but her hands clenched by her sides. Despite where we were, it seemed to be the fact I'd lied, let her down and called her a stranger that hurt more than anything else.

'You're my sister, whether you like it or not,' she said, with a defiant lift of her chin. 'I wanted to be a part of your life.'

'For God's sake, Ella, wake up.' I turned away, stomach lurching. I felt like throwing up. I wanted to scream in her trusting face that I wasn't capable of being a sister, or having a sister, that I didn't deserve one. The fact she was stuck here with me proved it.

I moved to the opposite wall, slid down to the floor, and buried my head in my dry and flaky hands. They smelt of bleach. I lowered them and picked at the dissolving stitches in my finger. My arm still hurt, but I wanted it to. Pain helped. *God, I need a drink.*

Silence followed. Ella stood by the wall on one leg, arms wrapped tightly around her body, stifling sobs.

'What's wrong with your foot?' I asked eventually.

She lifted her head and pushed her hair off her face. 'I hurt my ankle when he pulled me down the steps.'

Shit. 'Sorry.'

Her breathing slowly steadied. 'It's not your fault,' she said, brushing a hand over her face, but we both knew it was.

She didn't seem to have noticed the bucket and spade, or the notes from Jake – or if she had, she made no comment. She stared at me with the stunned air of someone emerging from a nightmare, then sank to the floor once more, chewing her thumbnail.

The rain had picked up again, pattering against the window.

I watched Ella for some time before saying, 'So how did Jake find you?' I tried to picture them bumping into each other, but couldn't. 'How did he know who you were?'

She massaged her temples with her fingertips. 'He didn't know who I was,' she said. 'Not at first. He was staying at the hotel and saw us together and later, after you'd disappeared, he approached me.'

'I knew he'd followed me to Sligo,' I said. 'He's been with me every step of the way.' I looked into her eyes. 'You know, he told me once he'd rather I died, than leave him.'

'Colleen, that's awful.' The look on Ella's face told me Greg would never speak to her like that. I thought of Jake's cold blue eyes, the way he always looked so composed, never a hair out of place. 'Words, that's all I thought they were,' I said. 'Words to keep me with him.'

'And now?' Ella's eyes were pleading. 'Do you think they're just words now?'

I shrugged. 'I don't know anymore. It's as though he's finally lost it. He sent me some bloody weird texts.' *And the lilies.*

Ella rubbed her ankle, grimacing with pain. 'He's going to

kill us, isn't he?' Her pupils were dilated. 'Colleen? He won't risk letting us go, because we'll tell the police.'

My blood froze. I'd gone down the scenario of Jake killing me so many times since he'd brought me here, trying to work out whether he was capable of taking a life. He was a surgeon, someone who saved lives, not extinguished them. Although it wouldn't be the first time a doctor had committed murder. I'd never pushed him like this before. I'd always done and said what he wanted. Good little Colleen, his pretty little puppet.

I looked at Ella's open, tear-blotched face. I didn't want to lie to her anymore, but avoiding the truth as I saw it, for her sake, wasn't the same thing. 'I'm sure he won't kill us,' I said, with more conviction than I felt. 'He's playing a game with me, that's all. Getting his own back for me walking out.'

'All the things you told me at the hotel,' she said after a pause. 'Was any of it true?'

I shook my head, made myself look at her. 'I wanted you to believe I had a good life, a life like yours. But the truth is, my whole existence has been a joke.' I tried to laugh, but it sounded rough. 'And when I finally find my father, look what happens.'

I was coming across as a pathetic victim. I wanted to slap myself, but to my surprise, Ella said softly, 'I'm so sorry, Colleen. I'm sorry you felt you needed to lie to me.'

'OK, now I feel *really* bad.' It was a lame attempt at lightening the mood. I lowered my head and pushed my hands through my unevenly chopped hair, missing the weight of it. 'I thought you'd run a mile if you knew the truth,' I said, but in all honesty, I hadn't thought about it much at all.

'You tried to kiss Greg, didn't you?' Her tone was cautious, as though she hoped I'd deny it. She waited and when I looked up, her expression hovered somewhere between hopeful and angry.

'My head is fucked, Ella,' I said. 'Don't you get it?'

'I'll take that as a yes.' She closed her eyes, as if holding back more tears.

'Nothing happened with Greg.' It was suddenly important she understood that. 'He wasn't interested in me.'

'But what if he'd responded?' Her eyes snapped open. 'What if he'd …?'

'Then I'd have done you a favour. You could have told him to piss off.' I buried my head in my hands again. I'd kissed her husband. The man she loved. I hated myself. But I still didn't know my motives, not really. Had I seen something in Greg that I felt she shouldn't trust, and wanted to show her she'd picked the wrong man? Well, he'd proved me wrong on that count. Or had I simply been pissed and jealous – wanted what she had?

'You're an awful person, Colleen.' She said it so quietly, I barely heard, but the sadness in her voice cut through me, deeper than I could have imagined.

'Sure. I agree. Tell me something I don't already know,' I said, with a flippancy I didn't feel.

Her chin trembled. 'I thought we might be alike, or you might take after Mum, but I don't even know who you are.'

'But isn't that the point, Ella?' I shrugged. 'We don't know each other at all.' I paused, searching for the right words, wondering why it mattered when we had far worse things to worry about. 'When you came looking for me, you were searching for something you lost when your ma died. You wanted someone to fill that void. You were doing it for you, not for us.'

Her eyes widened. 'What are you, a psychiatrist?' Her voice broke. 'It's not true.'

'Of course it's true.' I didn't mean to hurt her. I just wanted her to see things as they were. 'You knew pretty soon I wasn't what you were looking for; you even said you didn't want someone like me in your life, but you wouldn't give up, even when I tried to kiss your husband. And even when I disappeared, you didn't go home. You needed me to fill that gap your ma left.'

Ella burst into tears. 'She was your mum too.'

I shook my head. 'Anna wasn't my mother.' The words hurt

201

as I said them, but they felt true. 'You have to earn that status. Whatever she might have called it at the time, she abandoned me.'

'So did your father,' Ella fired back, brushing tears from her cheeks with the heel of her hand. 'Yet you couldn't wait to meet him.'

My insides twisted at the mention of Reagan. It was doubtful I'd ever get to see him now. 'I can't explain it, but that was different,' I said. 'And yes, I know he was years too late, and probably wouldn't have bothered hanging around once he got to know me, but still.'

Christ, I was playing the victim again. But it was true.

Ella was biting her lip so hard it had turned white. 'Colleen,' she said at last. 'There's something I need to tell you.'

'Sure, fire away.' I felt suddenly weary. 'Go ahead,' I added, when she looked like she'd changed her mind. 'It's not like I'm going anywhere.'

'I texted Reagan.'

'What?' My head shot up and I stared at her. 'My father?'

She nodded, her expression oddly defiant. 'You left your phone at the hotel. I read your messages. I thought there might be a clue to where you'd gone. I was worried about you …'

'And?' My pulse raced. I moved over and gripped her arm. 'Go on.'

'There was a message from Reagan and I replied to it,' she said, not pulling away from me. 'And you had a text from someone called Alfie.'

'Alfie?' A jolt ran through me. I hadn't expected him to get in touch.

She nodded. 'He sounded like someone who cares about you.' She paused. 'Are you having an affair with him?'

'No.' I felt hot all over. 'Why would you say that?' But there was something inside me that half-wished the answer was yes.

'Sorry.' She paused. 'I'm afraid I pretended to be you, and I told him where you were staying. I was hoping he might help me find you.'

'You impersonated me?' I let go of her and reeled back, unsure whether I was annoyed or impressed. 'Sweet Mary mother of God.'

'No, no, well, not with Reagan. Not when I met him, anyway.'

I stared at her, astonished. 'You met up with my da?' A moment of anger, or envy, that she'd met him first, dissolved into curiosity. 'What's he like? Did he talk about me? What did he say?' I sounded desperate.

Ella raised a weak smile. 'He seemed nice,' she said. 'He regrets not being in your life, and wants to meet you.'

Jesus. It was more than I could have hoped for.

I was about to speak, when a sound brought me tumbling to earth. There was a slice of movement outside the door and another labelled key was thrust underneath.

'Is he out there?' Ella stumbled up and joined me as I shot forward. 'Jake?' she called.

'No point shouting, I've tried. He doesn't do small talk.'

She stared at the key. 'What's it for?'

'Box number 3,' I said, in a parody of a TV announcer, picking it up and turning it over in my hands. On the reverse of the label there were two brief sentences that made my stomach clench.

This is for the final box, Colleen. Then it's all over.

Chapter 27

Ella

It was just a key, but Colleen's expression frightened me. Her freckles were stark on her ashen face and her bravado had fled.

'He's trying to break me.' Her voice was barely a croak. She looked around, and for the first time, I registered a bizarre array of items scattered across the floor: a blonde wig, an apron, a pair of wrinkled stockings and a bucket and spade.

Panic forced fresh tears to my eyes. 'Colleen, what's going on?'

She'd dropped to the floor again. She was barefoot, one skinny knee drawn up, and she was staring blankly at the label attached to the key. 'He's playing mind games.' Her voice was heavy with dread. 'Making me dress up to clean this crappy room. Offering reminders of Bryony's death, as if I needed reminding.' She flicked me a dark look through her lashes. 'Bryony was the sister before you. She died, a long time ago.'

I wanted to tell her I knew, but it didn't feel right. I remembered her expression when I told her I'd met Reagan: a painful mix of anger and jealousy. She was like a child in some ways, rousing a protective instinct.

'But why would he do that?' I pressed a hand to my aching head, which was throbbing in time with my ankle.

'I don't know.' She tipped her head back and screwed her eyes shut. 'I didn't realise he had it in him to be this cruel.'

She didn't elaborate, and I dropped beside her on the cold hard floor and rested a hand on her knee. Reagan had told me that Celia wasn't the same after Bryony's death, and although I didn't know the circumstances, it was clear Colleen blamed herself.

Her eyes flew open, startling me. 'He's watching, you know.' She pulled away from my touch.

'What?' I looked to where she was pointing and noticed with horror a small camera in the corner, a red light winking.

'He'll be enjoying the effects of his tragic behaviour.' Seeming to revive, she flipped her middle finger at the lens, then slid the key and its label across the floor. 'I'm not looking in the box, Jake,' she called. 'I refuse to play.'

I stood up, wincing at the wrenching sensation in my lower leg, and moved to look closer. We'd had a camera like it rigged up at home for a while, after a spate of break-ins along our road, but I'd hated the way the lens seemed to follow me around and had it removed. 'Please let us go.' I stared at the camera, my throat clogged with tears. 'We won't say anything. We just want to get on with our lives and—'

'He doesn't want us to get on with our lives.' Colleen got up and stood beside me, hands on hips. 'That's why we're here, isn't it, Jake?'

I imagined him staring back at us coldly, and thought about pleading again – appealing to his better nature, assuming he had one – when the sound of a door banging outside made us jump.

'What was that?' I looked at Colleen, heart leaping.

A car engine revved, and there was the sound of tyres spinning.

'He's leaving,' she said, crossing to the stack of boxes.

She clambered clumsily up on them, attempting to peer through the window. 'He's probably panicking now you're here,' she said, jumping down again. 'Your hire car's at the hotel, isn't it?'

I was gripped with hope as I hobbled towards her. 'But that's good,' I said. 'I mean, I haven't checked out of the room yet. Surely people will wonder if I don't go back? Someone will report me missing.' *Would Greg notice, if I didn't get in touch?*

'He's probably got that covered.' Colleen's tone was resigned. She didn't look at me when she added, 'He's clever, Ella. He won't leave anything to chance.'

I tasted acid in my mouth. My eyes roamed the floor, and I lunged for the key and the label that Colleen had discarded. *This is for the final box, Colleen. Then it's all over.*

The words made me shiver. 'Let's look inside,' I said. 'There might be something in there we can use to get out.' I sensed her tensing. 'You said he's playing mind games.'

'And?'

'Well, maybe this is some sort of challenge. He's driven off and isn't coming back, and we have to find our way out.' Even as I spoke, I didn't really believe it. 'It'll be our word against his,' I said. 'He could easily get away with it.'

'For Christ's sake, Ella, you're living in Enid-Blyton-land.' She shook her head, her expression almost pitying. 'This is *real life*. Why would he give us the opportunity to get out when it's obvious we'll turn him in?'

I realised her earlier reassurance that he wouldn't hurt us had been an attempt to placate me, and now she'd abandoned the pretence. I couldn't accept this was it; that we were stuck here, at Jake's mercy. 'Which box is it?' I said, filled with a grim determination.

Colleen released a long sigh and gestured with her foot to the smallest wooden box, underneath the window. 'That one.' It had a padlock, and a number 3 roughly carved into the wood.

'He's really thought about this,' I said, repulsed. I almost didn't want to touch it; didn't want to imagine the thought processes behind such sick behaviour.

Colleen stayed where she was while I unlocked the box, but came over when I lifted the lid, as if she couldn't help herself.

What little light there was outside was fading, making it harder to see as we peered inside.

'What is it?'

'It's a photograph,' I said, lifting it out. It was an enlarged copy of the half of the picture Jake had shown me at the hotel, of a younger Colleen, standing by a motorbike.

Her expression was hard to read – shock or puzzlement, I couldn't tell. 'Why the hell's he put that in there?'

'Look at this,' I said, not taking in her words. There was another picture: a grainy photo of a naked couple sprawled on a rumpled bed. Only the man's back and shoulders were visible, and a strip of his fair hair, but clearly recognisable beside him was Colleen. She was on her back, her eyes closed, one arm flung over her head, frowning in her sleep, as though troubled.

She snatched the picture off me and held it to the fading light. 'Jesus Christ.' There was a pause, then her lip curled with disgust. 'He was watching us.' She scrunched up the photo and flung it back in the box. 'We were on the ground floor,' she said, her eyes wild as she squatted down, clutching her hair with her hands. 'The curtains were half open when I woke up.'

'What are you talking about?' There was a cold feeling in the pit of my stomach. 'What *was* that?'

She shook her head. 'After I left Jake, I had a stupid one-night stand with an old boyfriend.' Her voice was filled with self-loathing. 'He was someone from way back I thought I'd loved. I hadn't seen him for years.'

'But you met him again?'

'I bumped into him in Sligo when I was searching for some-where to stay.' She sounded tired. 'I'd travelled by train for most of the day and my head was all over the place. He suggested we go for a drink, for old time's sake, reminded me he saved my life once.' Her voice dropped an octave. 'I'd gone up the cliffs at Aughris Head, intending to throw myself off, join Bryony at the bottom of the ocean, but he followed me up there. He said I should take some drugs to ease the pain instead, that they'd make me feel better.'

She shook her head, as if clearing the memory. 'Anyway, I said no at first, told him I didn't drink anymore, but he managed to persuade me.' She started shaking. 'I've been knocking back the booze ever since.' She raised her head, looking hollowed out, her eyes blank and staring. 'I can barely recall the rest of that night, but I knew the next morning it was a big mistake and got out as quick as I could.' Her eyelids lowered like shutters, her hand trembling as she held the photo. 'Jake must have followed us, taken this picture …' Her voice broke off.

'Oh, Colleen.' I could see it all: the jealous, controlling husband, finding his wife in the arms of another man – worse, someone she'd loved before him. 'How could he do this?' I scrolled back to my conversation with Jake at the hotel, racking my brain for clues. He was obviously a brilliant actor, because I'd truly believed he cared about Colleen. 'He seemed so concerned.'

'Psychopaths are good at being charming – it's part of their profile,' Colleen bit back. 'Look at Ted Bundy.'

As she stood and began pacing, I slammed the box shut and straightened, flexing my ankle. 'We can't just do nothing,' I said, wishing she'd stop moving in circles.

'Have you got any bright ideas, Sherlock?' She threw me a look, her eyes bright with unshed tears. 'You're the clever one, aren't you?'

My laugh sounded more like a sob. 'Why would you think that? I photograph food for a living. How's that going to help?'

She shrugged. 'We're fucked then.'

My eyes swept the walls, as if a secret door might have

materialised, or a portal that would transport me back to my old life. 'Could there be another way out? You must know this place well.'

'Why would I know it?' There was a crease between her eyebrows. 'I haven't a clue where we are.'

'Jake said you came here years ago.'

'What?' She pulled her chin in. 'If I did, I can't remember.' She looked around, as if seeing the gloomy room with fresh eyes. 'I'm sure I wouldn't have forgotten,' she said, but didn't sound certain anymore.

'He implied you had happy times here, when you first got together.'

'Did he?' Her mouth opened and closed. 'Well, I wasn't really myself when I met Jake. Those first few months are a bit of a blur, to be honest.' A moment later she added reluctantly, 'Drugs,' maybe seeing a question in my expression. 'Long story.' She paused. 'I admit there's something familiar about that view though, what I could see of it.' She shook herself. 'It doesn't really matter now, anyway. We're not going anywhere.'

My spirits dropped even lower. 'Don't say that.'

'What am I supposed to say?' Any fight she'd had seemed to have flowed out of her. 'I'm just sorry I got you involved.'

My stomach growled, loud in the sudden silence.

Colleen looked at me. 'There's no food,' she said drily. 'There's water in the tap if you're thirsty, and you'll have to pee in the bucket.'

The incongruity of her words struck us both, drawing reluctant smiles.

'Oh, and there's no electricity, so I hope you're not scared of the dark.'

'I'm not.'

'This is crazy,' she said, whirling around and kicking one of the boxes with her bare foot. 'Ouch!' She hopped about before sitting on the edge of the biggest box, her chin propped in her hand. 'It sounds awful, but I'm kind of glad you're here.' She gave a fleeting smile. 'Makes the thought of my imminent death a little easier to bear.'

'We're not going to die.' I almost believed it for a moment. 'I've a husband and daughter, and a father who loves me, and a brand-new sister I want to get to know.'

Her eyes swivelled to me, but she didn't speak.

I looked around again. 'Maybe one of those keys will fit the door.'

'Worth a try,' she said. 'I tried the first one, but maybe one of the others?'

I could tell by looking they were too small. We tried anyway, Colleen passing them over. I slid each one into the lock and jiggled it around, but none of them worked.

Infuriated, we rattled the door, taking it in turns trying to break it down, me with my shoulders, Colleen by kicking it, her legs lashing out like swords.

'It's hopeless,' I said at last, breathless and sweating with the effort. We moved back into the room, which was almost dark now, and sat on a smelly patch of carpet near the sink.

'I don't want to die,' said Colleen. 'At least, not before I've met my father.'

'Me neither.' My voice cracked. I didn't want to think of home, of Maisie growing up without a mother, but I couldn't help it. I remembered with perfect clarity the day she was born, how I'd cradled her in my arms, vowing never to let anything bad happen to her. I thought of Greg, raising our daughter alone and of my father, endlessly walking Charlie, alone in his grief. Tears pressed behind my eyelids.

'What was she like?' Colleen said, close but not touching me.

'Who?'

'Your mother, of course.' She hesitated. '*Our* mother.'

Snapshots of Mum flooded my mind, unbidden. Not her final days, when her spirit was fading, her skin stretched tightly over her bones, but from way back. Her look of concentration when she was painting, a wrinkle between her eyebrows; her comical despair when she baked me a birthday cake that sank in the middle; the way her eyes crinkled when she laughed; the feel of her hand around mine as she walked me to school, pointing out birds and trees; the way she held me when I wept after falling out with my best friend.

'She was lovely, the best …' I began crying, great hiccupping sobs, my arm across my face. 'I miss her so much,' I managed at last, aware Colleen's hand was on my back, stroking in little circles.

When I could breathe again, I dragged my sleeve across my face. 'I thought there'd been some big romance between her and your dad, some drama, but it wasn't like that,' I said. 'She wasn't ready to have a child, but knew how much Celia wanted one. She thought you'd have a good life with her.'

'I did at first; it was so perfect. I mean, she was always a bit too hot on the old religion, but things got really bad after Bryony …' She paused, but there was no real animosity behind her words. I sensed that, despite her outburst at the hotel, she had no bitterness towards my mother – hadn't given her much thought at all. Her focus had been on Reagan. She wasn't yearning for the woman who'd given her up – she wanted her father. 'It can't have been easy, finding out she'd kept this big secret from you.'

Tears welled again. 'I've been telling myself she must have had her reasons. That she believed it was for the best.'

'It probably was,' Colleen said, but it was hard to believe she meant it.

'I wish I'd known you as a child.' It felt easier to say in the gathering darkness, when I couldn't see her face properly, knowing mine was swollen and damp. 'I always wanted a big sister.'

She didn't respond right away, and I wondered if she was thinking of Bryony, but out of the blue, she said, 'You're young to be married with a kid. These days, I mean.' Her hand was still on my back, warm through my jacket.

'Greg and I knew pretty quickly we wanted to get married,

and we both wanted children,' I said, wiping my face again. 'When we found out Mum's cancer was terminal, we brought everything forward.'

'You couldn't have been sure you'd get pregnant.'

'No,' I admitted. 'But I did.'

'Does he get along with his parents? Greg, I mean.'

I nodded. 'His father died of a heart attack a couple of years ago, and his mum lives abroad now, but they were a close family. I suppose we've led charmed lives, compared to you.' I began to weep again.

'Jesus, Ella,' Colleen reached round to lift my hair off my face. 'You're a regular cry-baby, so you are.'

I managed a snotty laugh. 'It's funny you should say that, because I rarely cry normally.' I blotted my face on the sleeve that wasn't soaked. 'I have to keep things together for Maisie.'

'It won't do her any harm to see her mammy sad now and then,' Colleen said. 'And your lives don't sound that charmed to me.' She took a breath. 'Sounds like you've had a lot on your plate, what with his da dropping dead, and your mam getting sick and dying. Nothing charmed about that.'

Her words settled around me like a cloak. 'When you put it like that …' I said, remembering, with a bolt of guilt, Greg's choking grief over his father's death. I should have made more of an effort to console him. I'd been too distracted, still hoping they'd find a cure for Mum. 'Greg slept with a woman at work.' I wasn't sure why I was telling her. I'd never talked about it to anyone. 'It was all my fault.'

'Rubbish,' she scorned. 'He should have kept it in his pants.' I suspected her experiences with men had made her more than a bit cynical, but she surprised me by saying, 'It's obvious he loves you, Ella.'

With her words, I felt a loosening of the constraints that had been holding me back since Greg's infidelity. 'Thanks for saying that.'

'You're welcome.'

For a second, I imagined Colleen and me growing up together, sharing confidences into the night. Perhaps it would have been like this.

'Here,' she said, tugging the hem of my jacket. 'You should take this off – you're boiling.'

It was true. My face was slick with sweat. I could feel it under my armpits and gathered at the backs of my knees.

Colleen wriggled away while I pulled my arms out of the sleeves, and as I folded it neatly, wondering why I was bothering, a sound floated through the gaps around the window; the distant, but unmistakable sound of voices. 'Did you hear that?'

Colleen stiffened, head cocked. There was a shout, followed by laughter. 'Hikers,' she said, almost to herself. 'They must be lost if they're all the way out here.'

As the implications sank in, we turned to face each other.

'If we can hear them, they might be able to hear us.' Colleen was on her feet, yanking me up. 'Come on.'

We moved to the wall by the window and began to holler.

'HELP!'

'We're over here!'

'HEEEEEEEELP!'

We cupped our mouths as we shouted again, in an attempt to amplify the sound, but the words seemed to travel no further than the surrounding walls.

Pausing, breathing heavily, we waited. There was no response; just another faint shout, more distant this time. Whoever they were, they were moving away. I imagined a group of young people with backpacks and ruddy cheeks, looking forward to camping out. Or, lost, trying to get a phone signal, but finding it hilarious, part of the adventure. I wished more than anything we were out there with them.

'They've gone,' I said, still panting. I couldn't seem to get enough air in my lungs. 'No one's going to hear us.'

'I'm not giving up.' Colleen clumsily scaled the boxes and pressed her mouth as close as she could to the frame, shoving the window as wide as it would go. She screamed at the top of her lungs and I joined in, almost scared by the feral sound. I'd never imagined a scenario where I'd make such a terrible noise.

We took it in turns, pausing after each bout of yelling and screaming to wait for some sort of reply – anything at all – until I was hoarse and whimpering.

'You're right,' Colleen croaked at last, shoulders slumping as she let the window drop shut. 'No one's going to hear us.'

I clutched my sides and doubled over, disappointment as acute as stomach ache. 'Let's try again.' They could be on their way, running towards the building, one of them calling the police.

'It's pointless, Ella.' Colleen's words, flatly spoken, punctured my last bubble of hope. 'They were probably miles away. Sound carries out here, if the wind's blowing in the right direction.'

'Shame it wasn't blowing the other way.' I wanted to cry again, overwhelmed with helplessness. 'I can't believe this is happening.'

She jumped down, falling against me, and we held each other for a long moment.

'I'm thirsty,' I said, still close to tears. 'And I need a wee.'

'Me too.' Her voice was thick with emotion.

We released each other and I felt my way to the sink to drink from the tap, and left it running for Colleen.

'After you,' she said, directing me to the bucket in the corner. It didn't feel odd to be tugging my jeans down in front of her; it was so dark now. And nothing was normal anymore.

When we'd finished, Colleen emptied the bucket in the sink, then clattered it back to the floor. 'Not very good room service here.'

'No point ordering a sandwich then.' I sounded slightly hysterical and took a deep breath in an effort to calm my breathing.

I could barely make out anything in the room. There wasn't so much as a sliver of moon outside the window to relieve the

214

darkness, just a patch of ink-black sky. I thought of Maisie, spending another night without me, and I wanted to howl.

'We'll just have to wait it out,' Colleen said, reaching for my hand. 'I'm so sorry, Ella.'

Tears leapt to my eyes as her fingers linked with mine. 'It's OK.' The truth was, from the moment I'd known she existed she'd become my sister, and despite her belief that this was all her fault, she was just as much Jake's victim as I was and had been for a long time. If he were to come back and offer me my freedom at Colleen's expense, I wasn't sure I would go. 'Let's try and sleep.'

'Fat chance of that,' she said. 'A prison cell would be comfier.'

Buoyed up by the thought that help might be on its way, I felt around in the darkness for my jacket. 'We can use this to lie on,' I said, arranging it into a makeshift pillow.

We shuffled together and in a weird way it was nice having her beside me, the warmth of her body seeping into mine. Her breathing quickly deepened and, drained by the last twenty-four hours, my eyelids drifted shut.

Hours, or maybe minutes later, the purr of an engine reached my ears and a yellow beam swept across the room. I jolted upright. In the brightness of the headlights, I saw Colleen's fearful expression and knew it reflected my own.

'He's back,' she said.

Chapter 28

Colleen

Car headlights bathed the basement in an eerie glow, the throb of the engine invading the oppressive silence.

'Oh God, what's he doing?' Ella whispered. Her face was ghost-like, shadows heavy around her eyes as she peered up at the window. 'Why isn't he getting out of the car?'

'I've no idea.' I sensed a tremble in my voice, and took a deep breath. 'Mind reading isn't one of my many talents.' I sounded blasé, but my heart thudded, and my stomach twisted into a painful knot. 'Sorry, I'm acting like a dick.'

She grabbed my painful arm, and I winced. 'Do you think he's waiting for someone?'

Well I do now. 'Please, Ella, this is bad enough.' I pulled my arm free and stood up.

'But think about all the killers in history who've worked in pairs, Colleen.'

'I'd rather not,' I said. 'Anyway, Jake is more than capable of doing this alone.' I tried to hold back tears. 'He isn't a team player,' I continued. 'He has no friends. Even his father doesn't like him that much, despite Jake moving here from America to be with him.'

'But …'

'One person wanting us dead is enough, surely.'

'Sorry,' she said, dragging a hand over her face. She hadn't taken her eyes away from the window, and I could see the fear in them.

The rumble of the engine seemed to go on for ages. We waited, my neck aching from staring up at the window.

'Jake!' I cried, finally, though I knew he'd never hear.

'What the hell is he doing out there?' Ella scrambled to her feet. 'This is torture.'

'He's playing with us,' I said as the engine cut out, and the basement plunged into darkness. The hairs on my arms rose, and my heart picked up speed. There was no doubting I was scared. 'He wants to make me suffer for leaving him, for not being his perfect woman, for sleeping with Gabriel—'

'Gabriel?'

'The bloke in the photo.' The thought of Jake outside that guesthouse window taking photos made me sick to my stomach – and worse, I couldn't even recall that night. Why the hell hadn't he stormed into the room and confronted Gabriel? Dragged me home to Waterford?

My body tingled with fear as I tried to pick out the sound of Jake getting out of his car. But the quiet was total, apart from the intermittent hoot of an owl.

'What if we die, and Maisie never finds out what happened to me?' Ella's voice was a whimper, and I knew the thought must have occurred to her many times over the last few hours.

As I picked up on her sniffs and gulps, I fumbled in the darkness for her hand and entwined my fingers with hers. It was as though we were forming a barrier against Jake, and for a moment, I wondered if we could face anything together. But deep down I knew there was no barrier strong enough to protect us. He had control – as always.

I wanted to tell Ella we weren't going to die, that the Gardaí were on their way. But I didn't believe it, and it seemed futile to give her hope. A waste of the little energy I had left. *The grim reaper is on his way, brandishing his scythe*, would have been more appropriate, but I didn't say that either.

The car door slammed. 'He's coming,' I said, my voice a croaky whisper. *This is my comeuppance.* It should have been me that day, not my little sister. *I deserve to die.* Despite almost wanting to close my eyes and accept my fate, I knew Ella – the sister I never knew I had, but now wanted more than anything – deserved to live.

'Help me up,' I said, releasing her hand. The torchlight was enough to guide me onto the boxes once more.

'What?'

'I have to talk to him.' I grabbed her arm and eased myself up, crying out as I jarred my arm, the pain bringing fresh tears to my eyes.

'Careful,' Ella said.

'I need to try to make him see he has to let you go.'

'He has to let you go too.'

'No, no, it doesn't matter about me,' I said, reaching the window. Peering through it, I could just make out his legs in the darkness, and my mind drifted for a moment to the man who had picked me up off the streets of Dublin; the man who'd got me off drugs and drink. The man I'd loved and thought loved me. *If only he hadn't wanted to control me.*

I fumbled with the window and managed to push it open. 'Jake,' I called. 'Jake, *please*. Ella doesn't need to die.'

Everything plunged into darkness. He'd extinguished the torch and was on his feet, his heavy footfalls getting closer to the window. I dropped down off the boxes in fear as he kicked the window hard.

'Oh God,' I cried, expecting glass to shatter everywhere. Ella pulled me to her and hugged me close. 'Oh, Ella,' I said, tears rolling down my face. 'Ella, I'm so sorry. I'm so, so sorry.'

'My darling sister,' she sobbed into my hair, 'this is not your fault.' But I knew it was. Just as it had been my fault that Bryony lost her life.

We lowered onto the floor, wrapped in each other's arms, our faces buried into each other, curling like hedgehogs against danger.

What Jake had planned for us, I didn't know. That it ended in our deaths, I was certain. I could almost feel my life force draining away already, as though he'd sucked it from me. But then, the spark had gone out a long time ago – many years before Jake came into my world.

Some time later – although how much time had gone by, I wasn't sure – I heard the creak of a car boot opening, and the yellow light of his torch cast a beam across the basement once more.

'What's he doing?' Ella's voice was a broken whisper as she straightened up and moved away from me, and the gaping hole she left made me feel vulnerable once more. 'Where's he gone?'

A sudden noise of cans bashing together, sloshing liquid inside, carried on the still night air, made us both jump.

'Oh God!'

'What?' Ella sounded terrified, as I rose and pulled her to her feet.

'Get up,' I ordered, as two or three cans hit the ground, and the boot slammed shut. 'He's going to set fire to the cottage.'

Ella was so close I could feel her hot breath on my face. 'No, no,' she said on a sob. 'How do you know?'

Fear crawled over me. 'You just need to get up to that window and out.' I sounded stronger than I felt. 'It's your only chance.' I twisted round. Ella's face was a mask of terror. 'You have to try, now,' I cried, stumbling as I guided her towards the boxes. 'Before …' The sound of liquid splashing the walls of the farmhouse was unmistakable. Jake's heavy footfalls as he thumped around the building were terrifying.

'Come on!' I shuffled the boxes closer to the wall, and Ella hauled herself onto them, crying out in pain as she bashed her ankle.

A flash of blinding light was followed by a whoosh.

'This is useless,' Ella cried. 'We've tried reaching the window before. There's no way out.' She fell back to the floor, and covered her face with her hands. 'Maisie.' It came out as a tortured groan. 'Oh God, Maisie.'

Outside, I thought I heard Jake laugh, but perhaps I was imagining it.

The car engine started up once more, and rumbled for a while, as though he was sitting at the wheel, admiring his handiwork – before speeding away with a screech of tyres.

'*Nooooo!*' I screamed, breaking into a sob.

The crackle of spreading fire jolted me into action, and I rose once more, as though I could still find a way out – as though I could still save Ella.

She coughed as smoke seeped in around the window frame and a faint orange light from the flickering flames distorted her anguished face. 'We should lie on the ground,' she said, eyes watering. 'Carbon monoxide is lighter than oxygen. I remember that from school.'

I didn't argue, and dropped down next to her.

We flattened onto our stomachs, heads turned to look at one another. Tears seeped into her hair and I awkwardly put my arm around her. 'We can't just lie here,' I said through gritted teeth. 'We have to do something.'

Ella succumbed to another coughing fit. 'Shall we try the door again?' she said, when she'd caught her breath, but I knew it was pointless.

'Soon,' I said.

My limbs felt heavy, and my eyes were stinging too much to keep them open. The heat was unbearable.

Smoke drifted in, thick and toxic, filling our lungs, and

somewhere in the logical part of my brain, I registered it wouldn't be long before our bodies gave up the fight.

We kept coughing – an automatic reflex.

Ella shifted and my eyes jumped open. She was wrapping one sleeve of her jacket across her mouth, indicating I do the same with the other.

'We should wet it,' I said, placing it across my nose and mouth, aware of a rawness in my throat. 'I saw that once in a film.'

Her mouth lifted in a sad attempt at a smile. 'Oh, Colleen,' she rasped, between coughs. 'I don't want to die.'

The words were so heartfelt, a sob ripped through me. 'I'm going to try the window again.' I pushed myself onto my knees, but before I could stand, Ella's head lifted, and her red-rimmed eyes widened.

'A car,' she said, her voice weak and hoarse.

I'd heard it too, approaching fast.

'Why would he come back?' My voice was muffled through the sleeve.

'Maybe he's changed his mind and he's come to save us.' Ella sat up, then doubled over in a choking fit, her eyes streaming. 'Maybe that was his plan all along,' she managed. 'He wanted to scare us, not kill us.'

It seemed unlikely. 'Maybe Greg called the Gardaí.'

The car pulled to a screeching stop, faint headlight beams reaching through the smoke.

'Help!' Ella and I cried, but our voices were so weak, and the raging crackle of flames had reached a crescendo. Whoever was out there wouldn't hear us.

Even so, I couldn't help yelling. 'We're in the basement.' I got to my feet, but the smoke was too thick, and I dropped back down again.

'Help!' Ella cried again, dropping her jacket as we crawled across to the door, but her voice was weak and thin.

On our knees, we bashed on the wood, screaming, until Ella sank to the floor, eyes rolling back in her head.

221

'HELP US!' I shrieked, my sore throat protesting at the effort. Footsteps clattered down the stairs. 'The handle will be hot,' I shouted, hoping whoever it was had come to help.

Then I heard his voice. 'Colleen, you are one stupid, fucking bitch.'

My blood chilled.

He was back. *Jake.*

I heard a key turn, and the door flew open. He stood there, shrouded in smoke, giving the illusion he was part of the fire. I couldn't make out his face, but his ice-blue eyes seemed to pierce my skin.

'Bastard!' I yelled, and with a burst of adrenalin, I thrust myself at him. He fell back with a grunt of surprise and cracked his head on a step. As he lay groaning, I reached down and grabbed Ella's hand. She was only just conscious, as limp as a ragdoll, but with a strength I didn't know I had, I managed to drag her up the steps.

'Come *on*,' I urged, muscles straining as I pulled her after me, through the writhing smoke, towards the front door I could see standing open in front of us.

'Colleen!' Jake's shout gave way to a coughing fit.

'Keep away from us, you sick bastard,' I yelled, hooking Ella's arm around my shoulder and heaving her outside, half carrying her towards a copse, away from the burning building, the air stinging my streaming eyes.

We collapsed in a heap on the grass, hidden by a bank of trees, and I watched as flames licked the roof of the house, and sparks of orange flew into the night sky. *I know this place.*

Ella convulsed and retched, barely conscious. I rose once more and hoisted her up with my good arm, but she was a dead weight. I couldn't move her.

Suddenly, Jake appeared through the door of the farmhouse in the distance, his arm across his face as flames leapt up the walls around him, and the sound of timber cracking and smashing cut through the air. 'Colleen!' His voice was snatched away by the breeze that had sprung up, fanning the flames. 'Colleen, where are you?'

Ella crumpled back to the ground with a cry of pain. 'I can't run, Colleen.' Her voice was an anguished whisper. 'My ankle – I think it's broken.'

'Colleen, you can't hide forever!'

I tried to pull Ella to her feet before Jake could reach us but it was no use. She was drained of colour, her eyes bloodshot, her hair plastered to her head with sweat. She winced as her breath heaved noisily in and out of her lungs. 'I won't leave you,' I said. 'Put your arms round my neck. Please.'

'I can't, Colleen,' she gasped. 'Please. Just go and get help.'

My heart galloped as Jake headed off in the wrong direction, his strides long and purposeful. 'I know you're out there some-where.' His tone was unthreatening – as if he thought I might give myself up.

'Go.' Ella's voice was weak and her eyes fluttered closed.

'Ella!' I shook her. 'Ella, wake up!' I started to sob. How could I leave her? *This is my fault.* I'd already lost one sister. I wasn't about to lose another. I would kill Jake if I had to.

On my hands and knees, I scrabbled around for something to use as a weapon, but my hands only met wet grass.

As I cast my eyes about, I heard sirens getting closer, and shot to my feet. The Gardaí were fast approaching, and a fire engine drew up like a miracle, blue lights flashing.

Jake had stopped moving now and was a menacing black shape, silhouetted by the fire.

'Help me!' I cried from the trees, cupping my hands around my mouth in an attempt to direct my weakened voice. 'Over here!'

A couple of Garda got out of a car and raced towards me through the flame-brightened darkness, while the firemen leapt from the engine and unwound their hoses.

'My sister needs help,' I cried, hysterically, dropping back beside Ella.

'We'll need an ambulance,' said the officer, flashing a torch over to where Ella was, and began talking into the radio on her collar.

'It was him.' I pointed through the trees to where Jake stood motionless, my words disjointed through the sobs racking my body. 'He locked us in the basement and set the house on fire.'

The Gardaí exchanged looks, and moved towards him. I heard their muffled conversation, but couldn't pick up what they were saying.

'She's crazy,' Jake yelled, his voice carrying towards us. 'Always has been.' He was twisting his head, trying to seek me out in the darkness. 'Look into it, if you don't believe me. She let her sister drown and did nothing to save her. She's a drug addict. A drunk.'

Oh Jake, how could you?

'You'll need to come with us, sir,' said one of the officers, loud and assertive.

'She's set me up.' His protest was loud and clear. I'd never seen him this rattled. 'You're one crazy bitch, Colleen!' he yelled, as the Gardaí escorted him away. 'If I never see you again it'll be too soon.'

Once he'd been bundled into the police car, I squatted down and stroked Ella's hair from her face. 'Please be OK,' I said over and over like a mantra. Minutes later, an ambulance arrived, and a couple of paramedics rushed over.

'Can you hear me, love?' said one, bending to examine Ella, and when she didn't respond, he covered her face with an oxygen mask.

'Is she going to be all right?' I asked, clinging to her hand as she was stretchered inside the ambulance. Her hair was tangled around her face, which was pale beneath patches of dirt, her lashes sweeping her cheeks.

'She'll be fine.' The paramedic helped me up the step, so I could go with her. 'Looks like you've both been in the wars,' he added.

As the ambulance doors closed, I glanced back at the farmhouse.

The flames had been extinguished, but a pall of foul-smelling smoke hung in the air. In the light from the fire engine, I could see the place was a wreck, but I knew I'd been here before.

I shivered. It wasn't the first time I'd almost died in that farmhouse.

None of it seemed real.

As the ambulance pulled away, I turned to Ella. 'You're safe now,' I whispered.

But as we sped away, me clasping Ella's hand while the ruddy-faced paramedic kept up a stream of cheerful chatter, I didn't feel safe at all.

Chapter 29

Ella

Tuesday

My eyes drifted open. I was in bed, a soft pillow beneath my head. The remnants of a dream slipped away.

I'm alive.

I was immediately flooded with a sense of well-being. From now on, I was going to make my life count – no more working long hours, or pretending I didn't mind Dad barely talking to me. I wanted to go on holiday with Greg and Maisie and have another baby. I wanted to photograph landscapes, not food.

Soft light filtered over my face. I could just make out a slice of duck-egg-blue sky through the slats of a blind covering a large, square window. *A window.*

My ankle throbbed, jerking me properly awake. I tried to swallow, but my throat was raw and I coughed. Turning my head, I smelt something acrid in my hair and saw a thin tube, snaking from the back of my hand to a drip by the bed.

I was in hospital.

Memories crashed back; crackling flames, heat burning my lungs. Colleen, half-lifting me out of the farmhouse, my ankle screaming in agony; smoke swirling into the sky and Jake shouting. Gulping air, then falling onto wet grass, Colleen's face, wavering above me; the sound of sirens in the distance. Then … *nothing*.

I awkwardly shifted position and lifted the sheet. I was wearing a blue regulation gown and my ankle was heavily bandaged.

Panic rose. I was alone, and the door in front of the bed was closed. I peered at the small, glass panel and saw a figure move past and then double back.

Jake.

My breath jammed in my throat. It couldn't be him, but there was his face, looming at the glass, his piercing blue eyes pinned to mine.

A scream began to rise. I struggled upright, groping for a panic button, but when I looked again, he'd gone.

I stared at the glass and blinked, my breathing rapid and shallow.

There was no one there.

I shrank back feeling shaky and sick. Either the smoke I'd inhaled, or whatever drugs I'd been given were playing tricks with my mind.

My eyes skimmed the room. There was a TV fixed to the wall on one side of the bed and a locker on the other, a green plastic chair beside it with a blanket draped over the back, as though someone had thrown it off. *Colleen?*

As if on cue, the door opened a fraction, and when Colleen's head poked round, my body flooded with bright, hot relief. 'Thank God.'

'You're awake,' she said, edging inside, carrying a cardboard cup of steaming liquid. 'I was just getting some coffee.' Her dress was filthy and ripped at the armpit, and her legs were covered in scratches. 'How are you feeling?'

'Tired,' I said through a gigantic yawn, trying to shift into a position that didn't hurt. 'I can't believe I've been sleeping.' I didn't tell her I'd just hallucinated Jake, certain it was the last thing she wanted to hear.

'They gave you something.' She came over, gestured at the drip. 'You were out of it, in shock, they said. They're keeping an eye on your lungs. You inhaled more smoke than I did.'

'Are you OK though?'

'My shoulder's sprained, but otherwise, I'm fine.' She put her cup down on the locker, and bent to rearrange my pillows behind me. She smelt of smoke and sweat, mingled with hospital anti-septic, and I longed for Maisie's sweet biscuit fragrance and Greg's spicy aftershave – even Dad's mingled scent of leather and dog. 'That better?'

I sank back and nodded, battling an overwhelming tiredness. 'Is my ankle broken?'

'Hairline fracture.' She moved away, running a hand over her rumpled hair. She looked tired and shaky, eyes wide and blood-shot, her face smudged with dirt. 'They said it'll be painful, but should heal on its own.'

'Jake?' My heartbeat accelerated just mentioning his name.

'He's been arrested.' I felt a fresh spurt of relief, that the face I'd thought I'd seen moments ago couldn't have been Jake's. 'The Gardaí took him, thank Christ. He can't hurt us now.' She crum-pled onto the plastic chair, as though she didn't trust her legs to hold her up. 'Can you believe he's protesting his innocence?' Her voice hummed with anger. 'What a joke. He was the only other person at the farmhouse.'

Something pulled at my memory and floated away and my fingers plucked at the sheet, pleating and unpleating. I couldn't bear to examine what had happened, but images forced their way in: Jake's silhouette through the smoke in the basement doorway, flames leaping behind him, smaller than I remembered. In my mind he'd grown bigger – a monster instead of a man. 'Do you think he changed his mind?'

Colleen's head lifted. 'What?'

I hesitated, not sure I should say out loud the thought that had occurred to me. 'It's just … we'd have died in there, if he hadn't come back and unlocked the door.'

The word *died* vibrated the air and fear pressed into my bones. It didn't seem possible our lives could have ended so brutally, yet it had almost happened.

'More likely he was checking we were dead,' Colleen said. She rubbed one eye with her knuckle, and her sigh seemed to come up from the soles of her feet. 'Listen, Ella, I'm so sorry you got mixed up in my crap.' Her eyes caught and held mine, and although she'd said it before, I could see she meant it. 'If anything had happened to you because of me—'

'You wouldn't have known,' I broke in, with a slightly hysterical edge. The thought of being burned alive, of never seeing Maisie, or Greg or my father again, was too much to take in. 'You'd have been dead too.'

Colleen's eyebrows shot up. 'True,' she said, with a ghost of a smile. 'But I'm still sorry. For everything.'

'Like you said, I chose to come to Ireland.'

'But you didn't sign up for all this.' She scanned the room, hands pressed between her knees. I noticed she was wearing a pair of black plimsolls at least a size too big.

'Stylish, eh?' Seeing me looking, she waggled her foot for effect. 'One of the nurses found them for me. Couldn't have me running around the hospital in bare feet.'

I was struggling to keep my eyes open, still in the grip of whatever medication I'd been given. 'I need to call Greg.'

'He's on his way.'

I made a noise of surprise.

'I gave the hospital his name and they found his number and called him, but he was already on his way.'

'He's coming here?'

A smile illuminated her face. 'He was worried about you, after

229

calling your phone and getting no answer, then the hotel, and realising you weren't there. He jumped on the first available flight and should be here soon.'

Hot tears leaked down my face and I couldn't summon the energy to wipe them away. I wanted Greg here now, to feel his arms close around me, for him to reassure me that everything was OK. I wanted to hold Maisie and listen to her uncomplicated chatter.

As if sensing my turmoil, Colleen got up and perched on the edge of the bed, pulling my hand into hers. 'He'll be here soon,' she said, even though I hadn't spoken. 'The hospital let me speak to him, so I could let him know you were OK. He was seriously pissed off with me.'

The matter-of-fact way she said it brought a smile to the surface. My fingers tightened around hers. 'It's going to be all right now, isn't it?' I laid a hand on her cheek, feeling the sharpness of her cheekbone beneath my fingers. There was a feathering of blonde at her temple, and I wondered if she would let her true colour come through now she didn't have to run from Jake anymore.

She was silent for a moment, eyes searching my face, reading the things banked up in my chest that I wanted to say, but couldn't. 'Sure.' She placed her hand over mine, gaze softening, as if she was seeing the possibilities play out. 'It won't be easy, mind.' Pulling away, she stood and stretched. 'I'll have my work cut out winning over your husband, for a start.'

'You don't have to worry about that,' I said, with more conviction than I felt. The truth was, I had no idea how Greg would feel, after everything that had happened.

'And there's stuff to sort out here,' Colleen went on, as though I hadn't spoken, pacing around the bed, hands fluttering. 'We're not going to be playing happy families right away.'

'I know that.' My stomach plunged, and I saw that I'd been childish and naive to assume I could acquire a sister and absorb

230

her into my life without any ripples – as though she'd been waiting all these years for me to come along and complete her.

Her life was messy and complicated; she was bound to her past and Bryony's death, Jake, and whatever had happened in that farmhouse. It would be easier to walk away, back to my old life, to forget about her. I'd only known her a week or so, after all.

My mind swept through everything that had happened, flicking back and forth. I thought of the chain of events that had led me from home, to Colleen, to that basement, looking for a meaning.

If I gave up on her now, it had all been for nothing.

Watching her eyes dart to me and away again, a burst of frustrated affection brushed aside my fatigue. 'Listen,' I said, sitting forward. 'Mum wanted you to be happy, whether you care or not, and she wanted me to find you. I know she'd be glad that I came, in spite of everything. We can't change what's happened in the past, but you can have a different future if you want one.' I paused. 'With Reagan, with me. Your family.'

She stopped pacing and looked at me unblinking, her head tipped, as if listening to a distant voice. She opened her mouth, but before she could speak the door opened and a pink-checked, smiling nurse bustled in, bringing the sounds of the hospital: a trolley clanking, voices rising and falling from the corridor.

'Nice to see you're back with us, Mrs Matthews,' she said. 'You and your sister have been through quite an ordeal. She's barely left your side all night.' I caught Colleen's eye. Her mouth lifted at the corners before she looked away.

The nurse took my pulse and checked my blood pressure. 'There's been a lot of press interest,' she said, adjusting the drip. 'Reporters were hanging around for ages. It's all over the local news. Oh, and the Gardaí want a statement when you're up to it. I saw a couple of officers out the front.'

'Give us a few more minutes,' Colleen said, retrieving her cup of coffee. She took a sip and winced. 'As for the reporters, the vultures can wait a bit longer.'

I guessed there'd been press interest when Bryony died and felt a swell of sorrow for her. 'Yes, they can wait,' I echoed.

The nurse nodded briskly. 'Breakfast's doing the rounds,' she said. 'I'll get someone to bring you a decent cup of tea and some toast.'

The door had barely swung shut when it opened again, and a red-faced woman with an old-fashioned, rattling tray came in and doled out two cups of strong tea and a plate of toast, without asking whether we wanted either. 'It should be soft enough to spread now,' she said, adding a few pats of butter and a knife. 'Shall I put the TV on for you?'

She'd already picked up the remote and aimed it at the screen, before leaving with a distracted smile, and for a second, we stared at a stiff-haired newsreader with a serious expression, mouthing silent words.

Colleen snapped back to life and reached for the remote on the locker. 'I don't know about you, but I'm not in the mood for breakfast TV.'

'Wait …' I said, shuffling up the bed. 'I think it's the local news. There might be something on there about … about Jake.' I doubted I'd ever be able to say his name without a tremor of fear. 'There might be an update.'

'We'll get an update from the guards,' Colleen said, but after turning up the volume, she lowered her arm. An image appeared of a film-star handsome man with piercing blue eyes in a strong, tanned face, smiling from a slightly grainy photograph.

'Jake Harper, forty-two, a surgeon at the Whitfield Clinic in Waterford,' the newsreader was saying earnestly, 'was arrested in the early hours of this morning, charged with two counts of kidnapping, and attempted murder, after setting fire to the house where he'd been holding his ex-wife and her sister in the basement.'

'Bastard,' muttered Colleen through gritted teeth. Her pale cheeks had sprouted two red splotches. 'I hope they throw away the key.'

232

I looked from her to the screen, but the image had gone and the newsreader was talking again. 'That wasn't Jake,' I said.

Her head shot round. 'What?'

'That man.' Icy fingers touched my spine. 'It wasn't Jake,' I repeated. 'They must have used the wrong photo.'

'Of course it was Jake.' Colleen's bark of laughter held no humour. 'I should know, I was married to the psychopath.'

I pressed a hand to my pounding chest. 'I don't get it.' My gaze crept back to the screen, but the news had moved on; something about knife crime. 'That's not the man I spoke to at the hotel,' I said. 'That wasn't the man who brought me to the farmhouse.'

'Ella, what the hell are you talking about?' There was an edge to Colleen's voice; a mix of anger and fear. 'You saw him last night,' she said. 'We watched him being handcuffed. Or at least, I watched.' Her expression grew grim. 'I wanted to make sure they'd got the lying, murdering bastard.'

I sank against the pillows as a recollection flew back: Jake, shouting after us as we fled the burning farmhouse.

'Colleen, you are one stupid, fucking bitch.'

His accent. That was the thing that had been bothering me, earlier. 'I didn't know he was American.'

'What?' Colleen's brow creased. 'I don't see what that has to do with anything.'

'The man who brought me to the farmhouse,' I said, feeling as if I'd blacked out and missed something crucial. 'He was Irish.'

Colleen's face was a mask of confusion. 'Why the hell would Jake pretend to be Irish? He never lost his American accent. He was proud of it.'

'That's what I'm saying.' I desperately wanted her to make sense of something I didn't understand myself. 'The man who locked us up … it can't have been Jake.'

We looked at each other for a moment and something dark crept into Colleen's expression. 'What did this *man* look like?'

233

Her voice sounded odd, as though someone had their fingers on her windpipe.

'He was, I don't know ...' I tried to think, to remember my initial impression. 'Tall, dark hair, blue eyes. Good-looking, I suppose.' I swallowed. 'He was smartly dressed, wearing a white shirt, smart trousers, nice shoes.'

'That sounds just like Jake.' Colleen caught her lower lip between her fingers, eyes cast down, as though seeing something written in the bedcovers. 'Tall, you say?'

I nodded. 'About six-two.'

She raised her eyes. 'You're sure?'

'Yes.' My voice was too high. 'I'm sure, Colleen. Greg's about the same height.'

Her features tightened. 'And he knew all about me?'

'Of course he did.' I ransacked my brain for details. 'He even showed me that photograph he had, the one with you next to the motorbike ...' I stopped as she pushed her hands in her hair, shaking her head.

'That definitely sounds like Jake, yet you're saying it wasn't him.' Her eyes were pools of confusion. 'You're absolutely certain?'

'Positive.' The air jumped and crackled with electricity. 'I ... I think I saw him, Colleen.'

'What?' Her tone sharpened. 'When?'

'When I woke up.' I hesitated. 'I thought I saw Jake ... no, the man who *isn't* Jake, but he was gone so quickly, I thought I'd imagined it. But, what if ... what if it was *him* and he's here?'

'Oh my God.' She was backing towards the door, her face bleached of colour.

I sat up. 'Wait! Where are you going?'

'To find him,' she said.

234

Chapter 30

Colleen

'Colleen!' Ella called after me.

'Press the alarm. Get a nurse to stay with you.' My voice was shaking. 'Tell them Jake didn't do it. That whoever it was could be in the hospital. I'm going to get the Gardaí.'

I left the room, my head spinning, Ella crying out after me to wait.

I passed a coffee shop – shutters down, too early to open. 'Stupid, stupid,' I muttered as I hurried along the hospital corridor, the plimsolls flapping the vinyl floor.

Jake saved my life. How the hell had he known where I was? And who the hell had brought Ella to the farmhouse?

Hearing footsteps behind me, I looked back and caught my breath. It was only a doctor. He slipped past me like a ghost, head down.

I was jittery, my senses heightened through lack of sleep and shock. I paused for a moment, waiting for my heartbeat to slow, but it kept on thumping. If Ella was right, they'd arrested the wrong man and Jake was innocent – of that, at least. And whoever had locked Ella and me in that cellar – whoever had set it alight and left us to die – was still out there.

A woman looked up from the hospital reception desk. I must have looked peculiar in the filthy dress, and flapping shoes. 'Are you OK?' she called. 'Let me fetch someone to help.'

I ignored her, my mind racing. Who would have had a photograph of me as a teenager, and that awful one of me stark naked in the guesthouse?

The realisation slammed into me like a punch. 'Christ!'

The automatic doors shuddered open and I plunged through them, the cold morning air hitting my cheeks. I leaned against the wall, and buried my head in my hands. 'No!' I cried, shaking my head, not wanting to believe it, even though I knew it was true. 'It was Gabriel.'

*

Gabriel had pushed me to take drugs all those years ago, promising I would feel amazing. 'You'll never cry again,' he'd promised. 'They'll take away your memories of Bryony – you'll forget all about her.'

And I had, for a time.

Gabriel dealt in the big stuff, but I hadn't cared. He manipulated me, and I let it happen. I loved the risks we took, the stupid reckless things that made me feel I was leaving myself behind, no longer Colleen, or Bryony's big sister.

Gabriel had been at the farmhouse the first time I almost died. His grandfather had passed away a month before and left him the old place. We'd driven there, already high, planning to stay for a bit. Gabriel had wanted us to lie low – said the police were after him.

That night he'd looked at me differently. It was as though the loss of his grandfather had made him see me properly for the first time. He said he loved me, loved the way I couldn't give a shit whether I lived or died.

At the time, I hadn't.

When I overdosed he panicked. He called an ambulance then fled, and I never heard from him again.

After a stint in hospital, I lived on the streets of Dublin. That's where Jake found me. He offered to buy me coffee and we ended up talking for ages.

He told me he'd left America after the death of his mother, and was hoping to reconnect with his father. I didn't say much, but listening to him as I sipped my strong, sweet coffee had felt good. He was older than me, attractive, but that wasn't what drew me in. It was how kind and supportive he was, a good listener. I felt safe being close to him. I was ready for something different. I needed him.

He was a surgeon, he said, in a private hospital. He liked saving people.

He saved me. Then almost destroyed me.

But he didn't lock me in that basement and try to kill me. Gabriel did.

*

There was no sign of the Gardaí, so I crossed the road into the car park. Perhaps they'd parked up behind the hedge. As I walked, my mind flashed back to the half-empty bottle of black hair dye I'd left at the guesthouse. Had Gabriel used it to colour his hair, so he looked like Jake?

I reached the overgrown hedge, and peered round. The area was deserted, and I suddenly felt sick and dizzy. I doubled over, hands on my knees, and coughed until I retched. Everything was catching up with me. I felt scraped out. Empty.

The early morning silence settled around me, and the rising sun had turned the sky apricot. I straightened and wiped my mouth, noticing a doctor and nurse walking into the hospital. I was wasting my time here. There was still no sign of the Gardaí.

As I turned to head back, a car that had been parked some distance away drew up beside me, its silvery colour half obscured by mud. A man jumped out of the driver's seat, and before I could react he'd slung an arm around my shoulder, and pressed something sharp against my back. 'Don't scream,' a low voice hissed in my ear.

Despite the bulky fleece, and baseball cap pulled low, I knew who it was.

'Get off me,' I yelled.

'Shut up, bitch.' He grabbed my throat, and I felt my necklace break and slip away. 'Get in the car.' He moved the hand with the knife to ease open the back door.

Twisting my head, I looked at his bright blue eyes – eyes that had attracted me years ago, when I was a teenager, still mourning the death of my sister.

His arm tightened across my throat like a vice, and he yanked me close to his body, his breath hot on my cheek. He stank of petrol and sour sweat and my stomach heaved.

'I heard on the news how you and your sister survived. How about that?' He barked out a laugh. 'A sister who survived! Things are looking up.'

I tried to kick him, but he had me pinned to his body, the knife close to my throat now. My eyes darted about. *This is a hospital, for Christ's sake, in broad daylight. Where is everybody?*

With a sudden, deft movement, he manoeuvred me into the back seat of the car and jumped in beside me, slamming and locking the doors. He removed the baseball cap and wiped his forehead with the back of his hand. 'I hope you liked the wreath, and my messages, Colleen.' His breath was foul.

'But the texts were from Jake.'

He shook his head. 'When I dropped off the lilies, I saw your phone charging. No password, you silly cow. An unexpected

238

bonus.' He sounded almost proud. 'I deleted Jake's number and added mine next to his name.' He paused. 'My mother would have been proud of my ingenuity.' Now he was being sarcastic. I remembered his parents had disowned him when he flunked his chemistry degree. He didn't miss them, he'd said. But he'd loved his grandfather. 'The only person who cares about me,' he'd once told me.

'It didn't take long to work out which hospital you were at.' He trailed the blade of his knife down my cheek.

I flinched away, blood pounding in my ears. His chin was thick with bristle, his pupils dilated. I wondered if he'd taken something. The thought that I'd had sex with him a week ago made me want to vomit.

'I came here to find you, and you served yourself up on a plate,' he said.

'Why are you doing this?'

He seemed astonished. 'You knew I loved you, Colleen. I told you last week how I never got over losing you.' *Had he?* I couldn't remember.

'I nearly died of an overdose in that farmhouse, or have you forgotten?'

He replaced the baseball cap and tugged it down. 'I spent ages looking for you after I got out of prison,' he said, as if I hadn't spoken.

'You were in prison?'

'Over fourteen years for dealing, and you didn't once wonder where I was?'

Thinking back, it must have made the news, but I'd been in no fit state to know. 'It took me a long time to recover. I didn't—'

'It took me a long time to track you down,' he cut in. 'I guess I didn't have you pegged as a good little housewife.' He smirked. 'That husband of yours barely let you out of his sight, did he?'

'You know about Jake?' And then it hit me. 'You were following me.'

239

'Biding my time, Colleen. And it was worth the wait, because you suddenly took off to Sligo alone. Imagine how that felt.' He bared his teeth in a grin. 'In the end, it was almost too easy.'

'Gabriel, please.'

'You agreed to have a drink with me, you slept with me, you cried on my shoulder like a baby about your shitty husband. You told me you needed me, Colleen.'

I didn't. I wouldn't have. Did I? A shiver travelled up my spine. 'I don't remember.' My eyes trawled the car park. Someone had to turn up soon. *Just keep him talking.* 'I'd had too much to drink.' I struggled to keep my voice steady. 'It was a mistake. I didn't want to go down that route again. I've been sober for years.'

'You wanted it, Colleen.'

'No. No, I didn't.' My voice quavered.

'You betrayed me.' He ran his hand down my arm and across my thigh. My skin crawled. I wanted to launch myself at him, but knew he would overpower me.

I couldn't believe now how excited I'd been to see him in Sligo in a coffee shop, where I'd been sitting alone and scared, wondering if I'd done the right thing by leaving Jake. It hadn't occurred to me how much of a coincidence it was to bump into Gabriel, after so long. He'd seemed different at first, more mature, said he'd got a good job and had been working in England since he last saw me. All lies. He was a good liar.

Maybe I'd hoped, as we drank espressos, that somewhere deep down I still loved him. But I hadn't. I'd left that eighteen-year-old girl behind me.

When I told Gabriel how awful things had been with Jake, he convinced me to go somewhere for a drink for old time's sake, and one drink had led to another. He'd made sure of that. He'd always been persuasive. I wondered now if he'd spiked my drinks, and that was why I couldn't remember anything else about that night.

'I didn't know where you'd gone, Colleen.' His voice had taken on a pathetic tone. 'You left me in that room and brushed me off

with a text. You didn't care. I only had the film of you and me.'
He wet his lips with his tongue. 'Thank God I had the film.' He
gave a humourless laugh, and I remembered the laptop's blinking
light at the guesthouse, and how I'd assumed it was charging.
'Did you like the photo of us, Colleen? It's a still from the movie.'

Jesus. 'You're sick, Gabriel. You need help.'

Without warning, he rammed me hard and I began to scream.
'Shut up!' The flat of his hand collided with the side of my
face, before he pressed his fingers deep into the flesh of my arms.
'Shut up,' he said, softer, and I fell silent.

My ear throbbed with pain. 'You're hurting me.'

'You deserve it.' He stroked my cheek as I sobbed, before slamming my head against the door. The pain was intense and I fought
a slide into unconsciousness. He lowered me onto my back. I felt
the prick of a needle in my arm, before he covered me with a
blanket and launched himself into the front, starting the engine.

I touched my head, and my fingers came away bloody. I tried
to ease myself up, heart banging against my chest, but the pain
in my skull forced me back, and the car sped away.

Chapter 31

Ella

After locating and pressing the buzzer to summon help, it seemed an age before the nurse put her head round the door.

'What is it, Ella?'

'Have you seen my sister?'

She came in, looking me over. 'That's why you called?'

'She … I think she's in danger.' I threw off the blankets. 'The man who took her … took me, it's not who we thought it was. It wasn't Jake, and I think I saw the man earlier. He was in the hospital.'

I sounded breathless, and knew I wasn't making much sense. A frown gathered on the nurse's brow. 'They caught the man, and he's in custody,' she said, her voice kind. 'You've nothing to worry about; you're in perfectly good hands here.'

'But she's gone after him.' I swung my legs out of bed and the floor tilted towards me. 'I have to find her.'

'You can't get up.' The nurse placed gentle hands on my shoulders. 'You need to rest. You've been through a terrible ordeal.'

I shrugged her off, tears of frustration rising. 'Police,' I said. 'Get the police – I need to talk to them.'

Her face creased into anxious lines. 'You lie down, and I'll go and fetch someone.'

As soon as the door closed, I hauled myself out of bed. There was no way I could stay, while Colleen was God knows where.

There was no sign of my clothes. They were probably ruined, so I grabbed the discarded blanket off the back of the chair and threw it over my hospital gown before shuffling, barefoot to the door. Painkillers must have numbed the pain in my ankle, but it was difficult to walk with it thickly bandaged. My head was spinning and I clung to the doorframe, fighting the urge to cough. There was an abandoned wheelchair in the empty, strip-lit corridor. I hobbled over, checking the nurse wasn't on her way back, and collapsed into it, pins and needles prickling in my legs.

Pushing myself to reception, I kept an eye open for Colleen, but had no idea where to start looking. The sounds of the hospital were distant, as though everything was happening a long way away, adding to the sense that this was a nightmare I might wake up from any moment.

I followed the signs to a reception area, where a woman at a desk behind a glass panel was sitting in front of a computer. 'Excuse me, have you seen my sister – small with short dark hair, very pale?' My voice didn't sound as strong as I'd have liked and it seemed to take the woman an age to drag her gaze in my direction.

'Actually, yes, she was in a bit of a hurry,' she said, a frown in her voice. She pointed the pen in her hand at a pair of glass doors. 'She went outside.'

I wheeled myself to the exit, fighting for breath, ignoring a curious glance from a cleaner mopping the floor.

The doors were automatic and silently parted, and I shot through into what looked like a car park, though it was practically empty. No sign of any reporters, or the Gardaí the nurse had mentioned were waiting. Perhaps they'd gone for breakfast. Then I spotted a sign with an arrow pointing to the main entrance, round the side of the building, and realised there was more than one way out of the hospital.

'*Shit.*' Colleen could be anywhere. She might even be back in my room, wondering where I'd gone. About to reverse back inside, I saw something lying some distance away on the tarmac. Pushing forward, arms straining with effort, panic clutched at my throat as I drew closer and saw what it was. It was the necklace she always wore – the cheap chain with the letter 'B'. She'd constantly fiddled with it at the hotel. I bent to pick it up. *Colleen had been out here.*

I frantically looked around, as if she might be hiding, and thought I heard the roar of a car, pulling away from the hospital at speed.

Turning so fast the wheelchair almost toppled, I shot back inside, where the startled receptionist was talking to a colleague. 'Call the police.' My tone was urgent and they exchanged a look.

'Should you be out here?' said the woman I'd spoken to before. 'You don't look at all well.'

'Please,' I said. 'It's important. My sister … I think she's been taken.'

'There you are.' It was the nurse, a harried look on her face as she hurried towards me. 'Where do you think you're going?'

'I'm trying to find Colleen.' I tried to get out of the wheelchair. 'I have to talk to the police,' I said. 'Where are they?'

'Stay where you are.' The nurse pressed me down with a firm, efficient movement. 'I'll take you back to your room.'

'Please, you don't understand. My sister—'

'I know after what's happened you don't want to let her out of your sight, but I'm sure she's just gone to clean up, or to make a call and will be back before you know it.'

'She was going to look for him.' Why didn't she understand? 'Please, you have to help.'

'The doctor will talk to you.' The nurse wheeled me fast, her shoes silent on the floor. 'And the Gardaí will be back soon to take your statement.'

244

My breath was coming in gasps. 'I need to talk to my husband. Can I call him?' Greg would know what to do. *But Greg was on a plane, on his way to see me.*

'Of course you can,' said the nurse, her voice soothing, as though talking to a difficult child. 'I'll bring you the phone, once we've got you settled again.'

I wanted to scream, but knew if I did, it would make everything worse – make me less credible than I already was. As far as she was concerned, the man responsible for putting me in hospital was safely locked up and I had nothing to worry about. She probably thought I was suffering from post-traumatic stress.

As the nurse left me sitting on the edge of the bed, promising to return with a phone, panic pushed at my chest. *Where are you, Colleen?*

I let out a cry, as something came back to me – something Colleen said when she was telling me about the ex-boyfriend she'd bumped into and ended up sleeping with – *what was his name?* Gabriel, that was it.

He saved my life once. Her low voice came back to me. *I'd gone up the cliffs at Aughris Head, intending to throw myself off, join Bryony at the bottom of the ocean, but he followed me up there. He said I should take some drugs to ease the pain instead.*

Five minutes later, with the phone in my shaking hand, I pressed in the number for the police, but my words tumbled out in the wrong order and as the officer at the other end asked me to start again for the second time, I yelled at them to get to the hospital as quickly as possible, hung up and rang directory enquiries. 'Can you get me the number of the Strandhill Hostel in Sligo?'

Reagan had told me to call if I needed anything. I needed him now.

Chapter 32

Colleen

I couldn't say how long Gabriel had driven for, but when he finally stopped the only sound I heard was the racket of seagulls, and distant waves crashing against the shoreline.

Whatever Gabriel had injected me with was wearing off, and the spinning sensation I'd had throughout the journey had left me with a thumping head, and a weak feeling in my limbs. Or perhaps that was from where he'd thumped me against the door. But one thing I knew for certain: he hadn't intended to kill me with whatever he'd put in the syringe, or knock me out for long. He had a plan.

He got out of the car and slammed the door. Within moments, he'd flung open the back door, and was pulling back the blanket and yanking me out. We were at the edge of a roughly gravelled car park, and I had no strength to fight him as he pulled me away, through long grass, my legs like rubber.

He stopped and let go of me, and I dropped to the ground as if my bones had melted. 'Get up!' he ordered.

I drew my knees up to my nose, and wrapped my arms over

my head in a pathetic attempt to protect myself. The slam of his foot in my side was agonising.

'I said, get up!'

I raised my head, my eyes meeting his, as I cowered like a frightened puppy. I was witnessing evil. I wouldn't come out of this alive. *Perhaps it's meant to be.*

Above him the sky was a clear blue, and the sun shone, the seagulls I'd heard earlier circling like black spectres, cawing. *Would they eat human flesh?*

I glanced to my right. I was so close to the cliff edge, the sound of waves crashing below merging with the pounding in my chest. 'Aughris Head,' I whispered, recognising where we were with a horrified lurch in my stomach.

'Very good, Colleen.' Gabriel slow-clapped, before grabbing my wrists and yanking me to my feet. He turned me to face the sea, inches from the edge, and tears spilled down my cheeks. 'Do you remember?' His voice was a rough whisper. 'You wanted to drop into the ocean to be with Bryony. And I saved your life.'

I stayed silent.

'Colleen!' His voice was a roar.

'Yes. Yes, I remember.' Tears came faster.

'Well, I've decided you can now end what you started all those years ago.' He was calm again. 'You can be with Bryony. She's waiting for you.'

'Why are you doing this?' It was an effort to push the words out, and pointless anyway. He'd got it all worked out.

'I'm doing you a favour, Colleen.' He was behind me, large hands tight around my upper arms. One push and I would crash down onto the rocks.

'I want to live.' I was sobbing now. 'I've been given a second chance with Ella, and I don't want to leave her.'

'Fuck's sake, Colleen!' His laugh was harsh and loud. 'Do you honestly think that stuck-up little cow wants anything to do with the likes of a tramp like you? She hardly knows you, and she certainly won't miss you.'

'You're wrong.' I'd never felt this pathetic and weak, even when I was with Jake. Whatever Gabriel had injected into me was still making my legs wobble, and I knew if he let go of me, I would fall.

A sudden determination flooded my body. With as much strength as I could muster, I rammed my elbows backwards into Gabriel's stomach, catching him unawares. He released me, and I turned to see him stagger backwards and crash to the ground. I teetered close to the edge of the cliff, before falling backwards on top of him.

He grabbed my hair and threw me away from him like a bag of trash, and I wondered how he'd ever covered up this side of him. There was no trace of the charmer I'd bumped into in Sligo. The man I once knew. 'You fucking bitch,' he spat.

I scrambled to my feet and began to run. It was useless. He was behind me in seconds, one hand closing around my ankle, and as I hit the ground the breath slammed out of me. He flipped me over and climbed on top of me. 'I loved you once, Colleen,' he said, stroking my cheek with his sweaty hand.

I needed to change tack. I had one more chance.

'I loved you too,' I said, through gulps for breath. 'Why are we doing this? You were everything to me … you can be again.'

He lifted his hand from my cheek, and furrowed his forehead, staring into my eyes. His were cold, but filled with tears.

'We could be together, Gabriel,' I went on, forcing myself to touch his face, my skin crawling. 'Like before.'

He dashed his forearm across his eyes.

'We were so good together, weren't we?' I continued.

I wasn't sure when he stopped believing my words, or if he ever thought they were true, but he clenched his fist. The pain as he struck my face made me reel.

He rose, and hauled me up like a rag doll, saying nothing. I'd made things worse. Now I was going to die.

'Colleen!' For a second I was transported back to that terrible day – Bryony in the sea, Celia rushing into the waves. But it wasn't Celia. *Ella?*

I was disorientated, dizzy as Gabriel dragged my useless body back to the cliff edge.

'Colleen!' A male this time, closer.

Gabriel turned towards the voices, his grip on me loosening. I could just make out two figures, one much closer, the other falling behind.

'Colleen,' the man cried again.

Gabriel seemed to unravel. He hadn't planned for this, and his grip on me loosened further. So much so, I pulled free.

Gabriel turned back to me, his hands like claws as he went to grab me once more. But he knew. He knew I now had the upper hand.

One push sent him over the cliff edge, and his body twisted and writhed, as he tried to grab hold of something that wasn't there, before smashing against the rocks below. His scream would haunt me forever.

'Colleen?'

I turned. 'Reagan.' He yanked me away from the edge. 'I killed him,' I said, my voice raw.

'No. He fell.' There was something definite about Reagan's words as he wrapped his arms around me. 'He was too close to the edge and he fell.'

Reagan's words settled into me, as Ella stumbled towards us.

'Thank God,' she cried, taking hold of my hand, as I drifted into unconsciousness. 'Thank God you're safe.'

Chapter 33

Colleen

My vision cleared. I was on a stretcher, being carried towards an ambulance. Someone leaned in, and I instinctively shrank back.

'It's OK. It's me, Reagan,' he said, as he walked along beside me. 'I can't believe I almost lost you back there, before I'd had a chance to get to know you.'

'Gabriel?'

'The Gardaí are looking for his body.'

Once inside the ambulance, I saw Ella there too, attached to a drip, her bare feet and bandage filthy. 'You should be in hospital,' I said.

She held out her hand and I realised she was clutching something. 'Here.' She dropped Bryony's necklace in my open palm – the necklace I'd worn every day since I lost her. 'It was in the car park.'

I felt its warmth in my palm and tears prickled my eyes. 'Thank you,' I said. 'And not just for this.'

Ella's eyelids were drooping. 'I had to find you,' she whispered. 'You're my sister.'

*

I wasn't there to see Greg greet Ella later that day. Once I'd been checked over, I'd discharged myself, despite the doctor suggesting I stayed in overnight. I knew Ella would want to be alone with her husband. She'd insisted on paying for my room at the hotel until I'd sorted myself out, so I'd headed there.

She was being kept in for another night for observation, until they knew her lungs were clear, and she gave me her key-card, insisting I borrowed some clothes from her hotel room. If I'm honest, they weren't really me – too much like the clothes Jake used to want me to wear, but I found a plain T-shirt and some jeans that fitted once I'd rolled up the hems. I would wear them tomorrow. For now, a towelling robe would do.

After I'd showered, I lowered myself onto the bed, my body crying out with pain. I was covered in bruises, the worst on my face, but they were all superficial. I would eventually look like me again.

I'd lost my phone, but Reagan's email was etched on my mind, and I kept thinking of his arms around me on the cliff top – the first time he'd held me since I was a baby – and how, just for a moment, I hadn't wanted to move. I would contact him again in a few days, and see where it took us.

I thought about Alfie. I'd lost his number too, but it was for the best. I wasn't ready for a healthy relationship. Maybe one day I'd go to that pub in Sligo and search him out. I smiled to myself, remembering him hosting the quiz night, and how much I'd laughed.

My eyes grew heavy and I drifted into a dreamless sleep, waking at six the following morning. It was the best night's sleep I'd had in years.

I left my room just before ten. I'd ordered a taxi to take me back to the hospital, but as I tried to exit the hotel, a figure blocked my way, and my heart leapt into my throat.

'Colleen?'

I looked into the man's face. 'Oh God, Alfie.' He looked happy to see me, though I could see concern on his face, as he studied me. Applying some of Ella's foundation to my bruises clearly hadn't worked. I found myself taking him in – his tousled sandy hair and black-rimmed glasses. How much his smile made me want to smile back. But now wasn't the time. 'You scared the shite out of me,' I said, pushing past him, heart still thumping.

'Hang on.' He followed me out and laid a gentle hand on my arm. 'I heard about what happened. I'm so sorry.'

I stopped. 'It's fine,' I said, not trusting myself to look at him again.

'If you ever want to talk …'

I shrugged. 'I don't know, Alfie. Maybe.' I shook him off and continued towards the taxi, feeling his eyes on my back.

'Call me!'

'I've lost my phone and your number,' I called back.

He raced after me, and I waited while he borrowed a pen from a woman loading the boot of her car with suitcases and scribbled his number on an old receipt. He handed it to me and I took it without a word, and carried on walking towards my taxi, glancing over my shoulder once, to fix his image in my mind.

'Call me,' he repeated.

'Sure,' I said, and realised I was smiling.

*

It wasn't until I got back to the hospital that I understood how Jake had known we were at the farmhouse.

'Greg told him,' said Ella, as I sat by her bed munching crisps, hungry for the first time in ages. Greg was nowhere to be seen, and I could tell he was giving me a wide berth.

'But how did he know where to find Jake?'

'He'd looked him up before we even came here,' she said. Her hair was pulled back into a ponytail, and she had colour in her cheeks. I guessed the medication had finally left her system,

252

and she'd told me her lungs were fine, that she could go home. 'He contacted him at the hospital where he works before he left Ireland, and told him where you were staying.'

'Jesus.' I dropped a handful of crisps back into the bag.

'You have to remember you told us you loved him.' She looked apologetic. 'And Greg had his doubts about you – you know that.'

I sighed. 'So Greg told Jake I was staying at the hotel?'

'Yes.'

My mind spun. 'And Jake saw Gabriel there and followed him to the farmhouse?'

'It looks that way.' A shadow crossed her face. 'Thank God he did,' she said, with feeling. 'Your dad's been here all night, wanting to talk to you,' she said. 'I'd never have got to you without his help, you know.'

'How did you even know where to look for me?'

'It was something you said in the basement. You mentioned that place, and how you nearly died there once, and that guy – the one you bumped into and slept with – had saved your life by offering you *drugs*.' She gave me a look of disbelief. 'I mean, that's so messed up,' she said. 'It made me wonder if ... you know, he was the guy, and I just ... I don't know how I knew, but I had this feeling ...' She shook her head, her smile a little awkward. 'I'm not saying it was sisterly telepathy, or anything like that.'

'Oh, I think you are,' I said, in a teasing voice I almost didn't recognise as my own. 'But whatever it was, thank you.'

'And Reagan?' Ella hesitated. 'You really should talk to him.'

'I know.' I nodded. 'I think I'm ready now.'

Chapter 34

Ella

Colleen left to see Reagan and I sank on the edge of the bed trying to imagine the scene. Part of me wanted to go with her, but it was their moment – one that, this time, didn't involve Gabriel's body flailing over a cliff top and hitting the rocks below.

I'd watched in horror, but couldn't bring myself to look – to see if he was dead – even if my ankle hadn't felt on fire, and my lungs about to burst. The only important thing at that moment was that Colleen had been safe, huddled in Reagan's arms. She'd said something to him, her words carried away by the wind, and he'd murmured back as I'd stumbled forward to take her in my arms.

When Reagan turned up at the hospital in an ancient Volvo, he'd found me waiting in the car park, half-slumped against the wall, clutching the hospital blanket around me, and the necklace I couldn't seem to let go of, trying not to be spotted by nursing staff.

'I knew something wasn't right,' he'd said, after bundling me into the passenger seat with a worried glance at my grubby bare feet and bandaged ankle, and before I could put on my seatbelt we were heading at speed towards Aughris Head. 'In fact, I called Celia after I saw you at the café, but she didn't know any more than us.' Deep lines of stress were etched into his forehead. 'Then I saw on the news about the fire at the farmhouse. It kills me I wasn't there to help my girl.'

I'd gripped the sides of the seat as Reagan swung the car towards the cliff road, sweat breaking out on my forehead, feeling sick with panic and pain. 'I hope I'm not wrong, that's all, because I don't know where else to look … What if we're too late?'

'They'd better lock up that sick bastard and throw away the key,' he said, his voice a growl, eyes dark with anger as we pulled into a car parking area. There was only one car there, its back door swinging open. 'If I get my hands on him …'

I jolted back to the moment as Greg strode in with my bag, bringing with him a warm, clean scent of sunshine. 'I thought you might want to get changed before we leave,' he said.

'Did you see Colleen?'

His smile faded. 'I waited until she'd left the hotel room.' His voice had cooled. 'I wouldn't have known what to say.'

It filled me with sadness that he was avoiding her, but seeing it from his point of view, I could hardly blame him.

He dropped the bag and drew me into his arms. Since his arrival he'd barely let go of me. He kept tracing my face with his hand, his eyes searching mine. It was as if he hadn't seen me properly for a long time.

'I shouldn't have gone home,' he said for the hundredth time. 'I'll never forgive myself for that.'

'You weren't to know, Greg.' I wrapped my arms around his waist, enjoying the solid feel of him, and the tickly sensation of his newly grown beard on my cheek. All the barriers had come down. 'I shouldn't have accused you of lying about Colleen.'

'I can't really blame you after … after what happened before, but I promised you, Ella, I would never do anything like that again and I meant it.'

I moved back and looked at his face, saw lines of strain between his eyebrows and a smudge of worry in his eyes. 'I know,' I said. I remembered the feeling of well-being I'd had waking up in hospital the day before, so glad to be alive. 'Things are going to be different,' I said with conviction. 'We need to spend more time together, stop working so hard. At least, you do.'

He didn't hesitate. 'I agree.' He rested his forehead on mine. 'All this has made me realise what's important. I don't want to be a partner at work; I want to spend time with my family.'

'Oh, Greg.' I rested my head on his shoulder, absorbing his warmth. I thought of our losses – his father, my mother – and the grief that had bent our relationship out of shape. 'I'm sorry I kept pushing you away,' I said. 'I think subconsciously I was trying to keep you at arm's length. Maybe I was scared of getting hurt again.'

'I know.' His arms tightened around me. 'Maisie can't wait to see you,' he said, a break in his voice.

Hearing my daughter's name pulled something tight in my chest. I couldn't wait to see her. Something else occurred to me; something I'd been putting off.

'I need to talk to Dad.'

Greg let go of me with obvious reluctance and pulled his phone from his pocket. 'Do it now,' he said gently. 'I'll wait outside.'

My heart shrivelled as I found Dad's number and pressed Dial, wondering what I was going to say to him. To my surprise, he picked up right away. 'Dad, it's Ella. I don't want you to worry, but …'

I explained what had happened, but even though I edited out the worst details, he grew angry and upset. 'I'm coming over,' he said, before I'd finished.

'There's no point, Dad, we're coming home today.'

'I found the letter.' His voice was brusque with emotion. 'I knew you were going over there. I should have stopped you.'

'What?' My heartbeat faltered. 'Dad, did you know about

Colleen all along?' I hadn't planned to say it, but there didn't seem much point holding back after everything that had happened.

There was a brief silence, then a short exhalation of breath. 'Your mum told me about her, not long after we met.' He sounded hesitant now, unlike his usual self. 'I admit I didn't react well. We agreed not to discuss it again, that it was all in the past. I don't know if she ever thought about her after that.' His voice was pained, and I guessed it was hard to say things he'd kept buried all this time. 'Or him,' he added.

I knew he meant Reagan. 'Oh, Dad.' I realised he must have wondered, as I had, whether she'd secretly yearned for Reagan all along.

'She loved you,' I said firmly. 'She loved us both, but I think she wanted me to find Colleen and that's why she asked me to clear out her wardrobe. Why she kept saying sorry before she died.'

'I wish you hadn't found her.' His voice roughened. 'She's trouble. She nearly got you killed.'

'That wasn't her fault, Dad.' A flame of defensiveness ignited. 'She's had a difficult life, and that's partly because Mum didn't keep her. I feel I owe—'

'I don't want to hear it.' His words cut through mine. 'I don't care about her. We don't owe her anything. If you want to stay in touch that's your business, but I want no part of it.'

'Dad …'

'I miss you, Ellie. I just want you home where you belong.' In contrast to the start of our conversation, his feelings flowed into words more easily than they'd ever done. 'I love you,' he said.

I bit back a swell of feeling. 'I love you too, Dad.' Silence fell, but for once, it didn't feel awkward. 'We'll talk properly when I get back.'

'I don't think it's going to be easy,' I said to Greg, once I'd beckoned him back into the room, pulling a floral skirt and a clean white top from my bag. The clothes I'd been wearing at the farmhouse had disappeared, but I didn't care. My ankle was reminder enough, along with the flashbacks, and the self-recrimination in Greg's eyes. 'I don't think he'll ever accept Colleen as my sister, because it reminds him Mum wasn't perfect – that she had a past that didn't involve him.'

'It won't be easy for any of us,' Greg said, and I wondered whether he was talking about himself. He glanced at his watch. Our flight was booked and we couldn't wait to get home. I knew I might have to return to Ireland once Gabriel's body washed up, when the police would want to speak to us again – but I didn't want to think about that now. When it happened, I'd be with Colleen. We would get through it together.

I washed and dressed in the adjoining bathroom, brushing my hair until it shone and crackled with electricity. I detected a hint of smoke, as if I'd absorbed it through my skin – or maybe it was my imagination.

In the mirror, my face was lightly tanned, my complexion clear. There was no outward sign that anything had happened, except perhaps a faint shadow in my eyes, but my world had been shaken like a snow globe, and everything had settled slightly differently.

When Greg thrust open the door to tell me the doctor was waiting to discharge me, my heart gave a painful thud.

'Just coming.' I gripped the edge of the sink for a moment, breathing deeply until my pulse slowed.

After the doctor had been reassured I could use a crutch, and my lungs were clear of smoke, he wished me luck and Greg and I made our way to the visitors' room.

I was aware of curious stares, and hoped that back in England interest in our story would be less intense. We'd had offers to talk to the media, to tell our side of the story, but Colleen had brushed them off.

'I had enough of the press hanging around after Bryony drowned,' was all she said.

She and Reagan were sitting side by side, their heads close, talking in low voices, but stood up when we entered. Colleen looked different, and not because she was wearing my clothes, which didn't quite fit, or because her hair looked soft and shiny, catching the light from the window. She looked less brittle, her features smoothed out, her eyes lit from within. It was as if meeting her father had wiped out some of the bad things that had happened – some of which I didn't want to examine. Like whether Gabriel had fallen, or Colleen had pushed him.

'We'll leave you to it,' Reagan said rising, his gaze not wavering from Colleen's face. His air was protective, fatherly. It was coming off him in waves and I was glad. Colleen deserved to have at least one good relationship in her life.

'Ten minutes,' Greg murmured, his breath tickling my ear. He didn't look at Colleen. I guessed he still held her responsible for everything that had happened and maybe always would, but I also knew he understood she was part of my life now – if she wanted to be.

'Look at you, Long John Silver,' she said with a grin that was almost shy, when Greg and Reagan had left the room, their voices mingling outside. 'Is it less painful now?'

'A bit,' I lied, hobbling closer. The room was functional, painted a soft, pale grey, with a sofa in a darker shade and a box of tissues on a wooden table. 'Looks as if things went well between you two.'

She nodded, eyes bright. 'Being kidnapped and almost killed …' She paused and inhaled sharply, as if the memory had hit her afresh. 'It certainly cut through the crap,' she went on. 'We just talked and talked. About everything.'

I groped for something meaningful to say. 'That's good,' was the best I could do. 'What about Jake?'

'What about him?' Her voice was filled with contempt.

'He saved our lives, Colleen.'

She laughed. 'More good luck than anything,' she said, her shoulders tensing beneath my T-shirt, which was baggy on her.

'You don't know that for sure.' I remembered the way he'd

259

called after her as we fled, the anguish in his voice. *Did he love her?* I reminded myself I didn't know him at all.

'You know what, I didn't think I'd care if I died,' Colleen said. 'But in that basement, and then on the cliff, I realised I bloody well did. I wanted to live more than anything.'

'Well I, for one, am glad,' I said, softly.

'You know what else? My da just told me it wasn't my fault. Not just that, but Bryony. That what happened to her was an accident.' Her eyes shone with tears. 'Nobody has ever said that to me before.'

'Well, they should have.' I felt an ache in my heart. If only Mum hadn't given her up, she'd have had a completely different life; a better one, I was sure of it. 'I'm so sorry, Colleen.'

She looked at me, as if she knew what I was thinking. 'What's done is done.' She arched her eyebrows. 'You said it yourself, remember? We can't change the past. And maybe if Anna had kept me, she wouldn't have met your dad and you'd never have been born.'

'I suppose so.'

She rubbed the back of her neck and shifted from foot to foot. She was wearing a pair of my sandals, with glittery straps, and her feet looked oddly childlike. 'I want us to move forward,' she said. 'But I still don't know if I can. If *you* can.'

'We can if we want to.' I closed the gap between us. 'What happened is over, Colleen.' Her face blurred as tears leapt to my eyes, blending with the sunlight streaming in. 'I want to be in your life, if you'll have me.'

'Sounds like a marriage proposal.' She reached out and traced the freckles on my arm with her finger. We stood for a moment, not speaking.

'I'm going back with Reagan, to see Celia,' she said at last, dropping her hand. 'She doesn't deserve it, but I guess she's had a shite time of it over the years. I should make my peace with her.'

Her words weren't a dismissal. They were an invitation. She

was including me in her plans for the future. 'That's great,' I said, tears sliding down my cheeks.

'Jesus, you're an emotional one.' Feigning exasperation, Colleen stooped to pluck a tissue from the box on the table and handed it to me, and it felt so much like something a sister would do that my tears flowed faster.

'Making up for lost time, I suppose.' I blew my nose and tried to smile. 'I'd better go.' I was aware of Greg waiting, impatient for us to leave, and Reagan, worried about his daughter. 'Take care of yourself, won't you?'

'You too.' Leaning over, she pressed soft lips to my cheek. 'Can you still smell smoke, Ella?'

'All the time,' I said. 'I see ... I see *him* too, going over the cliff.'

We fell silent, meeting each other's gaze, the space between us shrinking, and I knew in that moment she would never tell me exactly what had happened in those last few seconds – maybe didn't know herself – and I would never ask.

'I'll come to England soon,' she said, a catch in her voice. 'I'd like to see where she's buried. Anna, I mean.' She hesitated. 'Our mother.' Her eyes held a promise, and I saw a shadow of Mum in her smile and hoped that wherever she was, our mother could see her girls, so different, yet inextricably linked, and I hoped she was happy we'd finally found one another.

I reached out and took Colleen's hand. 'I'd really like that,' I said.

Chapter 35

Colleen

Two Weeks Later

I'd never thought, until now, how close I'd lived to Waterford Harbour, where The Three Sisters – The River Barrow, The River Nore and The River Suir – meet before joining the sea. But as I stood at the window of Celia's cottage, blowing steam from a mug of tea, my eyes focused on the river in the distance, I wondered if my destiny had always been mapped out to intertwine with Ella's. Our lives had appeared to be flowing in such different directions, miles apart, yet we'd found our way to the brackish waters of the same estuary.

It was cloudy but bright, and Reagan was digging up potatoes in the back garden, puffing and brushing sweat from his forehead. I would never have imagined him doing something as mundane as gardening, but it suited him. He smiled and raised his hand. I smiled back. *Can you love someone you've only just met?*

'You're quiet today, Colleen.'

I turned. Celia was spreading jam thinly on a slice of toast. She looked so small. Her hair was grey and unkempt, hanging past her shoulders. It had been such a beautiful chestnut shade when I was a child, but after Bryony died her appearance had no longer mattered to her. Nothing had.

Since Reagan and I returned from Sligo, she'd been making an effort with me. She was still vague, unable to shift fully into the real world, but Reagan's influence had made her try, and I'd tried too; after coming so close to death, holding on to old grievances didn't seem so important anymore.

'I never blamed you for Bryony's disappearance, Colleen,' she told me, the first night I arrived back. She'd wanted to get it out in the open, lay it bare, Reagan told me. But there'd been that word 'disappearance'. I wondered if she would ever accept Bryony was dead.

My eyes skittered around the kitchen for the hundredth time since I'd returned, seeing the wooden cupboards, the old-fashioned cooker, the dull-coloured paint on the walls, which were as they'd always been. My gaze snagged on a framed picture of Bryony tucked on a wooden shelf, then moved on.

I couldn't believe I'd been staying here for two weeks now, or that Reagan hadn't done a runner. I'd meant it to be a short visit, a few days and then I'd be on my way – though, where to, I had no idea.

'I was thinking about what the Gardaí told me,' I said, my eyes settling on Celia's face.

She fiddled with her teaspoon, breaking her gaze away from mine. 'Please don't worry your head about that, Colleen.'

'But they never found his body.' I'd been playing the thought over and over in my mind. I knew it was irrational. Nobody could survive that fall.

'He's dead, Colleen. His body lost at sea.' The irony was heartbreaking.

I pulled out a chair at the small kitchen table and sat down. It was covered with a plastic red and white tablecloth and I pushed my finger through a layer of crumbs, and thought about the fire. The Gardaí had worked out that Gabriel drove Ella's hire car to a cliff top a few miles away from the farmhouse, planning to make it look as if she'd thrown herself into the sea. He'd even put her bag on the front seat. He'd then walked back to the hotel, before driving to the farmhouse to set it alight. None of it made sense at first, but I realised he'd worried that Ella would be searched for, and that he'd been seen with her.

He hadn't thought for a minute that anyone would miss me. And the farmhouse was so out of the way, he must have felt sure nobody would notice it had burned to the ground. And if they had, Jake was the only suspect.

Reagan came through the back door and I smiled, still hardly daring to believe my da was here, within touching distance. He was heading off at the weekend, and had asked if I'd like to go with him. He'd been in touch with some old contacts, and they'd asked him to play some backing gigs in London. Music was still a big part of his life.

I'd said I would go. I would meet Ella too; she was taking some time off work. We'd decided to go for a pizza, just the two of us, and talk about everyday things, like what type of music we liked. It sounded ordinary, but it was a big step. We also planned to visit Anna's grave.

But first, I needed to see Jake. I'd half wondered if he would come looking for me, and had braced myself to confront him. I couldn't explain the urge to see him. Maybe I was looking for closure.

I got up and put my mug next to the sink. There was a dusty old bottle of whisky on the windowsill – one of Terry's leftovers. I'd seen it the day I got back, but hadn't touched it. I hoped I never would.

'It's weird Jake hasn't been in touch,' I said to Reagan. 'I mean,

I got him arrested, for Christ's sake. You'd think he'd be pissed, and want to have it out with me.'

Celia narrowed her eyes. 'Don't blaspheme, Colleen,' she said, in a voice I recalled from my childhood.

I stared at her, but didn't reply. We still had a long way to go.

'Get off your high horse, Celia,' Reagan said. 'Or you might fall off.'

I smiled. He'd defused the moment, as he had several times since our arrival, and she seemed to tolerate him better than anyone. 'I'm going for a walk,' I said, grabbing my jacket and heading out.

I walked down the quiet, tree-lined road, heading towards the house I'd lived in with Jake for fifteen years. It was the first time I'd been out alone since Sligo, and although there was nobody about, I found myself picking up speed. Every noise startled me, bushes morphing into Gabriel waiting to jump out. He'd left me a nervous wreck, and I wondered if I would ever be fully free while they hadn't discovered his body.

The house, whitewashed, detached and immaculate, rose up as I rounded the bend, almost tripping over a black cat on the pavement. I stumbled, and stood for a moment, trying to calm my heartbeat. I'd thought he might be at the hospital, but his Ferrari was on the drive, and I was tempted to turn and run. I'd played out this scenario in my head every day for the last two weeks, but now I was there I had no idea what to say.

I walked up the path, and rang the doorbell. It felt strange. *This was my home once.* The garden looked as neat as ever, the beds bursting with newly planted flowers, and I wondered if he'd replaced me already.

He opened the door and even now, after everything, I could see how he'd reeled me in that day in Dublin. His good looks were a punch to the heart: the thick dark hair brushed back from a chiselled face, dazzling blue eyes that seemed to look inside me, and a magnetic smile he could switch on and off at will. He was wearing a thin grey sweater I'd bought him over a shirt and dark grey jeans.

'Colleen,' he said. There was no smile today. 'You look awful.'

'Jake, can we talk?' I tried to ignore the way his eyes were examining my hair with distaste. It had already begun to grow out, blonde roots pushing through the blackness.

'What is there to talk about?'

That threw me. Why was I here? Did I want to say sorry for getting him arrested? Did he deserve my apology?

'There is nothing in here that belongs to you, Colleen.'

'I don't want anything. I—'

'I thought we were happy,' he cut in. 'And yet you spread lies about me. Why?'

My heart gave an uncomfortable thud. 'I never lied, Jake. You were a controlling bastard, you know that as well as I do.'

'I never …' He broke off for a moment. 'I loved you.' Another pause. 'You'd be dead if it wasn't for me. If I hadn't gone to the hotel, seen that prick Gabriel in the foyer and followed him, you wouldn't be here right now. I knew before he was halfway there, where he was heading.' Jake had known about the farmhouse. I'd never had any secrets from him. 'I called the fire brigade, and the police, and look how you thanked me.'

'Can't you see?' I said. 'Gabriel pretended to be you. He said and did things I thought only you knew.' *Things I'd told him when I was off my face.*

'You walked out on me, and didn't tell me where you'd gone. I was worried sick about you. If that Greg bloke hadn't called me …' He shook his head. 'I love you, Colleen, always will.' He stepped back into the house. 'But I can't do this anymore.' He began to close the door, but his final words reached me, loud and clear. 'Don't ever come back here.'

*

266

'They've found his body,' Celia called, as I stepped through the back door. I dashed into the kitchen to see her face brighter than I'd ever seen it. 'They found Gabriel. He washed up a few miles down the coast.'

I covered my face with my hands, relief surging through my body, tears filling my eyes. *I was safe. Ella was safe.*

'And a parcel's arrived for you, Colleen.'

It was on the kitchen table, flat and oblong, wrapped in brown paper and tied with string. Inside were several layers of bubble-wrap and a note.

Mum would have wanted you to have this, Colleen. I believe it's how she wished things had been. Ella xxx

I pulled free the wrapping and lifted out a small watercolour painting. It was a sea scene: two little girls on a golden beach with buckets and spades. They were blonde, with a sprinkling of identical freckles across their noses, smiling at each other as though they shared a secret. I turned it over to see the letters E and C on the back. My eyes prickled with tears. There was no doubting it was Ella and me. There was no doubting, either, that my mother, Anna, had painted it. Her signature was in the corner.

Celia hovered at my shoulder and my heartbeat quickened. I knew the painting would remind her of Bryony. I pulled it to my chest, but Celia prised it gently from my hands and placed it on the table. Her eyes focused on the sea, the frothy waves with whites and blues of every shade. She ran her fingers lightly over the picture, her dark eyes brimming with tears.

'So this is you and Ella,' she said, a tear splashing onto its surface. 'You look like you're having fun.'

'Mam.' My throat was choked with tears. 'Don't do this to yourself.'

'It's OK, Colleen.' She pulled a handkerchief from up her sleeve and wiped her face. 'I know Bryony's never coming back, that

267

the sea took her.' She reached for my hand and squeezed it. 'But you're still here, and I'm glad.'

I tried to speak and found that I couldn't. I placed my hand over hers and hoped it was enough.

Epilogue

Anna

Twenty-five years ago

'That's pretty,' says Andrew, peering over my shoulder.

I lower my brush and watch him take in the scene I've painted of two little girls on a beach, with buckets and spades, blonde hair streaming from sun hats.

'Who are they?'

'My sister and me.' He knows I'm painting a series of family pictures for an upcoming exhibition, and wouldn't suspect for a moment both girls are my daughters.

He doesn't see Colleen everywhere, like I do, the shadow sister who walks beside Ella, copying her every move. After I confided in him about the baby I gave away, not wanting us to have secrets, I'd promised never to mention her again.

My confession upset him, though he tried to hide it. I thought it was about what I'd done, or maybe he couldn't bear the idea of my daughter growing up without her mother. I'd wondered if he might suggest bringing her to England, but instead, he grilled me about Reagan, his eyes dark with jealousy.

He said he couldn't stand that I'd loved someone before him, so I lied and said I hadn't; it was a holiday romance that got out of hand, that was all. He was quick to believe me, to demonise Reagan, turning him into a rat who'd taken advantage and abandoned his responsibilities.

'His loss is my gain,' he'd said tenderly, drying my tears and pressing his lips to mine.

I closed my eyes and let myself believe it.

The truth was, I'd loved Reagan from the moment we met. I knew he wasn't the settling-down type. He had plans to travel, plans for his music. So I told him I had plans too.

Had I secretly hoped he would change his mind when I returned to Ireland to break the news that I was pregnant? I wanted to tell him so many times that I loved him, but knew he didn't feel the same. He'd already moved on, arranging to visit America later that year. He couldn't wait to go. His eyes grew distant when he thought I wasn't looking.

I would have given up everything, abandoned my life in England, to go with him, but he never asked. Instead, he asked that I let his sister raise our baby.

'That's a great idea,' I agreed, wanting to please him, a smile masking my pain. Poor Celia, so desperate for a child of her own. I convinced myself it was better that way. I couldn't terminate the pregnancy, but couldn't keep the baby either – it would have been a permanent reminder of Reagan's failure to love me. The child would have a good life with Celia, and I would get on with mine.

I handed her over under Reagan's approving gaze, and when Celia cried with joy, I was filled with a deep satisfaction that went some way towards easing the deep ache inside me. She would call her Colleen, if I didn't mind. I said I didn't. If I'd chosen a name, I would have been claiming the baby as my own – I would have been lost.

Back home, I acted like nothing had happened. Reagan left for America to pursue his music career. I returned to my studies and eventually started teaching art at the university, where I met Andrew.

My painting had been a lifeline. Andrew was older and had some contacts in the art world. I began showing my paintings in exhibitions. They sold well, and to my surprise I became quite sought-after. I was commissioned to paint some portraits, and families became my specialty. Ironic, really.

It wasn't until after Ella was born that I began to yearn for Colleen. The milky happiness of holding my newborn baby was shadowed by a sharp sense of loss. With everything I did for Ella came a reminder of what I'd missed with my firstborn.

How was she? I wondered. When I left Ireland, it didn't occur to me to stay in touch. There would have been no point. The child was Celia's now. Reagan had written once – not the love letter I'd hoped for when I left him my address, but a formal note, letting me know where Celia was living, along with a photo of me holding Colleen that I didn't remember him taking.

I hid them in a shoebox, along with the hospital wristband I'd kept, worried Andrew might find them, but when Ella was a year old, I dug them out and took a trip to Ireland. Andrew doesn't know. I told him I was visiting my sister Tess in York. I'd always been close to my sister and knew he wouldn't question it.

He was worried about looking after Ella on his own, but I thought it might help them bond. Sometimes, he didn't appear to like sharing me, even with his own child.

The trip was a mistake. Celia was hostile, fear in her flinty eyes.

Looking past her, I saw Colleen, playing in the hallway of the old house in Cork, the debris of a doll's tea party spread around her on the polished floorboards, the sun slanting through the doorway, turning her hair to gold.

She was an older version of Ella, her limbs elongated, pale and skinny where Ella's were plump and dimpled, but the dusting of freckles across their noses was the same. I pushed my foot over the threshold with a desperate desire to go to her, and Colleen rose, clutching a floppy blue teddy. There was something vulnerable in her elfin face and wide eyes that called to me. I wanted to pick her up and run. I lurched forward, but Celia pushed me hard, strong for someone so small – or, maybe fright lent her strength.

'Please, Celia, I just want to see her.'

'It's not what we agreed.' Her voice was harsh. 'You signed her away.'

Signed her away.

Those words rang in my ears all the way back to England, and I hoped Colleen hadn't heard or understood. I'd signed my daughter away. I'd forfeited my right to be involved in her life the day I gave her up. Celia was her mother now.

I had no idea if she was in touch with her father. I never heard from Reagan again, and gradually my love for him leached away, like colour from an old photograph.

This painting will be the last time I think of Colleen. I owe it to Andrew and Ella to be there for them, to be fully present in a way I haven't been lately. I can't alter the past, but I can be a good mother now. A good wife.

Andrew goes back to the house to make coffee, and I carefully add a sprinkling of freckles to the girls' noses with the tip of my paintbrush. This is how I will always picture Colleen: frozen in time, smiling, playing happily with her sister on the beach, as I once did with my own sister.

When I've finished, I turn the painting over and write E&C in the corner. I'll leave it to dry before putting it up in the attic with the others. I'll never show it to anyone.

I hope one day my darling Ella will find it, and the shoebox in the wardrobe. Maybe she'll be braver than I was and find her sister – bring her home.

I hope they know how very much I love them.

I hope they will forgive me.

Acknowledgements

There's a brilliant team behind every book, and we're lucky to have such a great one.

We'd like to thank our agent Kate Nash, and our editors Belinda Toor and Cara Chimirri who have all been amazing. Thanks to Helena Newton for copy edits, and Michelle Bullock for proof-reads. Our thanks also go to Anna Sikorska for a brilliant cover design, Jo Kite for her hard work in marketing, and everyone at HQ Digital who has helped bring our book to publication. It's been a wonderful journey.

Enormous thanks to the readers, bloggers and reviewers who continue to support us, and of course to our families and friends for their unwavering belief and support.

Special thanks to our husbands, Tim and Kev – we couldn't do it without you!

Hello!

Thank you so much for reading *The Secret Sister*. We hope you enjoyed it.

It was such a different experience to co-write a book, and we absolutely loved writing it together.

If you enjoyed *The Secret Sister*, it would be wonderful if you could write a review. It's always lovely to hear what readers think.

And we always love to hear from our readers. You can get in touch with either of us via our websites, Facebook pages or through Twitter.

Many thanks,
Amanda and Karen

www.amandabrittany.co.uk

Twitter @amandajbrittany
Facebook www.facebook.com/amandabrittany2
Instagram @amanda_brittany_author

www.karenclarkewriter.co.uk

Twitter https://twitter.com/karenclarke123
Facebook https://www.facebook.com/karen.clarke.5682
Instagram https://www.instagram.com/karenanne37/

Dear Reader,

We hope you enjoyed reading this book. If you did, we'd be so appreciative if you left a review. It really helps us and the author to bring more books like this to you.

Here at HQ Digital we are dedicated to publishing fiction that will keep you turning the pages into the early hours. Don't want to miss a thing? To find out more about our books, promotions, discover exclusive content and enter competitions you can keep in touch in the following ways:

JOIN OUR COMMUNITY:

Sign up to our new email newsletter: po.st/HQSignUp

Read our new blog www.hqstories.co.uk

: https://twitter.com/HQDigitalUK

: www.facebook.com/HQStories

BUDDING WRITER?

We're also looking for authors to join the HQ Digital family!
Please submit your manuscript to:

HQDigital@harpercollins.co.uk

Thanks for reading, from the HQ Digital team

DIGITAL
HQ

If you enjoyed *The Secret Sister*,
then why not try another gripping thriller
from HQ Digital?